LOUISE'S WAR

The first in a new series from the
author of the Simon Shaw books

1942. Louise Pearlie, a young widow, has come to Washington DC to work as a clerk for the legendary OSS, the precursor to the CIA. When, while filing, she discovers a document concerning the husband of a college friend, Rachel Bloch, a young French Jewish woman she is desperately worried about, Louise realizes she may be able to help get Rachel out of Vichy France. But then a colleague whose help Louise has enlisted is murdered, and she realizes she is on her own, unable to trust anyone...

LOUISE'S WAR

A World War II novel of suspense

Sarah R. Shaber

Severn House Large Print
London & New York

This first large print edition published 2012
in Great Britain and the USA by
SEVERN HOUSE PUBLISHERS LTD of
9-15 High Street, Sutton, Surrey, SM1 1DF.
First world regular print edition published 2011 by
Severn House Publishers Ltd., London and New York.

British Library Cataloguing in Publication Data

Shaber, Sarah R.
  Louise's war.
  1. United States. Office of Strategic Services--
  Employees--Fiction. 2. World War, 1939-1945--Washington
  (D.C.)--Fiction. 3. World War, 1939-1945--Jews--France--
  Fiction. 4. France--History--German occupation,
  1940-1945--Fiction. 5. Suspense fiction. 6. Large type
  books.
  I. Title
  813.6-dc23

ISBN-13: 978-0-7278-9845-6

Severn House Publishers support The Forest Stewardship Council
[FSC], the leading international forest certification organisation. All
our titles that are printed on Greenpeace-approved FSC-certified paper
carry the FSC logo.

MIX
Paper from
responsible sources
FSC
www.fsc.org FSC® C018575

Printed and bound in Great Britain by the
MPG Books Group, Bodmin, Cornwall.

For my precious grandsons,
Brandon and Nathan Lindsay

Acknowledgements

I couldn't begin to thank everyone who supported and helped me while I wrote *LOUISE'S WAR*, but I will do my best!

First I must thank my family, especially my husband Steve, and my children, Katie and Sam.

I owe so much to my writing buddies, Margaret Maron, Kathy Trocheck, Brenda Witchger, Diane Chamberlain, Katy Munger and Alex Sokoloff. Without our writing retreats and brainstorming sessions I never would have begun or finished writing this book. Our friend and bookseller without peer, Nancy Olsen of Quail Ridge Books, is our rock.

My agent and friend, Vicky Bijur, must be the most patient person on the planet!

I am fortunate to have among my fans and friends Christine Ghafoor, gifted English/French translator, who proofread the smidgen of French in this book and saved me from embarrassment.

My heartfelt thanks go to Severn House Publishers, who took a chance on my new series despite challenging times in the publishing industry.

And I remember with affection the late Ruth Cavin, of St Martin's Press, who bought and edited my first five books. I was privileged to know her.

A Note Concerning Language

Some readers of this book may question my use of the word 'colored' to describe African Americans, believing it to be disrespectful and derogatory.

I understand that it's uncomfortable for us to come face to face with the racial prejudice of pre-Civil Rights America.

But I also believe that this book wouldn't be honest literature if I didn't do my best to write about the 1940s as truthfully and accurately as I can.

Giving my characters modern sensibilities, putting words that didn't exist then into their conversations, would rob real people who were members of minority groups, who struggled and suffered, of the dignity and respect they have earned from their history.

Besides, as Carla Sims, communications director for the National Association of Colored People in Washington, D.C., has said, 'the term "colored" is not derogatory ... it was the most positive description commonly used at that time. It's outdated and antiquated but not offensive.'

9

'Colored', and Negro, were the words used by both races to describe African Americans during the time this novel is set, and so my characters use those words.

Prologue

June 1942
Marseille, Vichy France

Rachel grabbed Pierre's wrist before he poured the scoopful of lentils into her basket.

'That's not three hundred grams,' she said.

'Close enough,' he muttered.

'I paid for three hundred grams of lentils,' she said, 'and I expect to get no less than three hundred grams of lentils.'

'That little bit of gold doesn't buy what it used to,' he said.

'We had an agreement.'

'All right, I'll measure again.'

'And this loaf of bread, it has mold on it.'

'Cut it off.'

'I want another loaf, no mold.'

He didn't answer her, but replaced the bread. She knew what he was thinking. These Jews, they would bargain until their last breaths.

For one link of a gold bracelet she'd bought four eggs, a wedge of cheese, lentils, and potatoes. Her basket was not even half

11

full. Two years ago she would have come home from market with fresh duck, wine, asparagus, butter, and a bouquet of fragrant roses for the dinner table. After dinner she and Gerald would sit out on the terrace that overlooked the Old Port, sip a *digestif*, and watch the sun set over the Château d'If. And Pierre, he was once just a farmer who drove a dogcart and tipped his hat to her. Now he was draining her dry of everything she owned.

'Is there any soap?' Rachel asked Pierre.

'No soap today,' he said.

Little Claude dragged on her arm, whining.

'Don't,' she said, 'you know how that hurts Maman.' She arched back to relieve the ache in her back. The baby had settled low, right into the bowl of her pelvis. She felt like she was walking with a melon between her legs.

'Help Maman with the basket,' she said to Claude.

The little boy grabbed one handle of the basket with both hands and together they struggled home in the midday summer sun. Sweat soaked Rachel's body by the time they'd walked two blocks. Her threadbare cotton dress clung to her bare legs and outlined her bulging belly. Stringy damp hair plastered her head. And there was no soap at home.

At last she turned the last corner before entering her street, where the boarded-up *patisserie* once offered the most mouth-watering *pain au chocolat* in Marseille. The baker and his family fled to Switzerland weeks ago. Rachel's doorway beckoned to her, a short block away from where she stood resting, breathing hard, before taking her final few steps toward home. But then she spotted two policemen, leaning up against a lamppost, between her and her doorway. One of them noticed her, dropped his cigarette on the ground and crushed it with his boot. He pointed her out to his partner, and they both moved toward her. They would want to inspect her papers.

She set the basket down and clutched Claude's hand. Then she remembered, and fear filled her heart. Before she'd left home she'd forgotten to pin the yellow star to her breast.

ONE

June 26, 1942
'Two Trees', a boarding house
Washington, DC

I slept naked last night, like everyone else in this city. But despite lying flat out on my bed in my birthday suit with the fan blowing straight on me, I couldn't cool off enough to fall asleep.

The heat wasn't the only thing keeping me from my rest. The Top Secret document I'd locked in the office safe before I'd left work worried me to the point that I'd been fretting about it all evening and into the night. Before I'd slid the document onto the shelf inside the safe, I'd noticed the surname on the memorandum subject line: Bloch. My stomach seized and a shiver of apprehension scurried down my spine. It couldn't be Rachel's family, could it? Bloch was a common French surname, there must be thousands of families named Bloch trapped in France.

I managed to banish my worries for Rachel until morning, telling myself I could do

15

nothing until I got to work. But around two in the morning I realized that without relief from the smothering heat I might well be awake all night.

Finally I got out of the bed, slipped a cotton housecoat over my sticky body, pulled the top sheet off the bed, went into the bathroom, opened the bath tub tap, and soaked the sheet in thetub. I wrung out the sheet until it stopped dripping, carried it back to my bedroom, and stretched it between the tall bedposts at the foot of my bed, tying the corners to the bedpost caps so that the sheet hung its full wet length down to the floor. I turned the fan on high, trained it directly on the sheet and stretched out on my bed. Cool air brushed my body, drying my skin. For a few minutes I listened to fat June bugs popping and buzzing against my window screens and the rhythmic clicking of a loose fan blade, until, blessedly, I fell asleep.

The morning queue at the bus stop was so long I figured I had no hope of catching a bus anytime soon. So I walked the ten blocks from my boarding house on 'I' Street to the agency's headquarters in Foggy Bottom. I shaded my eyes from the harsh glare with a straw fedora and my first pair of prescription sunglasses, and soaked three handkerchiefs sopping up perspiration from my neck and any other part of my body I could reach without exposing myself.

The security officer at the front entrance to my building stopped me at the door. He was an army private who compulsively shrugged every few minutes to resettle his rifle on his shoulder, as if he wasn't comfortable with it yet. Private Cooper knew me well by now, but he still squinted at my ID badge. Satisfied that I was the same person I'd always been, the soldier opened the door to the anonymous building, a converted apartment house at the corner of 23rd and 'E' Street without a sign or a street number, and nodded at me to enter.

'Good morning, Mrs Pearlie,' he said. As he did nearly every day, he looked down at my feet, sensibly shod in cotton anklets and canvas shoes, and said, 'I know it's hot, but I wish you girls would start wearing stockings and heels again.'

I didn't respond. I'd decided a long time ago that it was best not to say out loud much of what crossed my mind. I could think what I liked, though, and I thought the guard would wait a long time before he'd catch me wearing stockings in one-hundred-degree heat ever again.

I was here to work, not be whistlebait for teenaged GIs.

The heavy wood doors that opened off the hall of the old apartment building weren't identified or even numbered. The first one on the right led to my office, which I'd worked in alone for the last few days, since the three girls who clerked for me got food poisoning at a USO picnic last Sunday. Doing their jobs as well as my own was exhausting, though it was a relief to have some respite from the incessant clatter of typewriters and mimeographs.

I switched both floor fans on low, to keep the breeze from blowing papers everywhere, and raised the shades in what was once the living room of a two-bedroom apartment, now crowded with four desks, banks of index-card file cabinets, and a massive Yale floor safe.

I went straight to the safe, entered the combination, twirled the dial and used both hands to haul open the heavy door. Top Secret files and papers crowded it. I extracted a thin file off one shelf and shut the safe door behind me. The lock engaged with a solid click.

As the only clerk in the Research and Analysis branch of the Office of Strategic Services with a Top Secret clearance, all documents referred from General Donovan's office came directly to me, stamped 'your eyes only' in red. Oh so secret, and oh so silly, as the pundits editorializing in the Republican newspapers often described our infant spy agency. I wished I could put those jerks to work in my office. I'd make them file index cards until their fingers bled!

The document I held had arrived at General Donovan's office from London OSS headquarters by way of a creased leather diplomatic pouch, but the message originated with an intelligence operative in Marseille, deep inside Vichy France.

The original French message was scrawled on a fragment of brown waxed paper, the kind a village *charcuterie* might use to wrap up a housewife's breakfast bacon. A typed translation, single-spaced to conserve paper, was clipped to the original. The message read: 'Met with Gerald Bloch, of the Marseille Hydrography Office, expert on the coastline of French North Africa, free to work with the Resistance if OSS evacuates his family to safety.' That was all. A memo from General Donovan's aides directed us to forward the file and any information about Bloch we could find to the Europe/Africa desk for further study.

Gerald Bloch. My dearest friend in the world, Rachel Foa, had married a Gerald Bloch after she and her father, an officer of the New York branch of a French bank, returned home to Marseille in 1933. I'd last heard from Rachel in the summer of 1940, when France fell to the Nazis. She wrote to tell me that her father had died of heart failure after the Nazis occupied Paris and seized his apartment and his bank accounts. She reassured me that she was safe in Marseille, but I was desperately worried about her.

The Nazis occupied half of France, including Paris. But France was supposedly free and independent with a president, Marshal Pétain, and an administrative center in Vichy. For political and diplomatic reasons it suited the Germans to allow a puppet French state to exist, for now, anyway.

I'd known Rachel was Jewish before I met her, since the Dean of St Martha's, the junior college we attended, wrote and asked me if I had any objection to rooming with a French Jewish girl. Of course I didn't. I felt so blessed to go to college, especially during the depression, I would have roomed with a Hottentot. As it happened the only thing about Rachel that appeared remotely Jewish to me was that she didn't eat bacon on Saturday and played mah-jongg obsessively.

Could the Gerald Bloch of this file be Rachel's husband? Surely it was a coincidence. I forced myself to stay calm and read the file as if the name Bloch meant nothing to me.

This Bloch must be Jewish, too, or he wouldn't be trading his expertise for his family's escape from Vichy France. And French North Africa would soon be the target of a massive Allied campaign, the first offensive in the Mediterranean theater since the United States entered the war six months ago. I'd even overheard its code name, Torch, whispered in the women's restroom. Outside OSS all us typists and secretaries and file clerks kept the nature of our work to ourselves or risked being shot. Inside we gossiped shamelessly. Besides, most of the scholar spies from the Europe/Africa desk had been camped out at the Library of Congress for the past few weeks, feverishly writing reports about Tunisian railway track gauges and Algerian tribal cultures. I'd have to be blind and deaf not to realize the Allies were preparing to invade French North Africa through Morocco, Algeria, and Tunisia, to join forces with the British Eighth Army, already battling Rommel in Egypt and Libya.

I pictured Monsieur Bloch desperately bartering his expertise for his family's safety, and it made my eyes sting. If I remembered the conversation at yesterday's coffee break correctly, he didn't have much time to close the deal. Internment of refugees and Jews had begun in Paris and the rest of Nazi-occupied France. How long before Vichy France followed Paris's example?

I knew Rachel's husband was a scientist, but the letters that Rachel sent me were one page, thin, almost transparent sheets folded in half and sealed, to save postage, and there wasn't much space for her to elaborate on her husband's work beyond using the French word to describe it, a word I hadn't bothered to translate. She wrote more about her baby son Claude, the view of the Old Port from her apartment balcony, and the diminishing supply of butter and cheese in

21

the local shops. But her family had been French citizens for generations, and since she lived in unoccupied Marseille, in Vichy France, that meant she was safe, didn't it?

Donald Murray rapped on my open door, interrupting my brooding, and I turned my attention to my work. Don was one of those perfectly nice people who make you cringe without knowing why. I think perhaps his slight Boston accent seemed snobbish to me, although many of the people I'd met and liked had heavier Yankee accents than his. A thirtyish economist from Yale, he wore the summer civilian uniform of male Washington bureaucrats, khaki trousers, short-sleeved white cotton shirt, and white wingtips. He wasn't bad looking by any means. He was slender, with blue eyes and light-brown hair. He wore tortoiseshell eyeglasses with rims the same shade as his hair and affected a military-style crew cut, as did most of the young men in Washington who didn't want to look like slackers. Betty, one of my junior clerks, was sure Don had a crush on me, and that the 'third' after his name meant he had money. She kept telling me I could do worse, but the way he hung around my office irritated me. On a slow day a few months ago I read one of his journal articles on file in the office. Then I understood why economics was called the dismal science.

'I need the London telephone book,' he said.

'Come on in,' I said to him.

I went to the safe, spun the dial, blocking it from Don's view with my body, and opened the heavy door again. I retrieved the telephone book and plunked it on the library table in the middle of the room and shoved the safe door closed again.

'Please,' Don said. 'Let me take it to my office.'

'Sorry,' I said. 'You know the rules. I can't let it leave this room.'

'You know I'll bring it back.'

'Stop grumbling. You know how scarce the London phone book is. If this one goes missing, we might not be able to replace it. We'll have to ask the London office for phone numbers by way of diplomatic pouch.'

Don sat down at the work table and went through the familiar ritual of lighting his pipe, knocking old ash into an ashtray, filling the bowl with fresh Captain Black, tamping it down, drawing his first mouthful of smoke and exhaling it slowly. He settled the pipe in a corner of his mouth and opened the telephone book.

I pushed the library ladder over to the 'B' index card stack and climbed to the top rung, keeping my skirt tucked close to my body. At work I wore a khaki dress with narrow lapels and no pockets, thanks to fabric shortages, hemmed at the knee. I'd heard rumors we'd be allowed to wear trousers to work soon, thank God. I already

23

owned two new pairs I'd bought at J.C. Penney. I was used to trousers, since I wore overalls while working at my family's fish camp, but I'd met girls here who'd never owned a pair in their lives.

My office contained a minute fraction of the acres of index files that filled entire buildings in Washington. Even so, small square wooden file drawers, holding thousands of five-by-eight index cards, climbed the ten-foot walls of my office to the ceiling, blanketing every vertical surface of the stripped kitchen, bathroom and two bedrooms.

The powers that be had left us the toilet and bathroom sink, a deference to our sex that I appreciated.

Sure enough, one Gerald Bloch, a hydrographer, had an index card in our files. This meant we had a subject file on him somewhere in the building. This wasn't as unlikely as it seemed. After the war began, my branch of OSS, Research and Analysis, asked every academic in the country to send us information on experts they knew, including foreigners, who might be helpful to the war effort. Later we collected even more names from the foreign publications our agents bought in neutral capitals like Stockholm and Lisbon. OSS had rooms full of file clerks to stow away the stacks of paper that found their way to the agency.

I paused at the door, on my way to the 'B' main file, and looked back at Don. He didn't even remove his pipe from his mouth. He tapped the phone book with his pencil.

'I'll guard it with my life,' he said.

TWO

Three floors up, in yet another gutted apartment, I pulled Gerald Bloch's dossier out of a file cabinet. The Manila jacket contained few papers, and I flipped through them quickly, until I saw a Bloch listed on the program for an international hydrography conference held in 1936. Must be the same man. How many French hydrographers named Bloch could there be in the world, and what was hydrography, anyway?

Back in my office I'd barely settled down to read the Bloch file when Don closed the London phone book with a final slap. After giving it back to me he took the pipe out of his mouth and leaned back in his chair.

'Louise,' he said, 'I was wondering. There's a cocktail party at Evalyn McLean's next week. I can get us in. Want to go?'

'Gosh, Don, I don't own a dress I could wear to a party like that.' Maybe Betty was right. Don must have social connections, and money, if he could wangle an invitation to Friendship House. I wanted to go, just for the fun of it. But that might encourage him, and I didn't want that, though I was supposed to be finding my second husband. My parents made that clear barely three months after Bill died.

'Girls wear anything to parties now,' Don said, 'even Red Cross uniforms.'

'I'll get back to you,' I said. 'Depends on work – whether my girls are back from sick leave.'

I'd be thrilled to go to one of Evalyn McLean's parties. All the rich, famous and important people in town went to her soirées. I read all about them in the society columns. Last week Gene Tierney and Oleg Cassini were in town and went to Evalyn McLean's and then on to three more parties in one night. Of course I'd met lots of celebrities already. John Ford directed our Field Photography Unit, and I once saw Sterling Hayden in the cafeteria, eating chipped beef on toast just like the rest of us.

After Don left and I'd returned the London phone book to the safe I sat down with the dictionary and the Bloch file. I had some privacy even when my clerks were in the office. My desk, as befitted my title, which entitled me to one hundred and eighty dollars a year more than my subordinates, sat apart from the others behind a partition knocked together from two-by-fours and plywood. I could even lock my desk drawers. When the desks were delivered to this room, government workmen pried out the locks on the others.

Hydrography was the science of charting the oceans, I learned. Wet geography. Humor aside, I figured that hydrography would be critical to winning a world war that was fought on the sea as well as on land and in the air.

Bloch's file contained a letter from an instructor in the geography department at George Washington University, one Marvin Metcalfe, who'd met Bloch at that international conference in 1936, and thought he fit the OSS description of a 'foreign expert'. He'd enclosed the program from the conference, which listed Bloch as a speaker.

That wasn't all. The file contained a photostat of a letter from Bloch dated in May of 1940, as the Germans advanced on Paris, to the American consulate in Marseille. My French, and his handwriting, wasn't good enough for me to translate it, but I did recognize the words *émigrer* and *demande de visa*. Bloch had been trying to escape France for some time. The final document in the file was an article from a Marseille newspaper, probably clipped by an OSS employee at the Bern office combing old French newspapers. The piece was brief and in French, of course. I gathered that Bloch received some sort of award. A photograph accompanied it.

Bloch was a slender, fair man with a thin mustache. His wife, holding their baby son,

27

stood next to him proudly. I felt my chest contract and my stomach roil. Bloch's wife was Rachel.

Waves of heat washed over me; darkness, pierced by flashes of light, dropped like a curtain over my vision. I just barely made it into the bathroom before I slid to the floor.

I revived to find myself stretched out full length on the cool tiles. For the first time in my life I'd fainted. I grasped the edge of the toilet bowl and pulled myself to a seating position leaning against the wall. After the room stopped tilting I was able to stand and brace myself on the sink. I soaked a handful of towels and sponged my neck, and opened my blouse and cooled myself under my arms and neck.

I waited for my panic to wane before I returned to my desk and let the hot breeze from the office floor fan dry what was left of the dampness I'd sponged over my face and neck.

Thank goodness I'd been alone in the office when I'd recognized Rachel in the newspaper photograph. Otherwise my girls would have made a scene and the whole office would hear I'd fainted. I detested attracting attention to myself. And fainting, like crying, was one of those behaviors that men thought confirmed women's weakness, their unsuitability for important work. I didn't want anyone to think for a second that I couldn't do my job.

I'd calmed myself down a bit before I looked at the photograph again. Rachel's dark hair was longer than when I knew her, pulled up in a matronly bun, exposing her long elegant neck. The picture was grainy and distant, like the memory of the last hours we spent together, on our graduation day, almost ten years ago...

'Oh, *zut!*' Rachel had said, in her excellent, but accented, English. 'Help me! Sit on this thing!'

I had perched on one of the bulging cases, squashing its contents, while Rachel fastened the latches.

'You'd better tie this case up with rope,' I said. 'If it bursts open in the hold of your ship, what a mess.'

'It's so mean of Papa, making me leave so much behind.'

'The other passengers on the *Majestic* need room for their luggage, too, you know,' I said.

My eyes filled with tears, and Rachel dabbed at hers with the edge of a lace cuff.

'I can't believe you're leaving,' I said, 'that I might never see you again.'

'Don't say that,' Rachel said. 'You'll come and visit me in Marseille, and Papa might be transferred back to the States again someday.'

I didn't answer her. I'd never have the money to go to Europe. Besides, I was getting married in three weeks.

'Remember our pledge,' Rachel said. 'We're going to name our daughters after each other. You'll have a baby before I do, though.'

I didn't respond to that either. Bill and I had already decided not to have children until the Depression was over. We simply couldn't afford it.

'You'll marry soon, too, I'm sure,' I said.

'Of course,' she said, smoothing the skirt of her new traveling suit.

'Rachel...'

'Yes?'

'Someday I'll repay you...'

Rachel interrupted me by placing her hand over my mouth. 'You promised not to speak of that again, ever. Besides, how would I have gotten through this year without you?'

After we finished packing we sat on my bare mattress and held hands, silent, afraid to speak for fear we'd burst into tears. At last the porter came to pick up Rachel and her luggage and take her to the train station.

'Goodbye,' I whispered to her.

'*Non*,' she answered, shaking her head. 'In France we don't say that. It's *au revoir*. Until we see each other again.'

After Rachel returned to France we wrote each other every week. We shared the details of our marriages, her baby son, our lives. Hers was infinitely more colorful than mine, and I longed to visit her, but my family didn't have that kind of money. As the thirties came to a close Rachel's letters described France's growing fear of Nazism. For months after I stopped hearing from her I wrote her every week, I begged the French embassy for help in locating her, and I pestered the New York office of her father's bank. I wrote dozens of letters and got not one in reply. After Pearl Harbor I stopped trying to find her, but I wondered every day whether she was homeless and hungry, or even alive. I didn't think I'd know what had happened to her until the war was over, if then.

But now I knew that Rachel, Gerald and little Claude were still in Marseille and desperate to get out of Europe. I felt just as desperate. And powerless. What could I possibly do to help them? I'd learned from reading the newspaper what financial resources were required to sponsor a Jewish European refugee for an American visa, and I didn't have them.

I felt thankful that I was alone in the office. I couldn't have hidden my emotions from anyone. I felt alternately feverish, freezing cold and shaky, as my body responded to my anguish. For a few minutes I thought I might need to rush back to the bathroom to faint again, or maybe spew. But I commanded myself to calm down. Giving in to panic would be useless.

What could I do to help Rachel? Could I

even admit to anyone at OSS that I knew her? Would that influence the decision to respond to Gerald's overture, or not? I'd never felt so helpless in my life.

I could think of only one option.

With Bloch's file tucked under one arm, I knocked on Bob Holman's office door and waited for him to call out for me to enter. Holman, the head of the Europe/Africa desk, was a very fat man. In this stifling heat he often stripped to his underwear to work, and he wasn't the only man in Washington who did so. After a bit of shuffling around he called out to me, and I went into his office. Holman, his round face red, forehead streaming perspiration, sat at his desk knotting his tie. A cot with a rumpled pillow stood in a corner. The files on his desk, weighted down with whatever he could find to keep them from being scattered about by the breeze from his Philco floor fan, lay stacked in piles all around him.

Holman would decide whether or not to forward Bloch's file to the OSS Projects Committee, which had the authority to direct Special Operations, the glamor boys and girls of OSS, to smuggle the Bloch family out of Marseille. Over the last six months I'd earned Holman's respect by recommending specific dossiers to him, and he'd asked me to flag material I thought could be important. He got the credit for whatever I suggested, which I resented, of course, but that's just the way it was.

Truth was, I knew as much about Holman's work, and what went on in OSS, as he did. The difference between us was, Holman got briefed officially along with the other men in our branch while I picked up what I knew from the papers I filed, gossip in the girls' restroom and coffee-break conversations.

'I've got a good prospect for you, Mr Holman,' I said, handing him the Bloch file instead of tossing it in his pending basket.

'Let's see it,' Holman said, taking the file from me after resting his thick Havana cigar on the rim of an overflowing ashtray. 'Wait a few minutes, Louise, I've brought fresh lemonade from home,' he said, as I turned to leave. He read through the contents of the file.

'A hydrographer familiar with the North African coast,' he said. 'Interesting. Might be very useful to us.'

Holman laid the file aside. He hadn't tossed it into his 'to be filed' box yet, which was good, but then again he hadn't stacked it in the Projects Committee box either.

'Take a seat,' he said. 'Have some lemonade.'

'Thanks,' I said.

Holman pulled a Thermos bottle from a desk drawer. He sat it smack down on the Bloch file, leaving a wet circle on its Manila

33

jacket.

He poured me a glass of lemonade, which I drank appreciatively. It was still cool.

'Where did you get the sugar?' I asked.

Holman chuckled. 'I have my ways,' he said. 'Or rather I should say, my wife has her ways. She's a resourceful woman.'

I drained my glass.

'Thanks,' I said. 'That tasted wonderful.'

'You're welcome,' Holman said, mopping his face with a fresh handkerchief. 'God, it's damn hot. The family and I are going to spend this weekend at a friend's camp on the Potomac,' he said. 'My wife's picking me up after work. Just thinking about getting out of the city makes me feel cooler.'

'I'm planning to relax on the porch with Agatha Christie's new novel,' I said. How lame. I was never good at small talk. I tried not to stare at the Bloch file, now pinned under Holman's fleshy elbow.

Holman mopped his forehead again and glanced at his watch. This was my cue that he was done being familiar with the help and I should leave him to his paper-shuffling and get back to mine. I ignored his signal. I crossed my legs, which are shapely, if not long, thank you very much, and settled in for a chat.

Holman was enough of a gentleman that he didn't directly ask me to leave. Instead he screwed the top back on his Thermos and stashed it away in a drawer. He took his cigar out of the ashtray and chewed it, dribbling ash on Bloch's file. My determination weakened. Holman smoked the smelliest cigars in the building.

'So,' I said, trolling for more conversation, 'is your wife still looking for a job?'

Holman harrumphed. 'Yes,' he said. 'Silly notion, to go out to work and hire a colored woman to look after the children. I don't think it will happen, thank goodness. She can't type worth a damn. She's flunked the test three times.'

'She could work in a factory,' I said.

'Over my dead body. I'd look like a sap, with a wife in coveralls. I won't allow it.'

Holman glanced at his watch again. I'd overstayed my welcome, I knew, but I wasn't leaving until I knew what he did with that file, one way or the other.

'So,' I said, 'what did you think of the file I brought you?'

'Oh, yeah,' he said, 'thanks for reminding me.' He picked up the file, waved it about to shake off the cigar ash and tossed it into the Projects Committee outbox. Rachel and Gerald and Claude now had a spark, only a glimmer mind you, of hope of escaping Marseille.

Back in my office I was again grateful to be alone.

Behind the closed door I put my head on my desk and wept.

I tried to console myself by remembering

that I wasn't by any means the only American with friends or family in Europe. And Rachel and her family were French citizens living in Vichy, unoccupied France, so they were safer than most. I couldn't dwell on them or I wouldn't be able to sleep or work. And I'd done everything I could for them, hadn't I?

THREE

At quitting time I joined the throng of weary government workers who streamed out of dozens of government buildings and waited on steaming sidewalks all over the city, hoping against hope to get a bus or trolley home. Many of us waited in vain. Capital Transit refused to hire Negroes to take the place of their drivers who were drafted into the military, despite newspaper editorials, government pleas and public demonstrations by both races. It astonished me that some people in this country didn't have the common sense to understand that if colored men could fight in this war, they could certainly drive buses. Fortunately most folks with cars picked up as many riders from the slug lines as they could on their way home. A girl I knew once got a lift from Eleanor

36

Roosevelt and rode home in the President's armored Cadillac limousine!

A big gray Packard drew up next to me. A young man wearing a straw panama hat leaned out of the window. 'Where are you headed?' he asked.

'I can walk from Washington Circle,' I said.

'Get in.'

I squeezed into the back seat next to a girl who couldn't have been more than seventeen and a baby-faced army private. They were holding hands and looked scared to death.

'These two are on their way to the magistrate to get hitched up,' the driver said.

The couple looked at each other as if they couldn't quite believe the driver's words referred to them.

'I ship out on Monday,' the young private said. 'And Clara here is going to work at the S&W cafeteria near the Capitol.'

'Senators and generals eat there every day,' Clara said, 'and the pay is really good.'

Wait until you find out how much the hot, tiny room you're going to share with three other girls is going to cost you, I thought. And try not to get pregnant tonight. One of the clerks who worked for me was already a widow with an infant. She shared a bathroom with twenty-one other roomers in a rat-infested boarding house. Her baby boarded at a cousin's home in Maryland somewhere. For goodness' sake, Clara, go to

37

Union Station instead of the courthouse, sweetly kiss Private Dogface goodbye, go home and finish high school.

'Congratulations,' I said instead.

'Here you go,' the driver said, pulling over at Washington Square and Pennsylvania Avenue.

I climbed out of the car and waved as it pulled away from the curb. Since I'd gone to work this morning a bogus anti-aircraft gun constructed of wood had appeared next to the equestrian statue of young Lieutenant George Washington in the grassy center of the circle. At least the gun wasn't manned by a couple of artillerymen scanning the sky with binoculars, like the fake ones on the roof of the White House.

I walked south to 'I' Street. My boarding house was just outside the 'K' Street boundary that separated the rarefied air of Dupont Circle from the middle-class environs of George Washington University. The brick row houses on our street were narrower than the elegant town houses further north, our back yards were smaller, and sometimes we could catch a whiff of the Potomac and the Heurich brewery from our porch on a breezy day.

I wasn't yet used to seeing my boarding house, 'Two Trees', named after the tall pecan trees in the back yard, without its wrought-iron fence and Juliet balconies. Henry and Joe dismantled them last weekend and added them to the towering pile of scrap metal at the end of the street, waiting for the scrap collectors to tote it all away. Henry said the war would be over before they got around to it. The pile ruined the looks of the street. Circled by a tall chicken-wire fence, the stack held all the scrap metal our block could scrounge, including an astounding number of kitchen pots and pans and a garden statue of a naked cherub meant to sprinkle a backyard fish-pond.

Inside the narrow dark hall I hung up my hat and breathed a sigh of relief, glad to be out of the sun. I quickly sorted through the mail on the hall table. None for me, thank goodness. Letters from my parents inevitably asked when I was coming home. They thought it was noble for me work for the war effort, but they assumed my life in Washington was temporary. I supposed I'd have to go home after the war, unless I remarried, but it made me cringe to think about it.

I dumped my purse on a frayed needle-point chair and walked back to the kitchen to get a glass of water.

Dellaphine, who didn't cook for the household again until Sunday, sat at the kitchen table with her feet up on another chair, nodding off to the sound of the *Dinner Music* show on WINX. Her radio, a big Silvertone that droned on and on all day, sat on the Hoosier cabinet next to the mixing bowls. Dellaphine started awake as I tiptoed over to the sink.

'Good evenin', Mrs Pearlie,' Dellaphine said, stretching her arms over her head. 'You're home mighty early.'

'I got a lift,' I said. 'I'm sorry I woke you up.'

I filled a glass to its brim twice from the faucet over the sink and drank my fill. The scarred white porcelain sink stood stolidly on iron legs, wide enough and deep enough to bathe a child in, and reminded me of the one in my parents' kitchen. I'd often watched my mother rinse beach sand off my younger brother in ours. I rarely felt homesick, but for some silly reason this kitchen sink caused an occasional pang.

'I wasn't asleep,' Dellaphine said. 'I was just restin' my eyes.'

Dellaphine Stokes was our landlady's colored cook and housekeeper. She'd worked for Phoebe Knox, or the Knox family, since she was fourteen years old. She had kin in Wilmington, which is how I came to live at Mrs Knox's boarding house. Lily Johnson, the colored woman who took in my family's laundry, sang in the St Stephen A. M. E. Zion Church choir with Dellaphine's cousin.

Dellaphine was a warm milk-chocolate color and so skinny she could wrap her apron strings all the way around herself and tie them in front. Once there were two other servants in the house, but they'd left when war broke out, the driver to a government

40

motor pool and the maid to a commercial laundry. Dellaphine and Mrs Knox ran the boarding house themselves, but the four of us boarders were more than happy to pitch in. We lived in tall cotton compared to most of our fellow war-workers in Washington.

As a genuine country girl I was in charge of the chicken coop and the Victory garden. On the back stoop I took off my shoes, put a straw hat on my head, poured corn into an empty coffee can and padded out into the yard. The dirt was hot and dry under my bare feet. I stopped at the outdoor spigot, filling a watering can with water. Though it rained most evenings, it wasn't enough to keep the garden green and growing in this heat.

Since I grew up in coastal North Carolina I had plenty of experience with heat and humidity, but I couldn't remember a June this withering even on the Cape Fear River. Heat waves shimmered over the facades of granite and limestone government buildings. The waters of the Potomac River, crowded with yachts, sailboats and houseboats docked two-deep, most serving as living quarters, lay still and reflective as a mirror. Men looked swell in white linen suits for about an hour after they dressed, until the linen sagged into wrinkles and dust coated their shoes. Squirrels gathered in the shade of the White House porte-cochere, splayed on their bellies, panting, not moving until Fala

41

was nearly upon them. One Sunday I'd read in the *Washington Post* that the British Foreign Office classified Washington as a tropical hardship post, which allowed the British ambassador, Lord Halifax, to wear khaki shorts and a pith helmet like his colleagues in South-east Asia and Africa. Fortunately for his dignity and ours, he demurred. A grainy newspaper photograph showed him going about his duties stiff-upper-lipped in a dark suit.

I rattled the door of the chicken coop, built in the shade of one of the pecan trees by Joe and Henry before I came to town, sending the chickens running and clucking to the other end of the wire enclosure. Once inside the coop I scattered corn on the ground and filled the water pan. Dellaphine collected enough eggs for breakfast and baking every day, and recently we'd been thinking about raising some chicks, too, because of rumors of food shortages.

I pumped water three more times from the well and toted it to the garden, drenching tomatoes, okra, beans and squash. I collected a few ripe tomatoes and went back to the house, washing my feet at the back door with a bucket of water I'd saved for that purpose.

'That brings back memories,' Joe said, in his fluent but accented English.

I hadn't noticed Joe lounging on a kitchen chair, his thumb between the pages of a book, in the shade of the house near the back door, and started.

'Sorry,' he said, 'I didn't mean to startle you. Seeing you reminded me of my grandfather's farm outside Prague. The milkmaids always washed their feet before coming into the kitchen with their pails.'

When I'd first met Joe I instantly thought he looked exactly like I'd always imagined Jo March's professor husband Fritz Bhaer from *Little Men* looked, except younger. He had jet-black hair and a neat beard, wore thick rimless eyeglasses and carried a handsome gold pocket watch on an intricate fob even when he lounged around the house in baggy flannels.

Joe didn't talk much about his past, except for an occasional remark like the one he'd made about his grandfather's farm. I did know he'd grown up in England and taught Slavic languages at George Washington University.

Henry Post, the other male boarder who shared a room with Joe on the third floor of the house, was positive Joe was a Commie pinko, all these refugees Roosevelt's crowd let into the country were. I didn't know if that was true, but I'd be Red, too, I thought, if the world had stood by and let Hitler occupy my country.

'Have you been out here long?' I asked.

'Oh, yes,' he said, 'watching you go about your pastoral duties.'

Don't blush, I told myself, don't blush. Joe

43

came out here to relax and read, not to admire you. You're way past admiring age. I took off my straw hat and stowed the watering can under a bench. Dark, heat-generated clouds had begun to gather to the south, so Joe followed me inside, bringing the chair with him and restoring it to its place at the kitchen table.

'After spending all day inside a classroom it was nice to be outside for a bit, even in this heat,' he said.

Dellaphine was downstairs changing for her Friday night women's sewing circle at the Gethsemane Baptist Church, so I washed the tomatoes and left them on the drain board.

'Want to go out to get something to eat?' Joe asked.

'Too hot, too crowded,' I said. 'And it looks like it might rain. I was going to make a sandwich. Want one?'

Dellaphine appeared at the door wearing a flowered shirtwaist dress, carrying her piece bag in one hand and white patent-leather pocketbook in the other.

'You all can have some of the leftover ham,' she said. 'And there's bread in the bread box. Miz Phoebe is upstairs in bed with a sick headache.' Phoebe Knox's two sons served in the navy somewhere in the Pacific, we didn't know exactly where. 'Miss Ada's playing at a tea dance,' Dellaphine continued. 'And I don't know where Mr Henry is.'

'I expect he stopped somewhere to eat, since you don't cook for us on Friday nights,' Joe said, teasing her. 'What we're paying forty dollars a month for I don't know.'

Dellaphine snorted. 'You be lucky to get Sunday dinner,' she said. 'I wouldn't whine no more if I was you.'

After Dellaphine left I fixed ham and tomato sandwiches, which Joe and I ate with leftover Waldorf salad made the right way, with lots of apples, nuts, raisins and Duke's mayonnaise, and tall glasses of cold milk. After we finished Joe took our plates and glasses over to the sink and washed them. He was the only man I knew who'd ever washed a dish. The first time I saw him do it I just plain gaped.

Whenever Joe and I were alone, I had a heightened awareness of him that was almost electric, like the tingle I felt looking out over a rough ocean before a thunderstorm. I'd never felt that way before, not even with my husband, although I told myself that was because I'd known Bill since we were children.

That must be what made Joe different from my husband, from any other fellows I'd had crushes on. Bill had been just a boy, and I only a girl, really, even when we married. Joe was a man. And I was now a grown woman, away from my family's, my neighbors' and my church's watchful eyes, emancipated by my widowhood and my move to Washington.

I didn't know what to make of my feelings and had no reason to think Joe noticed them. Besides, this, whatever it was, infatuation, desire, maybe just curiosity, embarrassed me. I flushed, wondering if everyone else in the boarding house noticed that Joe affected me so.

When alone, silence tended to fall between us. I never knew what to talk about with Joe. He was so well educated and worldly it tied my tongue, though he wasn't a bit conceited. I felt sorry for him, too, what with what was going on in Europe. Only yesterday we'd gotten news of a second Czech village burned to the ground by the Nazis in retaliation for harboring enemy agents. That made me think of Rachel and her family, and I had to remind myself to put them out of my mind, for the sake of my sanity. I'd done what I could for them.

Joe rescued us from silence.

'Want to go into the sitting room and listen to the radio?' he asked. 'Kate Smith is on. I've had enough news for a while.'

'Sure,' I said, 'but then I'll have to knit. I pity the GI who has to wear a pair of socks I've made.'

'It won't matter, as long as they're warm.'

A crack of lightning shook the house, and the heavens opened, discharging the moisture that saturated the air during the day. A few minutes later Henry Post burst into the kitchen, furling his umbrella.

'That was close,' he said.

'Have you had supper?' I asked. 'There's ham and stuff in the refrigerator,' I added quickly, so he wouldn't think I was offering to fix him something. Damn it, I paid the same rent Henry did and he could make his own sandwiches, the same as the rest of us.

'I've eaten,' he said. 'I waited in line at a diner for an hour. There was only one waitress. It was all she could do to take everyone's order. We had to pick up our own plates from the kitchen.'

Ada Herman and I lived on the second floor of Mrs Knox's boarding house, in Milt Jr. and Tom Knox's old bedrooms. We shared the floor's single bathroom with their mother, Phoebe Knox, who occupied the large master bedroom at the front of the house. Mrs Knox must have had some money left after the Depression, even though her husband tragically drowned – Phoebe's euphemism for his suicide – the day after the stock market crashed, because she managed to keep the house and raise her sons. And she could have squeezed twice the boarders she had into her home. Both Ada and I could have room-mates if we moved the boys' desks out of our rooms. Joe and Henry shared an old servant's room on the third floor, but the box room and cedar closet on the same floor could be converted to bedrooms. Joe and Henry's room had a cold-water sink, I figured, because the pipe that fed it ran up a corner of my room, near my bed. I didn't believe there was a full bathroom up there because both men took their baths in the copper tub in the laundry room, and I think they shared a chemical toilet. I'd seen one or the other of them carrying a pot out to the old outhouse on several early mornings.

Dellaphine's bedroom and bathroom, which she shared with her daughter Madeleine, were in the daylight half of the basement. The laundry was in the dark half at the front of the house. The Knox house was at the end of the block, so it had a porch and a bigger yard than its neighbors. I didn't know how anyone could live without a screened porch. If it weren't for the men, I'd sleep out there every night.

I was almost asleep when Ada came in, too late to fire up her record player, thank goodness. I was a fan of Frank Sinatra, who wasn't, but I'd heard 'Blue Skies' enough to last me the rest of my life.

After last night's rain shower it was cool on the porch, where I sat drinking coffee and eating a biscuit spread thinly with some of Dellaphine's last pot of home-made strawberry jam. The ceiling fan turned slowly overhead. I resolved to have a quiet day, stay

48

out of the heat, read *Five Little Pigs*, maybe fix myself a grilled cheese and tomato sandwich for lunch. And on Saturday night everyone in the house knew the radio in the sitting room was mine. *The Grand Ole Opry* was my only relief from Glenn Miller and his kind. Not that I didn't like swing and jazz, it's just that I missed hillbilly music.

Ada slammed the porch door behind her. Ada was a busty woman in her thirties with platinum-blonde hair arranged in a long pompadour she often contained in a snood. She never left her room without make-up, and always wore a dress, never trousers or a houscoat. She clipped her nails short to hide her nail-biting habit.

Ada came to Washington from New York City to play the clarinet with the house band at the Willard Hotel. Rumor had it that girl musicians made eighty-five dollars a week. I almost believed it, what with the number of cocktail dresses and record albums Ada owned. She often stayed out at night long after her set was over, and had gone through several beaux since I'd arrived six months ago. Henry swore she was a divorcée.

Ada flapped the morning newspaper at me.

'Guess what's happening today!' Without letting me answer, she burst out. 'Marlene Dietrich! She's going to be at Jelleff's this afternoon! We have to go!'

'Dearie,' I said, 'I'm not going anywhere

49

today. It's too hot.'

'Louise, we could meet Marlene Dietrich in person! All we have to do is buy a war bond! Besides, Jelleff's is refrigerated.'

'Not outside, where we'd be standing in line for hours, it isn't,' I said. 'I admire Miss Dietrich very much, but you'll have to go without me.'

'I swear, I'll never understand you,' Ada said, shaking her head. 'Oh, well.' She stood up, eyeing my empty plate. 'Is there any strawberry jam left?'

'One jar. Dellaphine says we can have a teaspoon each. And are you done with the paper? I haven't read it yet.'

'Can I tear out Miss Dietrich's picture? Maybe she'll autograph it for me. There's just a Safeway ad on the back.'

Ada left me with most of the newspaper and went off to the kitchen to fix her breakfast.

I opened the newspaper, where a headline on the front page caught my eye. 'Tragic Death in Foggy Bottom', it read. The story left me immobile with shock.

One Robert Holman had died of a heart attack in his office at an unnamed government agency early yesterday evening.

FOUR

I was so jolted I couldn't bring myself to finish reading the newspaper story. Instead I went into the kitchen for another cup of coffee to bolster my courage, adding sugar even though I had used all I should today. Back on the porch, while drinking my coffee and watching a trio of hummingbirds busy at Phoebe's bee balm, I tried, without success, to convince myself I'd misread the news article. After finishing my coffee I picked up the paper again.

According to the newspaper, Holman's wife, who'd been waiting for him with their children in the family car to go away for the weekend, discovered his body and raised an alarm. Must have been quite an alarm, I reflected, for word of a death at the OSS offices to find its way into the newspaper, even if OSS hadn't been identified by name.

How terrible, I thought, for Holman's wife, his children and anyone still in the office when the body was found.

Morbidly the article dwelled on the disheveled state of Holman's office, a file cabinet overturned, the desktop swept clean, papers and files tumbled onto the floor. The man must have thrashed about mightily as he died, perhaps struggling to get to his telephone or out into the hall. His corpse lay spreadeagled on the floor, in the midst of a heap of papers. Poor man.

I read the story twice before I absorbed the news and accepted it. Bob Holman was dead. My boss. I had seen him, what, an hour, two hours before he died? Stupidly, I felt saddened that the man had died before enjoying his weekend on the Potomac.

Bob's funeral was tomorrow, only two days after he died. That was fast. Of course, it was extremely hot this summer and ice was in short supply.

Ada Herman slowed her pace, pausing to check out the feature at the movie house on the corner of Pennsylvania and 21st – Walt Disney's latest cartoon, *Kipling's Jungle Book* – waiting for exactly the right moment to turn down the street towards her boarding house. During the week it wasn't difficult to intercept the mail. It came on the dot of ten o'clock in the morning, when everyone else was at work and Phoebe and Dellaphine were busy around the house. Ada worked afternoons and evenings so she was free to linger around the front door until the mail dropped through the slot. She'd quickly riffle through the envelopes before depositing the stack on the hall table. Sometimes Phoebe, hearing the mail drop, would rush to see if she had a letter from one of her sons, and wait impatiently until Ada was through.

Ada had told him never to write her again, never ever, and he hadn't so far, but every day she lived in terror that a letter bearing a foreign stamp addressed to her would arrive before she could hide it from the others in the boarding house. She endured a recurring nightmare that Phoebe, or Louise, or worst of all, Henry, got to the mail before her, and asked her why she received a letter with a return address in German.

Ada checked her watch. It was still too early. She crossed Pennsylvania and stopped at a cafe to look at the menu posted in the window. Tonight diners could choose from either fried chicken or liver and onions, with mashed potatoes and peas, and fruit salad, iced tea or hot coffee. A few people queued outside, waiting for the cafe to open.

On Saturday mail delivery was sporadic. It came any time in the afternoon when her fellow roomers tended to be in the house. She'd missed it many times, but so far her luck held. That didn't stop her from trying to get to it first whenever she could.

Ada cut through the block by way of a vacant lot and an alley and found herself across the street from her boarding house. Henry was out in front, his suspenders hanging down his sides, flipping through the mail. She was too late. He saw her, and raised his hand.

Head swimming with apprehension, she crossed the street.

'You need to look before you cross the street, young lady,' Henry said. 'You could get hit by one of these jalopies, people drive too damn fast these days.'

'Anything for me?' she asked.

'Nope,' he said. 'Not today.'

I didn't mention Holman's death to anyone. I didn't want to talk about it yet.

Ada returned from Jelleff's, thrilled with Marlene Dietrich's autograph. 'Miss Dietrich was so elegant,' Ada said, 'and so sweet. Sort of reserved, though, and not as tall as I thought she'd be.' She paused. 'Are you all right, dearie? You're awfully quiet.'

'Just tired and hot,' I said.

After dinner I skipped *The Grand Ole Opry*, pleading a headache. Upstairs in my room I stretched out on my bed to read my Christie novel, but found a few pages after I started that I hadn't comprehended any of it. I'd have to start over again. Instead I gave up and closed the book, tossing it onto my bedside table. The brass bookmark flew out from between its pages and slammed into the cold-water pipe that led to the sink in the attic. The bookmark was a thick, heavy rectangle I received as a prize for reading the most books in the sixth grade, and I must have flung the book, and the bookmark, rather hard, because the clang of brass against iron pipe resounded like a bell ringing. I hopped off the bed and retrieved the bookmark and stuck it back between the pages of my book. A minute later, I heard the echo of object on pipe sound above me, three taps, equally spaced, like Morse code. Someone in the bedroom upstairs was responding to me, striking the pipe with a metal object. Had to be Joe, Henry would never do such a thing.

I was mortified. Could Joe be thinking I'd signaled him intentionally? Please, no! What would he think of me, that I was flirting with him? I lay back on my bed, a pillow over my face to hide the heat of embarrassment surging into my face, even though no one else was in the room.

Don't answer back, I instructed myself firmly. If you don't respond, he'll know it wasn't intentional. A few minutes passed while my heart rate slowed. Okay, I was in the clear. But then another two clangs reverberated into the room. I couldn't help myself. I grabbed the brass bookmark and tapped back, twice. He responded, with one tap, and I echoed it, concluding our peculiar goodnight.

I was still mortified, but I convinced myself I shouldn't be, that our conversation by water pipe was a friendly, silly gesture, that neither one of us intended it to be flirtatious. Otherwise I wouldn't be able to look Joe in the face in the morning.

I slid into bed, the worn cotton sheets soft on my bare skin. I wondered if Joe was sleeping naked tonight, too.

FIVE

I spent a restless night, tossing and turning even after I again hung damp sheets between my bedposts and trained the fan on them, disturbed by worries more serious than what Joe thought of me. I brooded over mortality, the heartache of my husband's early death, Bob's heart attack, and I wondered how his wife and children would live. His wife wanted to work, and it looked like she'd get her chance. At least there were jobs for women now. During the Depression a man's death often left his family destitute.

Finally my thoughts turned to Rachel and her family. I recalled the newspaper story about the disheveled state of Holman's office, and I fretted over the whereabouts, in that jumbled office, of Gerald Bloch's file.

'We should have eaten more of the ham,' Joe joked, as he helped himself to creamed ham and peas before passing the platter.

Phoebe Knox, from her place at the head

of the table, dotted her plate with tiny servings of ham and peas, squash and sliced tomatoes. She'd left her room for the first time all weekend to go to church this morning, hiding her swollen eyes by drawing down the netting of her pillbox hat to hide her face.

'The real question is, what's for dessert?' Ada asked, reaching for the breadbasket for a second biscuit. I pushed the butter dish down the table towards her without being asked. It puzzled me that Ada wasn't fat. Must be all that late-night jitterbugging.

'You do realize,' Henry said, 'that there're no actual food shortages in the country, or gas shortages either. The government wants you to think there are, all the while using the gasoline for military purposes.'

'It amounts to the same thing, doesn't it?' I asked. 'Better the gasoline goes to the military than shipping fresh food all over the country.'

'It's not efficient,' Henry said. 'Not organized. The Democrats can't win this war. Roosevelt will have to bring in Republicans to run the agencies. You wait and see.'

General Bill Donovan, the Director of OSS, was a Republican. I hadn't noticed that he was better organized than anyone else. Not to mention President Hoover, who'd organized us right into the Depression.

'I don't mind missing dessert for years, if

57

that's what it takes,' Phoebe said.

'Not everyone is making the same sacrifices,' Henry said. 'That's what I resent. I'll bet you a dollar that roast beef and chocolate cake are on the menus at the Cosmo Club and the Willard Hotel tonight.'

'You're not living at the Willard,' Phoebe reminded him. 'We have to eat up our leftovers.'

Dellaphine shoved the dining-room door open with her hip and came in with a tray.

'Dellaphine,' Joe said, scraping the last of the ham and peas onto his plate, 'dinner was delicious. And those peaches look great.'

'Don't be flirting with me, Mr Joe,' Dellaphine said, holding the bowl for Phoebe to dish out the peaches into cut-glass bowls. 'There ain't no sugar.'

'Not even just a teaspoonful to sprinkle over the fruit?' Ada asked.

'Not even that,' Dellaphine said, the dining-room door swinging shut behind her.

I liked the peaches fine without sugar, myself.

'So,' Phoebe said, too brightly, 'what's everyone doing this afternoon?'

Henry intended to read the newspapers, Ada planned to wash her hair and take a nap and Joe said he had tests to grade.

'I'm going to a wake,' I said.

'Who died?' Joe asked.

'A man I worked with,' I said. 'It was in the paper yesterday.'

58

'Where is it? The wake, I mean,' Phoebe asked.

'A funeral home near Griffith Stadium.'

'Good luck finding a taxi,' Ada said.

'I've got a ride.'

I still owned the black dress I'd bought when Bill died. It was quality, cotton pique with a Peter Pan collar, and I saw no need to get rid of it because I wore it to my husband's funeral. I wasn't sentimental that way. Not that I didn't still get a catch in my throat when I thought of Bill. It was funny, we had been childhood sweethearts, and when I remembered him now, it was as a sunburned boy catching crabs off my parents' pier, not as the serious young Wells Fargo telegrapher I'd married. I'd hated moving out of the two-room apartment over the telegraph office we'd shared and back into my old bedroom at my parents' house, but there was no money left in our shoebox bank after I'd bought this dress and paid for the funeral. Now I made more than sixteen hundred dollars a year, myself, more than Bill dreamed of earning.

When I recalled the end of my brief marriage it was as if I was watching a sad movie, poignant and moving, but not immediate. In the five years since Bill died the world had become a different place, and I was a different person.

I fastened a single strand of cultured pearls

59

around my neck. I'd bought it shortly after I'd gotten my pay raise at OSS, and I'd felt horribly guilty at the time. They'd cost eleven dollars and seventy-five cents, seven dollars less than a twenty-five-dollar war bond. But owning my own pearls meant so much to me I had to have them. They reminded me of the first time I met Rachel...

All thirty-seven of us, the entering 1933 class of St Martha's Junior College, had lined up against the hallway wall, waiting to have our pictures taken. Each, as directed, wore a dark dress with a white lace collar. We'd washed and styled our hair, dusted our shiny faces with powder and gently blotted our red lips. We were like peas in a pod, with one glaring, shameful exception. The night before at dinner when the dean instructed us on what to wear for our photographs, she ended her remarks with 'don't forget your pearls'. Well, I didn't have any. I was the only girl at St Martha's who hadn't gotten a string, symbolic of reaching upper-class womanhood, on her sixteenth birthday. I wasn't a member of that social class. And there'd be a record of my low standing for all time preserved in the pages of the St Martha's Junior College 1933 yearbook. All the other girls decked out in pearls, while I wore my only necklace, a silver locket. I resented being set apart, spotlighted for all time as the middle-class girl.

Not that anyone seemed to care. All the

60

girls were chatting and primping, and included me in their silliness. If they didn't notice, why should I? But I did. I was the one who'd look like the charity case as long as yearbook paper lasted. Not to mention the big group portrait the photographer would make up, the one with each of our pictures in little ovals, that would go in the foyer of the Main Hall.

My maiden name started with 'S', Rachel's with an 'F', so she was done already. She leaned up against the opposite wall, chatting with the other girls who'd finished, waiting for us all to be done so we could file into dinner together.

Mary Orr went into the front drawing room, where the photographer had set up his tripod, lights and screen. I was next. And I was miserable.

Rachel appeared by my side, her own double strand of real pearls dangling from her hand. 'Dearie,' she said, 'here, wear these. Then we'll all be the same.' She fastened the diamond clasp around my neck. The pearls, cool and smooth, rested comfortably on my skin as I posed, head up and shoulders back, for my class photograph.

Remembering Rachel's kindness made me wonder again what had happened to Gerald's file since Bob Holman's death. Was it sent upstairs to the Projects Committee before he died? Was it lying on his office

61

floor? Had someone cleaned up and taken it back to the main files? I thought I'd been so clever getting Holman to refer it upstairs, congratulated myself for helping Rachel. Now I had no idea where the file was. I had to find out, I couldn't let it go. I owed Rachel so much, much more than the loan of a string of pearls.

I heard Joan's car horn as I finished tilting a black straw fedora at a fashionable angle and securing it to my hair with a hatpin. I'd called Joan yesterday afternoon. She was just as upset, and all right, I admit it, curious about Holman's death as I was. We conspired to go to the wake together and pick up as much information about his unfortunate demise as we could.

Joan Adams was one of General Donovan's two personal secretaries. She'd graduated from Smith College, so she fit in with the rest of Donovan's swank circle. We'd met in the security office on our first day at work, sharing a grimy towel after we had our fingerprints taken. We'd sworn the oath of secrecy together, and listened to the security officer's lecture. 'Remember,' he'd said, 'this town is crawling with spies. Anyone asks, you're a government file clerk, that's all. You keep your mouths shut about every single thing that goes on here, no matter how trivial, or people might die.'

Despite her family's wealth, Joan had no pretensions. Our first week in Washington

62

she'd invited me up to her apartment in the Mayflower Hotel for cocktails and to listen to records with her crowd. Thanks to my Southern Baptist upbringing, I'd never touched a drop of liquor before, but that afternoon I learned to like Martinis. Not that I drank them often. Too expensive. I splurged often enough to feel worldly and sophisticated.

The price of Martinis was not a concern for Joan. She got a hundred dollar a month allowance from her parents, in addition to her salary, which is why she picked me up in a green Lincoln Continental cabriolet. I'd only ever driven my parents' Ford Model A pickup. One of my secret fantasies was to own a car one day.

The coffin was closed, which surprised me, I must say. I knew the Holmans were Baptists, and Baptists do like to wring their hands over their dead. The widow, a short sturdy woman with salt-and-pepper hair, stood next to the coffin, resting a hand on it, while she received her guests. I didn't see Holman's children. Maybe his widow thought they were too young to attend his wake.

The room was crowded with familiar faces, but I didn't recognize anyone senior to our branch director, James Baxter Linney, once the President of Williams College. A scattering of army and navy officers wearing a respectable amount of chest hardware represented our agency's bosses, the Joint Chiefs of Staff. And I was sure the two men standing alone near the front door were FBI agents. You could spot G-men anywhere. They wore dark suits, white shirts and ties no matter the occasion or time of day. Hoover forbade his agents to drink coffee or alcohol or to accept meals, so they stuck out like sore thumbs when everyone else in the place held a plate and a glass. One of the agents, the one who seemed to be in charge, did manage to express some individuality. A tiny yellow feather poked out from his hatband.

I saw Don across the room with Roger Austine and Guy Danielson, who for once seemed to be speaking civilly to each other, and Charles Burns, the head of the Map Division. Don looked very surprised to see me. He nodded at me briefly before turning his attention back to the other three men.

Joan and I joined the receiving line behind Dora Bertrand, an anthropologist from the Far East Division who was the only woman at the wake who wasn't either a clerk or someone's wife. She was the first woman I'd ever met who had a PhD.

Dora told us she'd been in the office when Holman's wife found his body. We pried as many details as we could from her, keeping our voices lowered out of consideration of the somber occasion.

Dora whispered that she'd run down to

Holman's office when she heard his wife screaming, closely followed by Austine, Don and Danielson. 'The four of us were reviewing a report that General Donovan wanted to read over the weekend. That's why we were working late.' She'd seen the corpse and everything. 'He couldn't have been dead long,' she said. 'We'd all seen him alive within the last couple of hours or so.'

'It's not surprising he had a heart attack, as fat as the man was,' Joan said. 'His face was always red. That's a sure sign of a heart problem.'

'I'm amazed his death got into the newspaper,' I said. 'What with it happening at OSS and all. You'd think the government would have suppressed it.'

'When Mr Holman's wife screamed, well, the best word to describe it was piercing,' Dora said. 'Most of the civilian staff had gone home for the day, but security came running from everywhere. Our guards arrived first, then soldiers from the bivouac on Navy Hill, then the Capitol police, then the FBI. The soldiers kept us out in the hallway, but the office door was open and we could see Holman's body.'

'What happened next?' Joan urged.

'I'm not supposed to talk about it,' Dora said, lowering her voice, 'but I will say that when the FBI appeared, two agents and a deputy special agent, they ran off our security and the police. In fact,' she said, lowering

65

her voice even more, 'that agent over there, the one with the yellow feather in his hat band, he's the deputy special agent who was on the scene. Roger, Guy, Don and I had to stay at the office to be interviewed. For hours, without dinner. I about starved.'

'Was General Donovan there?'

'Sure. And Dr Linney. Watching the G-men's every move,' Dora said. 'It was quite entertaining. You'd never guess we were all on the same side.'

Dora was a socialist, but General Donovan made it clear he didn't care what anyone's political inclinations were as long as he or she could help defeat the Nazis. The same couldn't be said for everyone in the office. Generally speaking the economists were Marxists, the administrators were dollar-a-year Republicans and the historians, and most everyone else, were New Dealers. The foreigners at OSS ranged from exiled European royalty to Communists. If it weren't for the war they wouldn't be caught dead in the same room with each other.

'Around ten o'clock,' Dora went on, 'General Donovan came and told us that we could all go home, that the doctor had said that Mr Holman died from a heart attack.'

We stopped gossiping as we drew near to the head of the line. When it was my turn to speak to Mrs Holman, she gripped my proffered hand firmly. She looked tired, but her eyes were clear.

'So sorry about your husband,' I murmured. I really was. Even though I hadn't been close to the man. No one, especially someone with young children, should have to die in the prime of his life.

'Thank you, dear,' she said, but she didn't ask how I knew her husband, and her attention had already moved on to the next person in line.

Dora, Joan and I returned to the buffet. No one ignored free food in Washington, especially on a Sunday, when many restaurants were closed and boarding houses often didn't serve meals. Mine was an exception, but I still wouldn't get dinner at 'Two Trees' that night.

Joan reached over the platter of deviled eggs for a ham biscuit. She was a big woman, over six feet tall, with an appetite to match. She had a deep, easy laugh and a jolly sense of humor, which might explain why she had lots of friends but no beaux.

Dora left us to join a group of the branch researchers across the room.

'She has to watch herself,' Joan said. 'Can't hang out with us clerks too much. Doesn't want to be taken for one herself.'

'I admire her so much,' I said. 'She's got a real career. Of course she's not married, she couldn't do both.'

'You don't want to spread it around how much you admire her,' Joan said. 'You know she's a lesbian, don't you?'

'A what?' I asked.

Joan pulled me aside and explained.

'Good God,' I said. I knew there were men like that, but I'd never heard of a woman doing such a thing. 'How do you know?'

'It's not a secret. She taught at Smith before the war. I took her class on Asian cultures. I was shocked at first, but now we're great friends.' I glanced over at Dora. She didn't look like a pervert. She was a tiny woman with short coal-black hair and thick glasses, thicker than mine even, but a lovely smile.

'I want another ham biscuit,' Joan said. We went back to the buffet and reloaded our plates.

'Were you particularly close to Mr Holman?' Joan asked.

I took a chance on her discretion.

'Not really, but I left some important information with him the afternoon he died. I'm worried about what became of it. I read in the newspaper what a mess his office was.'

'How important is this information?'

'It's hard to say. Mr Holman seemed to think it should go to the Projects Committee.' I paused, wondering if I dared tell Joan about Rachel.

Joan noticed my hesitation.

'We can't talk about it here,' she said. 'You'll be in the cafeteria for coffee break tomorrow?'

'Probably,' I said. 'If my girls have recovered from food poisoning by then.'

The crowd thinned quickly, but the widow didn't seem to mind. She took her hand off her husband's coffin and breathed a sigh of relief.

All the mourners leaving the wake murmured about paperwork they had to get back to, but I knew better. The Washington Senators and Detroit Tigers game was about to start.

'Can you come over to my place for the rest of the afternoon?' Joan asked me. 'I've invited Charles and Dora too.'

'Sure,' I said. 'That would be fun.'

The funeral director mopped his face and under his arms with a damp towel. He was sure his shirt was ruined, the second one this week. He'd been a nervous wreck since Bob Holman's corpse arrived at his funeral home escorted by two FBI agents. He glanced out the window. The same two agents sat in a black Packard that waited at the curb, engine running, poised to follow the hearse to the cemetery for the deceased's burial. There wouldn't be a church funeral as such, only a minister speaking a few words at the gravesite. It'd had been like that since the country had gotten into this war. Not enough time or gasoline to drive all over town for separate services.

He'd embalmed and arranged Holman's corpse exactly as the G-men had instructed him, obscuring all evidence of the wound at the base of his neck. It was barely visible anyway. Puncture wounds closed quickly, leaking only a trickle of blood. He'd caked foundation a quarter of an inch deep over the mark and powdered it liberally, dressed him and settled the man's head into the deep folds of the thick silk pillow in the coffin.

Holman's widow was the last person to leave. The mortuary assistants lifted the heavy coffin onto a gurney, rolled it out to the curb and heaved it into the hearse. The vehicle pulled away from the curb, trailed by the G-men a few car lengths behind. He'd be glad when Holman was safely planted six feet deep. Then maybe he'd stop ruining shirts.

SIX

I'd visited Joan's studio apartment at the Mayflower Hotel a few times before. I wished I lived there and owned everything in it, from the Pullman davenport that opened into a bed, to the club chairs slip-covered in blue-flowered chintz, to the sculpted wool rug that perfectly matched the chintz, to the mahogany sideboard that held a china coffee service and a silver cocktail set. There was even a tiny kitchenette set into an alcove. A crystal chandelier that blazed with light hung from the ceiling, highlighting ornate Federal ceiling moldings. The apartment was refrigerated, but today Joan had left the tall casement windows open wide to a view of Pennsylvania Avenue.

The bathroom looked like something out of a Greta Garbo movie. It was lined, floor, walls and ceiling, with white marble, and spacious enough to accommodate the walnut vanity that matched the dresser in the other room.

Bill and I had lived in a tiny apartment over the Wells Fargo office where he worked, but it was nothing like this, and it wasn't really ours.

I'd been taught in Sunday school not to covet. Well, I coveted Joan's apartment and her car. And it was clear to me that living that well depended on money. I figured that to live on my own like Joan I needed to make twenty-five hundred dollars a year, and I wondered what on earth I could do to earn that kind of dough. Nothing, I shouldn't think. Another good argument for remarrying before I got too old to find a husband, I supposed.

Joan took my hat and hung it alongside hers on a coat rack near the door. She stuffed her pajamas, they were silk, I believe, into a dresser drawer, and rang the front desk for ice.

71

'What do you think about gin and tonics?' Joan asked. 'So refreshing in this heat.'

'Sounds great,' I said.

A knock on the door signaled the arrival of the ice. I quartered limes while Joan dumped peanuts into a silver compote and wiped down the cocktail table.

Dora Bertrand and Charles Burns arrived together. Burns was a tall, handsome man with an upper-class Yankee accent like Don's. He had a thin David Niven mustache. I'd run across him many times at work but didn't know him well. As a division head he was senior to the rest of us.

'Bless you,' he said to Joan, who greeted him with a gin and tonic. 'So nice to be here. Otherwise I'd be forced to listen to the baseball game with my room-mates. I don't know why, I just don't care for the sport. You ladies don't mind if I take off my jacket, do you?'

'Not at all, be comfortable,' Joan said. 'What's going to happen, I wonder, if all the baseball players get drafted?'

'I hear talk that women might form professional teams,' Dora said.

Charles lounged on Joan's davenport, and took a gulp of his drink.

'How silly,' he said. 'No one wants to watch women play sports. There some things women can do adequately while the men are at war, but not that.'

'I can't say I'd want to watch women play

72

baseball myself,' Joan said.

I wondered why Charles wasn't in the army, he looked healthy enough to me, but I decided that he might be too old. Or perhaps OSS needed his expertise.

'What shall we do?' Joan asked. 'Bridge? Monopoly? Chinese checkers?'

We settled on Monopoly.

Dora and I set up the board while Charles found a music program on the radio. Joan refreshed our drinks and we settled down to while away the afternoon. When we selected our tokens I reached for the red one. I saw a bemused look flit across Dora's face.

'What?' I said.

'My dear, you surprise me. I would never have guessed you would choose red. I took you for a blue person, maybe green.'

'Do you want the red one? You can have it.'

She shook her head. 'Don't give it up,' she said. 'Yellow is fine with me.'

We finished our drinks, had another, and concentrated on accumulating real estate. Inevitably, though, our conversation turned back to Bob Holman's death.

'I saw him,' Charles said, 'a couple of hours before his wife found him. He seemed the same as always to me.'

'He was terribly overworked,' Dora said. 'He slept at the office several nights a week.' She threw a six and moved her pawn to Park Place. 'This is the last time you see this block without houses, so be warned.'

'It's a mistake to spend all your money at the beginning of the game,' Charles said. 'What happens if you have to pay rent and you're broke?'

'I always buy the purple or green properties if I land on them,' Dora said, 'because one always passes "Go" shortly and collects two hundred dollars. I'll take two houses, please.'

'Did you see the corpse?' I asked Charles.

He shook his head. 'No. I'd already left for the day. Read about it in the newspaper.'

'Me, too. But Dora was there.'

'Was she?' Charles asked, glancing at her. Dora said nothing, counting her money.

'That must have been a shocking experience for you,' Charles said to Dora.

She shrugged, not rising to the bait.

I opened my mouth to speak again, but Joan noticed and gently nudged my foot. Okay, so I had asked Dora enough questions at the funeral home. I wished she would be more specific. I wanted to know exactly who had gotten to Holman's office when, so I could figure out who might have seen the Bloch file.

'I believe I've had enough gin for this afternoon,' Charles said. 'Can I get myself some water, Joan?'

'Of course,' Joan said. Charles sauntered over to the sideboard as if he owned the place and poured himself a glass of water from a cut-glass pitcher. He didn't ask if we wanted any, but we were still working on our highballs.

'Good Lord,' he said, when he returned, scanning the game board. Dora had acquired the most property, with Joan a distant second. I'd landed on both the income tax and luxury tax, not to mention going to jail twice, so I might as well be living in a Hooverville. Charles still had lots of cash, which was a good thing since he would need it to pay Dora's exorbitant rents.

While Charles pondered his strategy, Joan casually asked Dora the question I'd wanted to earlier.

'The newspaper said Mr Holman's office was a mess.'

'It looked like a tornado had struck it,' Dora said. 'Mr Holman didn't die tidily. He must have pulled the desk over, and he was face down, spreadeagled on the floor. Papers everywhere.'

Dora had us beat at Monopoly, and we all knew it by now.

Charles's failure to trounce us embarrassed him.

'Well,' he said, scanning the board. 'You girls aren't bad at this game. I should have been playing closer attention.' As if Charles lost because he neglected to play to his usual manly standard, the jerk!

Dora ignored him, quietly sorting her stacks of money and returning it to the Monopoly box.

The afternoon had passed comfortably, and now the sun angled low in the sky, pouring intense light into the room. Joan pulled the curtains closed to keep the glare out of our faces. Charles leaned back in his chair and took a cigarette out of a chased silver case. Dora fumbled in her purse for her packet of Lucky Strikes, and Joan reached for her cigarette box on the coffee table, but Charles insisted they each take one of his. They were elegant, quite long, with gold-wrapped filter tips, Sobranies, I think. He offered me one, but I demurred.

'Quite wise,' Dora said. 'Nasty things. Can't be healthy.'

Charles held his lighter for Dora first, then Joan. In that instant I saw Joan look at Charles with an interest that he didn't notice, much less return. I realized that Dora and I were there to chaperone Joan and Charles, without Charles's having a clue, and I felt sorry for Joan.

'Must go,' Charles said. 'The baseball game should be over, and I can return to my apartment and read the Sunday paper in peace. I'll have to find supper somewhere, unless one of my room-mates decides to scramble eggs. I don't know how to boil water, myself.'

'I'm going to order supper from room service,' Joan said. 'You could stay and eat with me.'

Charles shook his head. 'Thanks, ducks,'

76

he said. 'But I must go. Work tomorrow.'

How humiliating for Joan, I thought, that Charles would rather read his newspaper and eat eggs with his room-mates than have supper with her. She was a lady, though, and gave no indication that he'd hurt her feelings.

Charles said goodbye to all of us and pecked Joan on the cheek at the door.

'I must be going too,' Dora said. 'Gail always cooks a big meal on Sundays and she'll be expecting me.' Gail must be Dora's room-mate? Lover? What?

Pretty soon I'd be so darn worldly and sophisticated, if the folks back home could see me they would shake their heads behind my back, and talk about how I was putting on airs. But maybe they wouldn't be too surprised. I'd always been different. Peculiar, my mother said. More interested in reading than was healthy for a young girl. I remembered well my Great-Aunt Edna, who found me holed up in my room, reading *The Age of Innocence*, instead of outside at a family picnic pitching horseshoes like the rest of the kids. She'd rested her fists on her ample hips and shook her head. 'You're not like the rest of them, are you?' she'd said. I assumed she was being critical of me, until after she died leaving me a small bequest designated for my college tuition. Thanks to the Depression the money shrank until I had enough for just one year.

Joan hugged us both goodbye, but I could tell the afternoon hadn't turned out the way she'd planned.

Outside the hotel we found Charles waiting for us. He dropped his cigarette and ground it out on the sidewalk with his shoe.

'Louise,' he said, ignoring Dora. 'Can I give you a ride home? I've got my car. Perhaps we could find a cafe and have supper?'

I was so shocked I couldn't answer right away. The man had dismissed Joan's invitation, and not five minutes later he was asking me out? I ransacked my brain for a civil answer. I had to be careful what I said, the man was senior to me at OSS. I was expendable, he wasn't.

'Come on,' he said, 'you don't want to walk in this heat. And you've got to eat.'

'I've already offered her a lift,' Dora said, rescuing me. 'We live quite near each other.'

'I must go,' I said to Charles. 'You know how it is. Work tomorrow.'

Dora's car was a Model A, maybe ten years old, but it purred along Pennsylvania Avenue nicely. 'I take care of it myself,' Dora said, 'change the oil, inflate the tires, everything. I hate to rely on some man at a filling station.'

'Do we really live near each other?' I asked.

'You're on "I" Street, aren't you? Close to Washington Square? I've noticed you at the bus stop. I share an apartment with Gail in the Whiteville building.'

Dora and her Gail were two more women who earned enough to keep their own apartment. The place had a real kitchen, too, because Dora had mentioned cooking dinner. I swallowed my envy and changed the subject.

'Charles is a louse,' I said. 'Imagine being so rude to Joan.'

'Women like Joan grow up believing their lives are worthless unless they're married. They imitate their mothers, learning to be deferential and self-deprecating to attract a beau who'll become a husband. And most men behave accordingly, they can't help it, that's what they grew up expecting from women. Remember that remark Joan made about not wanting to watch women play sports? She was the captain of the Smith College field hockey team, for God's sake.'

I didn't say anything, but I thought that Dora could hardly judge Joan. Dora didn't want a husband, but Joan did, very much. Being self-deprecating was a tried-and-true way to attract men. That and having nice legs and a deep cleavage.

SEVEN

Dora dropped me off at my door. 'Come across the street and visit us sometime,' she said.

'Sure,' I said. 'Sometime I will.' And I wouldn't care who knew it, either.

Once inside I went upstairs and changed out of my black dress into blue jeans and a red checked shirt. The usual late-afternoon clouds gathered on the horizon, and I could feel the static electricity lift my hair as I unpinned my hat. Before I left the room I lowered my windows in case it rained, leaving them open a crack and turning on my fan to draw in some cool air.

Phoebe and Dellaphine were in the kitchen at the table planning menus. Grocery-store ads clipped from the newspaper covered the tabletop.

'Let's have beef twice this week,' Phoebe said to Dellaphine. 'Henry's been complaining. Ham once, chicken twice. Unless you see some nice fish.'

There was no such thing as 'nice' fish, in my opinion. They were all slimy and smelly. I'd cleaned and fried enough of them to know.

80

'What should I do about dessert?' Della-phine said. 'Everyone's tired of sliced fruit.'

Phoebe flipped through the pages of her Boston Cooking School cookbook. 'Oh, I don't know,' she said. 'Any ideas, Louise?'

'Can you find coconut?' I said, slipping into another chair at the table. 'It makes fruit taste sweeter.'

'There's always honey,' Dellaphine said. 'It's too close to the end of the month to find marshmallows.'

'I'll tell you what,' Phoebe said, 'see what you can find, coconut, honey, maybe there will be some condensed milk, and cobble together some desserts from that. We'll buy a real cake from a bakery on Thursday and have it Thursday night.' She slammed her cookbook shut.

'I wish this war was over and life would go back the way it was before,' Phoebe said. 'I understand that the men have to fight and girls have to get jobs until the war is over. But I hate all the rest of it. Girls wearing practically no clothes, crazy music, bad language, families living in trailers and tents, single girls living on their own, children growing up in day nurseries, no servants. It's not civilized.'

Phoebe reminded me of my mother – Southern and traditional in her outlook on life.

I'd expected Washington to be strange, even foreign, but except for all the war activity the city didn't feel much different from my hometown of Wilmington, North Carolina. The city's native residents I'd met drank iced tea with lots of sugar and fresh mint, ate fried chicken and ham for Sunday dinner, rocked and fanned themselves on their porches in the summer, inhaling the fragrance of wisteria and gardenia, and gossiped about politics and society with a soft drawl. I could see why, less than a hundred years after the city was founded, Abraham Lincoln stared out of his office in the White House across the Potomac into Virginia, and wondered how many Washingtonians would welcome General Lee with open arms should he invade the city.

These days, with the influx of politicians, soldiers, refugees, diplomats and 'businessmen' any Southerner would straight away spot as carpetbaggers, the city's Southern hospitality was stretched to the limit.

I wandered into the lounge to listen to the radio. Ada stood at the window, peeking outside from behind the dim-out curtain.

'What's up?' I asked.

Ada jumped, placing her hand over her heart.

'You startled me,' she said.

'I'm sorry,' I said. 'What are you looking at?'

'Soldiers across the street. Parked in a Jeep. They've been there for half an hour. What do you suppose they're doing?'

I glanced out the window. 'Smoking a cigarette, I expect, before catching the bus to Fort Myer.'

'They don't need the bus. They've got a Jeep.'

'Maybe they're drinking beer. They can't once they get back to base. Why?'

Ada drew the curtains closed. 'I hate seeing so many soldiers in the streets. It seems like—' She stopped short and glanced at me nervously. 'It's like living in an occupied country.'

'It's just because of the war.'

'I know, but how can we be sure, well, that things will go back to normal someday? I mean what if Roosevelt doesn't ever want to give up the Presidency? All these soldiers are used to taking orders from him.'

'Don't be silly,' I said, though I wondered myself sometimes. Roosevelt had already won a third term. What was to stop him from running for a fourth? 'Come and sit on the porch with me. It'll be nice and cool once the rain starts.'

'I'd rather stay inside,' she said. 'Have you seen my cigarettes?'

I went out onto the porch alone to watch the sky light up and blamed Ada's nerves on the dropping barometer.

Once tucked into bed that night I had nothing to distract me from my fears for Rachel. I'd have given anything to know how she was.

'We must do this,' Gerald said.

'I understand,' Rachel answered.

'I know what it means to you.'

'It's just a piece of furniture.'

Rachel couldn't remember a time that her great-grandmother's sideboard hadn't stood in her home, crammed with a couple of generations of family treasures. The treasures were long gone. She'd sold the Germaine monogrammed silver, the antique Limoges china, and the rest of the family *objets de valeur* for a pittance to buy food and fuel.

Gerald slipped the crowbar under the edge of the sideboard lid and leaned his weight on it. Old glue and dovetailed joints split with a crack, and he pried the heavy mahogany top from its base.

They worked by candlelight. Claude slept soundly through the racket in the bedroom they all shared. They'd stripped the extra rooms in the flat of furniture to sell, besides, she rested better with Claude beside her. They'd have the new baby in its basket in their bedroom too, squeezed between the suitcases they kept packed and Claude's cot.

Two nights ago a brick had sailed through their front window, and last night's sniper fire sounded closer to their street than ever. 'We have to find a way to bar the door,' Gerald had said. He constructed notches for the bars from the thick stretchers of an

Empire daybed. Only the sideboard was long enough to furnish the wood for bars.

Gerald laid the heavy sideboard across two chairs and Rachel held it steady while he sawed it lengthwise into three boards, one bar for the door and two for the front windows. The other windows had heavy shutters he'd nailed shut days ago. Rachel didn't miss being unable to look out over the Old Port to the Mediterranean. Nazi gunships filled the harbor and blighted the view.

Monday morning, the office buzzed with talk about Bob Holman's sudden death. The girls lingered longer than usual in the ladies' restroom to gossip while the men stood around the halls in little groups, smoking, no doubt speculating about who would get Holman's job. But there was a war on, so by mid-afternoon talk turned to the shocking news that had greeted us all in the morning newspapers – the arrest of a group of Nazi saboteurs at, of all places, the Mayflower Hotel.

My clerks had returned to work, thank goodness.

'Would you believe,' Betty said, throwing back her typewriter return with a clang, 'the U-boat that dropped those Germans off, it was only three hundred yards off the Long Island coast. Makes me shiver to think about it.' She stopped typing long enough to reapply bright-red lipstick and check her match-

85

ing painted fingernails for chips. Betty was boy-crazy, or as they said these days, khaki-wacky, but I tolerated it because she was an excellent typist.

'They'll all be dead before Christmas,' Ruth said. 'Hanging, most likely.' Ruth was a Mt. Holyoke girl who wore her pearls to work every day. Her typing wasn't much, but she could file faster than any of us. I swear she could recite the alphabet backwards in thirty seconds.

Barbara didn't join the conversation, as usual. She was a war widow on a mission. Each day she pored through the Washington newspapers, typing index cards for every person mentioned, her contribution to winning the war that had taken her young husband at Pearl Harbor and separated her from her child. She didn't allude to her background otherwise, but a tiny Star of David on a gold chain hung around her neck. Mostly she wore it under her clothes, but sometimes you could catch a glimpse of it if she wore a scoop-necked blouse.

Because of Barbara's absence her stack of newspapers reached from the floor to the top of her desk.

I didn't have to wait until coffee break to talk to Joan. She stopped by my office a few minutes after I arrived at work, appearing at the door and crooking an index finger at me.

'Mrs Pearlie,' she said.

'Yes, Miss Adams?' I answered, rising from

my desk.

'General Donovan would appreciate it if you'd help me straighten up Mr Holman's office this morning.'

'Of course.'

'Thank you,' I said, as we walked down the hallway together. 'Now I can look for that file.'

'Don't mention it,' she said, lowering her voice to an uncharacteristic whisper. 'Guess who's taking over Holman's desk?'

'Who?' I whispered back.

'Donald Murray,' she said. 'Isn't he your beau?'

'No,' I said, 'definitely not. I haven't got any beaux. Don't want any either.' That remark, about not wanting a beau, surprised me. It slipped out, and I wondered if I was just being defensive, or if I really meant it.

'Wish I could say the same,' Joan said.

I did allow the thought to cross my mind that Don's promotion might be useful to me, and then chastised myself for such a cynical thought. Anyway, I'd find it easier to talk to Don about the Bloch file than if Holman's replacement was someone I didn't know.

Don sat at Holman's desk, smoking his pipe. He nodded a greeting at us. 'Must have been some heart attack, huh?' he said.

The desk, which had been piled high with documents and folders when I last saw it, was almost bare. Files and papers littered the floor. A file cabinet lay on its side, its contents spilling out of open file drawers.

'Okay,' Joan said, all business. 'Why don't Mrs Pearlie and I go through the papers and sort them, reconstruct the files, then pass them to you so you can familiarize yourself with Mr Holman's work.'

'Sounds good to me,' Donald said.

Two hours later Joan and I had reassembled Holman's scattered files and stacked them on Don's desk. I'd rummaged quickly through the undisturbed file cabinets, too. The Bloch file was nowhere to be found.

Joan went to get Donald coffee. Now that he was a desk head, God forbid that he'd sit in the cafeteria with the rest of us.

'Mr Murray,' I said, as casually as I could.

'Yes,' he answered, without looking up.

'Friday afternoon I brought a file to Mr Holman. It concerned a hydrographer, a Frenchman in Marseille, an expert on the North African coast.'

'Sounds interesting. Where is it?'

'Mr Holman reviewed it and placed it in the Projects Committee box. I can't find it now.'

Don leaned back in his chair.

'Maybe he took it upstairs himself,' he said. 'Or changed his mind and sent it back to the main file. It'll turn up.'

'Do you want me to look for it?'

Donald frowned. 'If you have time,' he said, 'and it doesn't interfere with your other work.'

88

I didn't want to press the matter any further. He fiddled with a pen for a second before addressing me again, as if he was nervous.

'By the way,' he said, 'about Wednesday night. Can you come to the cocktail party with me?'

'I'd love to,' I said. I couldn't think of a good reason to say no, and since he'd asked me I'd gotten excited about going.

Joan came in with Don's coffee, and the two of us left him and went across the street to the cafeteria for our own coffee break.

We were later than usual, so we sat at a table by ourselves. Joan sipped from her cup, and made a face. 'I can't get used to drinking coffee without sugar. I'm going to buy a pound from Mr Black this weekend, and I don't care how much it costs or how unpatriotic it is.'

I poured cream into my own cup, watching it swirl around as I stirred it.

'That file I told you about is definitely missing,' I said. 'I've looked everywhere.'

'As much paper as stuffs this building it's not surprising.'

That was an understatement. The girls in my office needed ladders to reach the top rows of the card files alone, and those were just our branch's indexes. Many of the three-by-five cards contained only a couple of typewritten names or a single sentence that directed us to one subject file, others referred to dozens. Those subject files filled every available wall, nook and cranny in our building, including conference rooms, bathrooms, offices, stairwells, hallways and broom closets. Only six months after Congress declared war, our branch of OSS had already moved twice, from an annex at the Library of Congress, to an abandoned ice-skating rink, to our current quarters.

'You don't suppose the FBI lifted Bloch's file while they were in Mr Holman's office, do you,' I asked.

'Why would they? Europe's not their territory – they're domestic and South America. When are you going to tell me why you are so interested in this file?'

I scanned the nearly empty cafeteria, and lowered my voice. I had decided to tell Joan the truth. 'The subject of the file, Gerald Bloch, is the husband of a dear friend of mine from junior college. My room-mate.' How could I explain my friendship with Rachel to Joan? Rachel and I were both outsiders at St Martha's. Rachel because she was Jewish, me because I was 'middle class'. Oh, the other students and the faculty were politely kind to us, but we didn't fit in. For two years we just had each other. I got really good at mah-jongg, and Rachel learned to listen to the Carter Family singing 'Keep on the Sunny Side' without putting her fingers in her ears.

'Oh, no,' Joan said. 'I am so very sorry. You

must be worried sick.'

'It such a coincidence that I'd find Rachel's husband in an OSS file,' I said. 'Hard to believe.'

'Not really. Lots of us here have friends and family still in Europe. Did you hear what happened to Julia Cuniberti?'

'The clerk on the Italian desk?'

'Her family's Italian American, and she speaks the language. Well, she learned through the documents and cables she filed that the Nazis had commandeered her uncle's lodge in the Apennines and forced his family, including four children, to live in the attic! The Italian partisans identified the lodge as a Resistance target, and Julia could not do a thing to warn her uncle. All she could do was pray for them. The lodge was bombed twice! She had to file all the intelligence about it!'

'Oh, my God! What happened?'

'She has no idea. None of the reports mention her family.'

Neither one of us spoke for a few minutes.

'Maybe Mr Holman took your file upstairs himself before he died,' Joan said.

'Maybe.' I took a breath. 'Joan, could you look for it in General Donovan's office? He'd have to initial it, wouldn't he, before it could go to the Projects Committee?'

Joan crossed her legs and lit a cigarette, the flame leaping from an engraved silver Tiffany cigarette lighter.

'I must warn you, Louise.'

I knew what she was about to say.

'We can't let our feelings get in the way of our work here. There are thousands of unfortunate families in Europe. We can't save each one. Besides, going behind the backs of your bosses to help your friend could lose you your job.'

'I understand.'

'But I don't like the idea of files in this office going missing, for any reason. I'll take a look around General Donovan's office. Only a look, mind you.'

'Thank you. That's all I ask.'

It was easy for Joan to caution me. She couldn't possibly understand what I owed Rachel – so much more than friendship! But I'd promised Rachel never to speak of it to anyone, and I still felt bound by that promise.

EIGHT

I spent the rest of the morning mimeographing reports to send to agencies all over Washington, where undoubtedly they'd be filed in more file cabinets. I did slip out once to check the 'B' files to see if the Bloch file had found its way home. It wasn't there.

At noon Joan and I walked to the Water Gate Inn on Rock Creek Drive, where the huge, puffy popovers were heaven sent, for lunch. The dining room was hot and crowded, overhung with a fug of cigarette smoke, so we lounged outside at a picnic table by the Potomac River, shaded by a cottonwood tree drooping with thirst. A small colored boy fished on the riverbank below us.

'Much against my better judgment,' Joan said, 'I did check around my office for the Bloch file. It wasn't in the Project Committee's box. I got a look at the General's desk, too. Not there.'

She saw my speculative look.

'Don't jump to conclusions,' she said. 'What is that word? Don't get paranoid. That file may have been mislaid, thrown away even, we don't know what state Mr Holman was in before he died. He may have been quite confused before his heart attack. Who knows what he did with it.'

'I guess you're right.'

'Anyway,' Joan continued, 'I talked to Dora this morning, and she told me the whole story about what happened Friday. She didn't want to go into details outside the office. She, Don Murray, Guy Danielson and Roger Austine were having a late meeting about some report or another, and having their usual disagreements, when they heard Mr Holman's wife screaming bloody murder. They rushed to Holman's office and found him dead with our security guards standing over his body, guns drawn. The guards shooed everyone out of the office, including the widow, and waited there until three FBI agents showed up. The Capitol police arrived, but they weren't allowed into the office either, so they left. A while later a doctor arrived, examined the body, and then men from a funeral home showed up and removed the corpse.'

'What about the FBI agents?'

'Two went with the body and the special agent stayed behind in the office for a while, arguing with General Donovan and Dr Linney. The special agent was one of the G-men at the wake, the one with the feather in his hat. Finally everyone was allowed to go home. Dora said there were GIs still standing guard all around the building when she

94

left.'

The little colored boy, dejected, packed up his fishing gear, a bamboo pole and a tin can of worms, and climbed up the riverbank toward us.

'Any luck?' I asked him.

'No, ma'am,' he said. 'It's too hot.'

Joan watched the child walk off before she spoke to me again, her voice lowered.

'There is something else,' she said. 'Now don't work yourself up over this.'

'What?'

'We keep copies of every communication from the London office in General Donovan's personal files.'

I felt my pulse quicken. 'What do you have?' I asked.

'A typewritten translation of the original note from the Resistance operative and a carbon of the memo forwarded to your branch requesting what information you might have about Bloch.'

So there was still some tangible evidence of Gerald Bloch at OSS.

'I don't suppose,' I began.

'No,' Joan said, pursing her lips tightly. 'Absolutely not. I can't remove one of General Donovan's files. Only he and I have keys to the file room. I'd lose my job, at the very least.'

'Of course not,' I said, 'I wouldn't dream of asking you to do such a thing.' I would, actually, but I understood it wasn't possible.

'And I can't make photostats,' she said. 'They are terribly expensive and every use has to be authorized. Besides the damn machine takes up an entire room and has its very own guard.'

'Enough,' I said. 'I don't want you to do anything risky.'

Once back in my office I felt encouraged by Joan's discovery of copies of some of the Bloch documents in General Donovan's files. I wondered if even more information might be found elsewhere in the building.

I remembered the index card where I'd first located Gerald Bloch's name. I didn't recall that it had referred to any other file than the one I originally retrieved and gave to Holman, but I thought I'd double-check. I rolled out the library ladder and climbed up to the 'B' drawer. I drew out the drawer and leafed through it. Twice. Bloch's reference card was gone.

NINE

The only piece of Bloch's card that remained was a shred left behind when someone had ripped it from the metal rod that held it in place.

Oh, outwardly my world stayed pretty much the same. Betty, Ruth and Barbara worked away industriously below me, Betty smacking her gum while she forced a thick wad of typing paper and carbon paper into her machine, Barbara bent over her typewriter. The fan twirled overhead, moving bars of shade across the office walls.

But I gripped the ladder with white knuckles. Someone had deliberately stolen that card. I climbed down the ladder, cautiously, as I felt a bit woozy, and ducked behind my partition to think. It was conceivable that the main file had been lost in the commotion following Holman's death, but clearly, clearly to me anyway, the index card had been stolen from the file drawer.

Who had taken the card, and why?

I had no idea. And because I had no idea, I couldn't trust anyone at OSS. Not Don, Dora or even Joan. I didn't know what to do, but I had to do something. Letting this lie wasn't an option for me.

But I couldn't act rashly. I didn't know what I was up against. I'd go home, rest, think and sleep on it, then decide.

I could hear raised voices even before I opened the front door. Joe met me in the hall, finger to his lips.

'Dellaphine and Madeleine are at it again,' he said, 'and Mrs Knox isn't here to referee.'

Madeleine stomped into the hall, brandishing a folded newspaper. She was livid; I could see the flush rising up her dark neck into her face.

She shook the newspaper in my general direction, then at the ceiling, toward heaven, I supposed.

'It says right here,' she said, slapping the paper, twice. 'Secretaries wanted; high-school diploma only requirement. Does that sound to you like only white girls need apply? No it don't! I get to this office, and some prissy Miss Anne receptionist tells me all the jobs are full! Well, watch this.'

She picked up the hall telephone and dialed, tapping a pencil on the table as she waited impatiently for an answer.

'Good evening,' she said sweetly. 'I understand that you have secretarial openings? Yes? How many? Well how come when I was just down there you said they were full? Oh, you remember me now, do you!'

98

Madeleine slammed the receiver down.

'I'm sorry, honey,' I said.

Joe started to say something, but Madeleine gave him a look that would curdle cream, so he retreated into the lounge, taking his pipe out of his pocket as he went.

Dellaphine emerged from the kitchen.

'Sugar, you should have known them jobs weren't for you,' she said.

'Momma, please!'

'You got a good job.'

'Keeping children at a day nursery for white women who work the jobs I'm better trained to do!'

'You don't got to clean toilets or nothing, do you?'

'I graduated Dunbar High School with As in typing, shorthand and bookkeeping. I didn't spend all those hours studying to end up raising white people's children!'

'That's part of your problem, Maddy,' her mother said, one hand on her bony hip, waving a wooden spoon with the other. 'You come across as abrasive. You got to act humble and grateful.'

'Momma!'

'Honey, I know you'll find a good job soon,' I said. 'I see more colored girls working in government offices every day.'

'When this war is over, I'm going to go live in Paris, and be and do whatever I want – like Josephine Baker!'

'You do that, baby,' Dellaphine said. 'In the

99

meantime calm down, come get you a glass of ice tea and help me get dinner on the table.'

Madeleine rolled her eyes, and stomped down the hall after her mother.

I followed Joe into the sitting room, where he'd lit his pipe and lifted a stack of papers out of his briefcase.

I could think of no excuses, so I dragged my knitting basket from under the cocktail table. I raised the lopsided sock I was knitting to the light, and found a new dropped stitch. Resigned to imperfection I ignored it, and started the edging. Besides, if I didn't knit, I'd have to talk to Joe. Or worry about Rachel.

Joe had the radio tuned to some opera. He'd know everything about it, including the composer, the performers and how it differed from the interpretation he'd once seen in London, and I'd have to admit I didn't even know the name of the blasted thing, and I'd sound like I'd fallen off a turnip truck on the way through town.

'Like it?' he asked.

'What?' I said.

'*La Bohème*,' he said.

'The music is wonderful,' I said, pausing in my work, since it was all I could do to knit tolerably when I wasn't talking, 'but I know nothing about opera.'

'Would you like to go to a concert with me sometime? It wouldn't have to be the opera,

100

if you'd prefer something else.'

I choked on my heart in a way I hadn't when Don asked me to Evalyn McLean's party.

'Sure,' I said, 'I'd love to, and opera would be fine,' bending with new concentration over my knitting needles.

'How about Friday?' he said. 'Let me check the newspaper and see what's coming up.'

'Okay,' I said, lightly, I hoped. I thrashed around for something else to say.

'How was your day?' Lame, lame, lame!

'The usual,' he said. 'The students are distracted by the war. Most of them are waiting for draft notices or duty assignments. And your day?'

'I'm a file clerk,' I said. 'That pretty much covers it.'

We were silent again, until Dellaphine called us to dinner – fried haddock, creamed potatoes, more squash and honey cake. I pushed the haddock around on my plate so it looked like I'd eaten some.

After dinner I didn't go back into the sitting room with the others. I needed to think. Instead I settled into a wicker rocker on the porch and watched the heat lightning flare over the city.

I was convinced that something questionable was going on with Gerald Bloch's OSS file. It wasn't misplaced during all the confusion of Holman's death, because someone

101

had deliberately ripped out the reference card from the index files in my office. The two events had to be linked. And my files weren't secure from anyone in my building during office hours. With my girls out sick last week, anyone could have come into my office when I wasn't there.

I pictured the layout of our first-floor wing of the huge old apartment building that accommodated the Research and Analysis branch of OSS. Once it contained three apartments. The first, a two-bedroom unit to the right of the front door, housed me and my three clerks and our towering index-card files. On the left, what had once been a doorman's room was now our security office, staffed by the army. Most days one Sergeant Corcoran stayed in the office, checking the credentials of visitors; the front entrance was manned by Private Cooper, and the side door by a Private Herndon. Up the hall on the left was Holman's office, once a studio apartment. Further down the hall on the left a stairway rose to the upper floors. The side entrance to our hall, Private Herndon's station, faced the staircase.

Four researchers shared a two-room unit in the rear of our wing. Dora and Roger Austine crammed their desks into one room. Roger was a French-language professor from Tulane. His mother was French, and after his American father's death she and his sisters returned to southern France, where they still lived. His uncle was the Archbishop of Toulouse, so they were quite safe from the Nazis. At least for now. Roger was a fervent admirer of Charles de Gaulle.

Don, before his promotion to Holman's job, shared an office with Guy Danielson, a European historian from Princeton. Guy was older than most of us, more conservative, even reactionary. He and Roger despised each other. Fluency in French was the only trait they shared.

For months they'd been arguing about who should lead the French government in exile. Roger tried to convince Bob Holman that de Gaulle was the reincarnation of Napoleon, while Guy insisted that the Count of Paris, the old charlatan who claimed to be the King of France, was the man with the credentials.

A small bathroom served their offices, but Dora usually walked down the hall to use ours.

Once past the security guards, anyone who worked for the Research and Analysis branch, and any authorized visitor for that matter, had free access to all the offices in the building. Anything that needed to be restricted, like our precious London telephone book, was locked up.

The Research and Analysis branch of the OSS, which everyone in the know called R&A, was more like a college campus than a government office. Ex-professors wandered about laden with books and notes and documents, cooperated and argued in endless meetings, frequently decamping to the Library of Congress to do their research. They wrote thick reports, which we clerks typed, distributed and filed endlessly. When under a deadline our scholar/spies stayed up all night working, smuggling wives and girlfriends in to type. Often they took papers and files home to study.

Not until the end of the day did we stow away our stacks of papers, remove the pins from wall maps, secure secret files and lock our office doors. Much of the time we did that not only for national security's sake but to keep raiders from other government agencies from stealing our typewriters and mimeograph machines.

Bob Holman's heart attack presented an unexpected opportunity for someone to steal Bloch's file. How long had Holman been dead before his corpse was discovered? Who went in and out of his office before his wife raised the alarm? In the confusion that followed the discovery of Holman's body, could the thief have left our hall through the either of the two entrances that the guards abandoned when they rushed to Holman's office? Not to mention the staircase that led to the second floor. Of course, if the thief worked for OSS, which seemed likely to me, he could simply return to his office and hide the file amongst his own papers.

The words 'spy', 'traitor', 'quisling', and 'mole' crossed my mind for the first time.

And why Gerald Bloch's file? I wasn't sure that Bloch had any skills or knowledge that dozens of other men living on the French or North African coasts didn't have. Gerald, Rachel and little Claude were just flotsam and jetsam floating in the ocean of a world-wide war.

But this wasn't only about the fate of one French Jewish family. If Bloch's file was stolen deliberately, and I was sure it was, something larger must be at stake. I felt justified, even responsible, for trying to find out what more I could.

Who could I report all this to? Anyone at OSS could be the culprit. Don? He could have been in Holman's office after his death. Dora? Ditto. Joan? Should I trust her because she was my friend? What about Guy or Roger? Dr Linney, our branch head? If I went over Don's head to speak to Linney, everyone in the branch would know about it within minutes, and the culprit would be forewarned. Same thing if I went straight to General Donovan. Now that would really create an uproar and send the thief scampering underground. It seemed to me that the only way to find him was to keep quiet about what I suspected was theft of OSS information. Unless the file was lost or misplaced, in which case I would make a spectacle of myself.

Which reminded me that I had no independent proof that I had actually given the file to Holman in the first place, that it had disappeared, or that the index card had been stolen. I could have stolen the file and the card myself, and made up the story of their loss as cover!

I decided to keep what I knew to myself until I had more evidence that the file was stolen. Keeping my mouth shut was a specialty of mine.

I wondered if General Donovan would be at Evalyn McLean's party, and if I might have a chance to speak to him alone. I could tell him about the file without the entire office knowing I had talked to him. Would he believe me?

Thinking about the McLean party brought up the confusing issue of my love life. I had never been out on two dates in one week before, except the week Bill and I got engaged, when we went to our church homecoming picnic on a Friday and the movies the next day. And this week I had not only two dates, but I was going out with two different men! And that didn't count Charles Burns offering me supper and a ride home from Joan's. I didn't understand it. I was way, way past my prime, almost thirty years old.

'Beady little eyes' was a description that might have been invented just for J. Edgar

Hoover, General Bill Donovan reflected. Those black, tiny eyes set in the FBI Director's heavy swarthy face betrayed him as the autocrat he was. Donovan couldn't stand the man, but ever since Congress had passed the Hatch Act, giving the FBI the authority to search for spies and saboteurs within the United States, Donovan had been forced to work with him. They'd been meeting daily since Bob Holman had been found murdered at his desk. The murder had been hushed up successfully for now, but the murder investigation itself was going nowhere fast. Hoover's G-men and the OSS Security Office had clashed continually since the start of the investigation. They were meeting tonight at the Cosmo Club because it was neutral territory. Neither Hoover nor Donovan would agree to meet at the other's office.

A waiter appeared silently and set their drinks before them – smoky amber liquid in highball glasses filled with ice, grease for squeaky wheels.

Hoover sipped from his drink, set it down, and took a thick file from his assistant, Clyde Tolson. The nature of Hoover and Tolson's friendship had aroused gossip for years, but Donovan preferred not to speculate. He had more than enough to do spying on the Nazis.

Hoover tapped the folder on the table in front of him.

'What we know,' he said. 'Bob Holman was murdered, stabbed in the base of his neck, from behind, with a thin-bladed weapon, like an ice pick or a letter opener. Holman must have been working in his undershirt at the time, as was his habit, because it seems that his killer dressed him in his shirt and jacket to hide the fatal wound. Gave him a bit of time to cover his tracks, since we didn't know Holman had been murdered until the doctor arrived and examined him. We decided,' Hoover continued, 'to keep the murder a secret for now.'

'You decided,' Donovan said.

Hoover peered at Donovan over the sheaf of papers he was skimming. 'Maybe you don't care if the country knows OSS security is so lax someone could be murdered right under your nose, but I do.'

Donovan shrugged.

'Suspects,' Hoover continued.

Donovan's security chief, Colonel Ellery Huntington, shifted impatiently beside him.

'Let's hear what you have,' Donovan said.

'We've established that any number of people in OSS could have had access to the murder victim. Your internal security is laughable. Your people wander about like bees in a beehive. But there are three people who had a strong motive to murder Mr Holman, as well as access.'

'Go on.'

'Dora Bertrand.'

Donovan scowled. 'Why her?'

'She's a socialist and a lesbian.'

108

'Those aren't motives for Holman's murder.'

'Holman was head of the Europe/Africa desk, correct?'

'Yes.'

'He was a Republican. We all know that he opposed opening a second front in Europe this year. You don't think that Miss Bertrand might want to help her pals the Soviets by removing an influential opponent of a second front?'

'That's a bit far-fetched, don't you think?'

'Because she's a lesbian she's vulnerable to blackmail. Maybe her Red friends threatened her, forced her to kill Holman. You know my office has advised the clandestine services not to hire homosexuals.'

'Miss Bertrand makes no secret of her political leanings or her homosexuality. She is extremely competent. If she weren't a woman she would be a section head already. I don't care who she sleeps with, if she can help us defeat Hitler.'

Tolson flinched, but Hoover's expression remained inscrutable.

'Then we have Guy Danielson. Did you know his last name used to be Danielovich?'

'Several generations back, I believe.'

'He's a monarchist. He has contributed money to the political machine of the Count of Paris, the pretender to the French throne.'

'Which means?'

'That he might be amenable to killing

109

someone who favored de Gaulle as the head of the French state in exile. Holman was a de Gaulle enthusiast, wasn't he?'

Donovan didn't answer.

'Then, we have Roger Austine. He is engaged to a colored woman, a foreigner.'

'I know. I have met Miss Lebron.'

'We can assume that Austine is subject to blackmail, too.'

'He doesn't broadcast his engagement, but he makes no secret of it, either. Why should he?'

Hoover shrugged, gave the file back to Tolson, took a cigar out of his pocket and lit it, symbolically turning the floor over to Donovan.

'I see no reason to single out these three persons on the basis of their politics,' Donovan said, 'or their sex lives. We, as you know, have been conducting our own investigation.' He turned to Huntington and nodded.

Huntington opened his own thick file and cleared his throat.

'We've determined that Mr Holman was murdered less than an hour before his body was discovered. As you said, he was stabbed with a thin blade, like an ice pick or letter opener, in the back of his neck. We haven't been able to find the murder weapon.'

'You agree that a woman could have struck that blow?' Tolson asked.

'Absolutely,' Huntington answered. 'Now, we questioned our security officers and our

110

employees who have offices in the same hall as Holman's. Here is a list of personnel who were seen there during the hour before his murder.'

'We know all this,' Hoover said.

'Bear with us, please,' General Donovan replied.

'Guy Danielson, Roger Austine, Dora Bertrand, Donald Murray and Mrs Louise Pearlie. Their offices are all in the hall.'

Hoover shifted, impatient.

'Also, passing through on various errands, General Donovan's secretary, Miss Joan Adams, Dr Linney, the branch head, Mr Charles Burns from the Map Division, four Negro messengers, all with appropriate identification, and of course Mr Holman's wife,' Huntington said. 'And I must point out to you that others could have come down the back staircase and returned that way, so the sergeant wouldn't have seen them. His job is to clear visitors, not impede my staff.'

'I would suggest,' Donovan continued, 'that the motive for murdering Holman need not be political. Perhaps Mr Murray, who is an ambitious young man, seized an opportunity for advancement. Then there's Holman's wife. They are known to have argued because she wanted to work. She could have murdered him herself, and then sounded the alarm. My point, Director Hoover, is that we still have no idea who killed Bob Holman, or

111

why they did it. Until we do, we at OSS are keeping our minds open to all possibilities. And I must insist that you do not use this murder as a weapon of political persecution. I won't have it, not at OSS.'

Thank God for cross-referencing. I eagerly removed a file labeled 'International Association of Hydrological Sciences' from a file cabinet a floor away from where I'd found Gerald Bloch's file. It contained the program of the 1936 conference Bloch had attended and nothing more. But now I possessed proof that the man existed, and I intended to keep it safe from whoever had stolen the original file and reference card.

I tucked the empty file jacket back into the file cabinet and folded the program into an armful of other papers and strolled back into my office, the picture of nonchalance. Once behind my desk I locked the conference program away in my desk drawer. My heart pounded and I felt elated as I pinned the tiny key inside my bra. I suppose I fancied myself a real spy, a 'glamor girl', on a dangerous mission to unearth a spy within OSS and maybe save a few lives in the process.

At coffee break I carried my cup of steaming hot coffee, black, I'm sorry to say, over to the table where Roger Austine, Dora Bertrand and Guy Danielson sat. Guy and Roger must be speaking to each other today.

Coffee break was less hierarchical than other OSS events, so no one seemed too surprised when I joined them. Joan, at a table across the room, raised an eyebrow at me, a gesture that meant she knew exactly what I was doing, and she didn't approve at all.

'Hello, dear,' Dora said, scooting over so I could slide a chair next to her. If my parents suspected this middle-aged woman, mousy in a gray dress, was a professor, a socialist and shacked up with another woman, and that not only was I drinking coffee at the same table with her, but also that I admired her, they would link hands and jump off the roof of the First Baptist Church of Wilmington, North Carolina.

And what would they make of Roger Austine? He slicked his hair back with brilliantine and wore a flower in his lapel. Or of Guy Danielson, a cynical misanthrope who would tell anyone who would listen that a benevolent monarchy was the highest form of government, and the excesses of Hitler and Mussolini were entirely due to their low social origins?

Guy sipped from his cup and grimaced. 'Coffee should be like a beautiful woman,' he said, 'blonde and sweet!' That took Dora and me out of the running, but neither man noticed the gaffe, and we didn't care.

'I hear you received a stack of French underground newspapers this morning?' Guy asked Roger.

113

'Yes. You know, every day I think the news can't get any worse,' Roger said, shaking his head. 'And every day I stand corrected. Now that Pierre Laval is Prime Minister of Vichy France, I think that Vichy will be overrun with Nazis very soon. He's already ordered Vichy Jews to wear the yellow Star of David. So much for unoccupied France. What a charade.'

'Your family?' Dora asked.

'Still living in Toulouse,' Roger said. 'You know that my uncle is Monsignor Saliège, Archbishop of Toulouse. That protects my mother and sisters. They live with him in the archbishop's palace.'

'I understand that the Gestapo in Paris is deporting Jewish families to labor camps,' Guy said.

Roger wiped his face with his handkerchief before responding. 'Yes,' he said, his voice wavering. 'Aided and abetted by the French police. Thousands have been shipped east by cattle car.'

'I don't understand why the Nazis are sending women and children, too,' Guy said. 'What use will they be in labor camps?'

Dora clenched her fist in her lap.

'They need the women to take care of the men, and I suppose the men will work harder if their families are with them,' Roger said, shrugging.

I finished my coffee quickly and excused myself, taking refuge in the women's bathroom to collect myself. What had I been thinking? I wasn't a spy. I was a file clerk. What on earth could I do to prevent the Nazis from shipping Rachel and her entire family wherever they pleased?

Rachel and her father had always made so much of being more French than Jewish. I remembered my first visit to Rachel's New York home. We took a horse-drawn carriage down to the seaport, passing by Battery Park Place, where the Nazi consulate stood facing the green park lawn. A huge red flag, centered by a black swastika, hung over the door.

'Doesn't that frighten you?' I asked Rachel. 'The things the Nazis say about Jews are so horrible.'

'Papa says Hitler is a clown who won't survive another year as Chancellor,' Rachel answered. 'Besides, we're perfectly safe. We're French.'

Barbara and Betty might as well be chained to their typewriters, they were pounding the keys so intently to catch up from their absences. Ruth was gone, and so was our rolling file cart, so I assumed she was toiling in the file rooms. I sat down at my desk, unlocked my desk drawer and removed the file containing the program for the hydrology conference that Gerald Bloch had attended in Scotland in 1936. It was the only clue I had. I read every word over and over until my eyes ached. I had no idea that water aroused such scholarly passion.

I uncovered a couple of useful facts. The name of the George Washington University academic who sent in the materials about Bloch in the first place was one Marvin Metcalfe. If he still taught at GWU I might be able to speak to him. Even better, I saw that Joan's so-called friend from the OSS Map Division, Charles Burns, spoke at the conference. Here was someone under the OSS roof I could ask about Gerald Bloch, but I still had to be circumspect. I needed to question Burns in a way that wouldn't arouse his suspicion. The best approach, I decided, was to go to him just as myself, a file clerk with nothing more on her mind than an overflowing in-box. That wouldn't take much acting.

I trudged up two steep flights of steps to the Map Division. When I opened the door I was halted in my tracks by a frightening image, a world map tacked to the wall. Almost all of continental Europe was soaked in bloody red ink centered by a giant black swastika rolling west toward England. Portugal, Spain, Switzerland and Sweden were islands of neutrality scattered within the colossal territory already conquered by Germany. How long could they hold out?

Libya, an Italian colony also drenched in Axis red, pierced Africa between the French colonies of Algeria and Morocco, and British Suez. Japan's red ink oozed into China, the

116

Philippines and Indonesia and pooled a few short miles away from Australia. And someone had hand-drawn a black swastika over the capital of Brazil, a hot bed of Nazi influence in South America, in our own hemisphere.

TEN

That bloody map frightened me as much as any horrifying newsreel footage or shocking newspaper story about the war I'd seen yet. The preacher at our church in Wilmington consistently railed about the coming of the Antichrist and Armageddon. If Hitler and this war didn't qualify I didn't want to think about what nightmare conflagration would.

I inhaled deeply to steady myself and went into the office to search for Charles.

Lord knows I was accustomed to the mess caused by the massive influx of information OSS collected, but the chaos here flabbergasted me. A young clerk was actually climbing, or maybe scaling would be a better word, a tower of leather-bound folios that rose above his head smack in the middle of a huge room. He picked a volume off the summit, slid down to the floor, and carried it over to a work table where a dozen young men and women wearing green eyeshades and black cuff-protectors labored to catalog thousands and thousands of maps. Towering shelves, clogged with files, folios, books and document boxes, surrounded them, lining the walls. I hoped the shelves were screwed into the walls. They looked unsteady to me. If one fell it would cause carnage among the platoon of clerks.

I found Burns, pouring over a Shell Oil road map of Algeria. When my shadow fell over him, he grimaced.

'What the hell,' he said. 'Get out of my light. It's bad enough as it is.' He looked up and saw me, wedged between his desk and a bank of file cabinets, and softened his tone. 'Oh,' he said, 'sorry, I didn't recognize you. What is it?'

'I've been clearing up Bob Holman's office,' I said.

'So?'

'It was a mess. And I found this loose on the floor. It had your name in it, so I thought you might know what it's about, so I could file it properly.'

'Let me see,' he said, taking the 1936 conference program from me.

He leafed through the brochure.

'It's just what it says it is. A program from a hydrology conference. Listing presentations from expert hydrologists and hydrographers. Like me. Before I became a map librarian. I'm sorry, I don't have any idea

118

why this was in Holman's office.'

'You didn't send it to him?'

'No. Look, I don't have time for this. I've got to hand over a preliminary list of North African maps to a typist, if I can find one who's free, in an hour, and I have a God-awful headache.'

'Have we got any good maps of North Africa?'

'Not really. The British Admiralty charts of Egypt and the Suez Canal are excellent, but we need the French colonies, Algeria and Morocco. For them we've only got a National Geographic map, two oil-company road maps and some tourist guidebooks, only one in English. They show nothing of strategic value. We'll have to rely on the local Resistance for information, and those damn Arabs, they're almost as shifty as the Japs.'

I threaded my way between stacks of books and desks out of the office and into the hallway. What now?

I wondered if Marvin Metcalfe still taught at George Washington University and if I could invent a plausible pretext for visiting him.

Lying proved to be easier than I thought. I told my girls that I had a severe toothache and had to leave work to go to the dentist. No one questioned me when I left the building.

After waiting an hour for the bus, I gave up

119

and walked north. George Washington University was on 'G' Street, south of my boarding house, within easy walking distance despite the heat. Uniformed men of all ages and scores of businesslike young women crowded the campus sidewalks, hurrying to class. I envied those women. If the war had come earlier, if I was younger, or if my aunt's bequest hadn't shrunk during the Depression, I might be in a real college now, too, learning something meatier than secretarial skills. I stopped an army captain toting an armful of engineering textbooks and asked directions to the geography department.

Inside the squat stone building it was refreshingly cool and dark. I had to wait a few seconds while my vision adjusted from the intense light outside to the dim interior. A secretary seated at a metal desk kept watch inside the doorway. She was an older woman, at least forty, with minimal typing skills, as I could see as she pecked at the antique Remington on her desk.

She tilted her eyes over her reading glasses and looked me up and down. When she spotted my OSS badge she deigned to speak to me. 'Yes?' she asked.

'Can you tell me the way to Professor Metcalfe's office?'

'He's not a professor,' she said. 'He's an instructor. Down that hall, last door on the right.'

I saw right away why Metcalfe wasn't in

the military. He wore a brace on his left leg, which he stuck straight out along the side of his desk. Polio, I supposed, like so many. Otherwise Metcalfe lived up to my image of a college instructor. He needed a haircut, his collar was frayed, and the leather briefcase that rested on the floor was creased with wear. Metcalfe looked up from a stack of blue books when I tapped on his open door.

'And you are?' he asked.

'Louise Pearlie,' I said. Damn, I thought, should I have used an alias? I hadn't given a cover story any thought at all. And my OSS ID tag still dangled from my collar. I was stuck with myself. 'Sorry to interrupt you at your work,' I said, 'but my boss –' that was a stupid thing to say, please God, don't let him call Don – 'sent me to ask you some questions,' I said, 'about a hydrology conference you attended in 1936, in Edinburgh?'

'What, you people don't have telephones?'

'I was in the neighborhood anyway,' I said. 'On my way to the dentist.' Another mistake. I should have checked to see if there was a dentist's office nearby.

Metcalfe rolled his eyes, as if my inanity was the best he could expect from a female government clerk.

'Okay,' he said, 'what about it?'

I was ready for this question.

'One of our division heads died a few days ago,' I said. 'We found the program for a hydrology conference that took place in

121

1936 loose on his desk. Your name is listed as a participant. We don't know why it was on Mr Holman's desk, and we hoped you could tell us why it might be important.'

'It was the last international hydrology conference held in Europe. The 1939 conference was here, in Washington. Of course there won't be any more until this bloody war ends. Not that it matters. I have no time to work on my research, much less my dissertation, what with the teaching load I'm carrying. I sent the program to the OSS back when they asked our department for the names of important people in our field.'

'Did you know any of the other speakers well?' I asked.

'I've got another copy of the program. Let me refresh my memory.' He pulled a folder out of his desk file drawer, the program out of the folder, and glanced through it. 'This Burns fellow. He's with you people now. We shared an office one semester when he was in graduate school here. Somehow he managed to finish his dissertation before the war started. And Gerald Bloch, he's a Frenchman, but he speaks very good English. We had dinner in Edinburgh one evening. His wife was with him. Lovely woman. Can't remember her name. Bloch wasn't here at the 1939 conference. Couldn't get out of Europe, I suppose.'

'Might his wife's name have been Rachel?'

'Yes,' he answered, 'I believe that's correct.'

'And Bloch's expertise?' I asked. 'For our files, you see.'

'The Mediterranean,' Metcalfe said. 'The North African coast particularly.'

'Thank you,' I said. 'I appreciate your time.'

Metcalfe withdrew several brochures from the folder. 'Look here,' he said. 'I have some reprints of some of Bloch's journal articles. We all exchange reprints with each other at these conferences. Do you want them?'

'Sure.' I stuffed them into my bag.

I left the building with my stomach knotted into a tight ball. I'd been dangerously unprepared for my meeting with Metcalfe. He didn't seem suspicious, but if I planned to continue to investigate the missing Bloch file without OSS permission I needed to be more cautious. Ruthlessly I suppressed the apprehension that surfaced whenever I thought of Rachel and her family in peril. I couldn't help them if I was crippled by my fear for them.

It was nearly lunchtime, and my stomach growled. When I saw the foreign-languages building ahead of me I thought of a distraction. Why not drop in on Joe? My errand gave me a good excuse to be here, and we could go to lunch. Have a meal away from the boarding house and talk without anyone else around.

★ ★ ★

123

'I'm sorry, Mrs Pearlie.'

'I'm sure you're mistaken,' I said. 'Mr Prager teaches Slavic languages here. He's Czech, has a dark beard, medium height. Wears a gold pocket watch.'

The secretary, younger than the watchdog at the geography department but no less authoritative, closed her notebook with an impatient slam.

'There is no Joseph Prager working here,' she said. 'Not in foreign literatures, not in languages, not in the day or the evening colleges.'

'I don't understand,' I said.

'Perhaps this fellow fed you a line,' she said, as only a twenty-year-old blonde wearing a fraternity pin could say to an older woman with no ring on her most important finger and thick eyeglasses. I couldn't think fast enough to reply with equal condescension, and wound up leaving the building with a flush creeping up my neck.

I took refuge in Quigley's Pharmacy at the soda fountain. I ordered a grilled-cheese sandwich and a Coke, which was exempted from sugar rationing because the government considered it indispensable to the war effort. Right now it was indispensable to me. The ice-cold, sweet surge of flavor braced me to mull over what I'd learned.

So Joe didn't teach at George Washington. Why did I think he had? He said very little about himself, and he'd never mentioned his job directly. He talked about his students, read Czech books and wrote lectures, and I'd seen him grading papers. But, I realized, he'd never actually mentioned GWU. We all assumed he worked there, since our boarding house was so close to the university. Well, he must teach somewhere else. Perhaps Georgetown? But he'd let us all assume he taught at GWU. Which he might do if he needed cover? That had to be the answer. He must teach at one of the government or military language schools, and, like the rest of us working for the government, couldn't talk about it. Of course that was the explanation.

I relaxed and finished my sandwich. It was energizing to be sitting in a soda shop on a college campus, where students talked about books and classes instead of stuck in an office going deaf from the din of clattering typewriters and mimeographs, when a successful day was marked by a tiny dent in a mountain of paperwork. I let myself feel sorry for myself for a few minutes, before I reminded myself that I was doing crucial war work.

The other girls and I joked sometimes, calling ourselves 'secretaries of war', but really, the most massive army in the world would be helpless without the information we gathered. Besides, it could be worse. I could still be living in Wilmington, gutting fish and frying up slimy fillets in my parents' fish camp, putting in the same hours as my salaried brother, for room and board at my parents' house and two dollars at the end of any week the till wasn't empty, thankful for a roof over my head after my husband died.

When men began to leave their jobs to join the military, I got my chance to escape the fish camp. Oh, I didn't think of it that way at first. I was doing my patriotic duty, taking the place of a man who'd become a soldier.

I was one of the first girls in Wilmington to get a defense job. Since I had a junior-college business degree I had my pick of positions. I ran the office at the Wilmington Shipbuilding Company, and as long as I live I'll never forget my first paycheck. Ever. I went right out and cut my hair into a soft shoulder-length style and got harlequin-framed eyeglasses to replace my steel spectacles.

My standing rose within my family, too. I gave part of my salary to my mother for housekeeping expenses. And because of the importance of my job we got 'A' gasoline ration coupons.

I was very good at my job. Which meant not only running the office, but also keeping secrets. My company built ships for the navy. Any number of foreign governments wanted to know its business. But not one peep about my work escaped my lips. My mother didn't even have my office phone number.

My boss was a simple man who tended to

say the same things over and over, just in case you didn't grasp his meaning the first few times. 'Louise,' he would say to me, 'you ain't like most women. You know how to keep your mouth shut.' I could have reminded him that the last three employees we'd fired for talking too much had been men, but I knew how to keep my mouth shut about plenty that had nothing to do with military secrets.

My competence, and reticence, impressed a naval officer who visited the company shortly after Pearl Harbor. He voiced his regard to a friend who was an OSS scout, and I went to Washington soon after the Coordinator of Information became the OSS. I rode north by train sitting on my suitcase in the aisle the entire way, absorbed in my Esso map of the city, the address for 'Two Trees' safely tucked into my pocketbook.

I became the chief file clerk at my section within three months. My paycheck was so much bigger than anything I was accustomed to that I didn't tell my parents about it. I was independent for the first time in my life.

I'm not sure I would have had the nerve to leave Wilmington without the self-confidence I learned from Rachel. I remembered so clearly the day we climbed to the top of the Empire State Building on my first visit to New York. Clutching Rachel's hand I moved to the edge of the observation deck. I felt dizzy and my head swam. I'd never imagined being so high. I could see the entire city, even recognize parts of it. Ocean liners rocked gently in the Hudson River. A dirigible floated over Penn Station, off to the north. The cars, trolleys and people below us rushed around like sand fleas on a Carolina beach. After lots of encouragement I did manage to circle the deck, holding on to Rachel with one hand and the outer rail with the other.

'See,' Rachel said, 'that wasn't so bad. Besides, it's good training for you. We're riding the Cyclone roller coaster tomorrow.'

'I can't, I'm sure I'll be too scared,' I said.

'Don't be silly,' she said. 'I know you can do it.'

The next day I did ride that roller coaster. Twice, in fact, the second time with my hands raised high above my head.

Rachel's words sustained me through some tough times in later years. 'I know you can do it.' I could almost hear her voice.

I drained the icy dregs of my Coke and decided that my fictional toothache was a good enough excuse to take the rest of the day off. I wanted to go shopping, because I hated the hours-long wait in cashiers' lines on Saturdays. But I was afraid I might run into someone I knew who'd wonder why I was out of the office on a weekday afternoon. While I was in Quigleys I did buy tooth powder, face cream and the quota of three Hershey's chocolate bars from a fresh box a sales clerk had just placed on a shelf.

I decided to spend part of the afternoon at the public library, find a French–English dictionary and try to translate the journal articles by Bloch that Metcalf gave me, so I could see what kind of expert he was.

I was lucky. I caught a northbound bus right away. I got off at Mt. Vernon Square, where the vast neoclassic library building stood. Like many Washington public buildings, it mimicked a Greek temple, but one with 'Poetry', 'Science' and 'History' etched into the entablature instead of some stylized battle between ancient, weathered gods.

The library interior wasn't refrigerated, but stone walls and marble floors cooled it, and I felt refreshed the minute I walked inside. I found the reading room, such a relief from the hectic pace of a capital city at war. It was a long, vaulted space with tall bookshelves and polished mahogany tables reflecting the warm yellow glow of dozens of reading lamps. The only sound was the quiet murmur of bodies shifting in their seats, turning pages and an occasional clearing throat.

Nearly all the chairs were occupied.

The reference librarian told me that her one French to English dictionary was kept locked up, like our London telephone book, and I had to use it right at the librarian's desk under her watchful eye. Besides, it was

129

in use, and a couple of people were waiting their turns. I could sign a request, come back in half an hour and use the dictionary for fifteen minutes. I thought of flashing my OSS identity card, but figured that might not get me any sympathy, since OSS was probably responsible for requisitioning most of the library's dictionaries in the first place.

I slipped into an anteroom to read the latest magazines while I waited. I picked up *Life*, which fell open at a shocking scene of civilian suffering in Russia. A small child, a boy, perhaps two years old, lay frozen in death in a snow bank, an arm and leg contorted unnaturally. Nazi soldiers had flung him up against a stone wall and left him to die. His mother lay next to him, shot to death.

For a minute I thought I'd burst into sobs right there, in public, what I saw was so awful. And of course I thought of Rachel and Claude. If the Nazis were capable of such atrocities in Russia, they could perpetrate them anywhere.

I closed the magazine and did my best to compose myself. No more war news for me. I couldn't afford to be immobilized by fear.

I reached for another magazine, *Home Companion*, I think, but I quickly tired of its gee-whiz tone. The women in its pages bore no resemblance to anyone I knew. In its cheerful stories women skipped off to work in full make-up with neatly coifed hair pulled back in colorful do-rags, carrying lunch pails full of healthy home-made food. Their overalls didn't get dirty no matter how filthy the job. If they weren't married with an obliging mother at home caring for their children, they were engaged to a shop foreman or a military officer. None of them were war widows or lived in boarding houses or had to park their children in crowded day nurseries.

All the women's magazines told us women war workers that we must be willing to take on men's work until the end of the war, then gratefully return to our true calling, caring for husbands and children and homes. Funny how all those magazines were edited by men. And they didn't bother to tell those of us who weren't wives and mothers what we were supposed to do when peace returned, once we weren't critical to the war effort any more.

I was glad when my wait for the French–English dictionary was over.

I used it under the watchful of eye of the reference librarian, who kept checking her watch. Under those circumstances I didn't get through much more than the titles of Bloch's journal reprints. In French they were 'Gyres en Mer Méditerrannée et en Algérie', 'Un tourbillon en mer ouverte dans le bassin algérien' and 'Subduction sur le front Alméria– Oran'. It was a struggle, but I managed to translate them as 'An Open Sea

131

Eddy in the Algerian Basin', 'Subduction at the Algerian–Oran Front', whatever that was, and 'The Mediterranean Sea and Algerian Whirlpools'. At least, the closest I could come to the French word 'gyres' was 'whirlpool', although I suspected there was a better scientific term for it. Boring as the articles sounded to me, it was clear that Gerald Bloch was an expert on the Algerian coastline. His information could be crucial to the Allies' landing on the North African coast. This gave me, I reasoned, a legitimate reason, not only a personal one, to continue searching for Bloch's file.

The librarian had her hand extended for the dictionary before I'd finished closing the book. I handed it over to her and went outside into the heat.

When I got home the house was quiet. Dellaphine and Phoebe must have been napping through the hot hours of the late afternoon, resting up before the dinner rush began. I felt deliciously alone. I decided to sit out on the porch with my book and relax. I was worn out, and wanted to forget about Rachel, Claude, and Gerald and their fate for a while.

I went into the sitting room looking for *Five Little Pigs*, and found Joe napping on the sofa. A book with Cyrillic letters on its spine lay open across his chest.

His glasses lay on the floor where they'd

dropped from his hand. I bent over to retrieve them. Then, with the curiosity of all nearsighted people who want to know how blind someone else is, I held Joe's glasses up to my face and looked through them. The lenses were clear.

ELEVEN

Joe's eyeglasses didn't alter my vision at all. My book forgotten, I carefully laid the glasses across his chest and tiptoed straight upstairs to my room.

I closed the door softly and lay down on my bed to think. Okay, so Joe didn't teach at GWU and he didn't need glasses. He wasn't who he said he was. So what? Half the people in Washington had cover stories. None of my fellow boarders knew I worked for OSS. I was a government file clerk, one of thousands. Henry's job was equally vague. He'd been a reporter for a Chicago newspaper, so I figured he worked for one of the black or white propaganda agencies.

Wearing glasses with clear lenses wasn't much of a disguise, when you considered some of the lengths our agents went to change their appearances. Maybe Joe wanted to look different, older, for personal reasons, not wanting to be recognized if he crossed paths with someone he once knew in London or Prague. He might have friends or family still in Czechoslovakia.

The staff from the Axis embassies were under guard somewhere until our government could figure out what to do with them, some people said living it up at a resort hotel in Virginia, but that didn't mean there weren't plenty of Nazi spies in Washington. One couldn't be too careful. 'Loose lips sink ships' screamed at us from posters all over town. Blowing cover, your own or someone else's, was the worst sin an OSS employee could commit. Out in public, if I saw a familiar face from work, I kept my mouth shut. That person could be shadowing a foreign agent, or making a dead drop.

I knew what I needed to do. I wouldn't break Joe's cover. No questions, not even one. As of this moment I was uninterested in his past or what he did when he left the boarding house for 'work'.

Any thought that Joe was other than a refugee teaching Slavic languages somewhere in the city was ludicrous.

Joe Prager opened his eyes and lifted his glasses from his chest, shaking his head. He slipped them back on. So stupid. He'd objected to the eyeglasses from the start. From experience he'd learned that the most convincing disguises were the unobtrusive ones.

The beard, the books and papers, the worn, vaguely European clothing were simple to tack on to his public persona. But he'd never in his life needed eyeglasses, and now he had to remind himself constantly to wear them or carry them around. It wasted his concentration.

Louise was a smart woman. He didn't know what government agency she worked for, but he couldn't take any chances. When they went out Friday he had to have some explanation that would seem authentic to her, or his mission could be compromised. He'd worked too hard to allow that to happen. And he'd regret it if anything happened to her because of his carelessness.

'What?' I said. 'What is it?'

Conversation, and consumption, had stopped at the dinner table. Everyone stared at me. Ada was open-mouthed in astonishment. Feeling self-conscious, I lowered my forkful of meatloaf to my plate.

'Where did you say you were going, dearie?' Phoebe asked.

'To a reception at Evalyn McLean's, tomorrow night,' I said. 'A friend of mine asked me to go with him. My new boss at work,' I added hastily, with a glance at Joe, who'd gone back to his meal.

'My goodness,' Phoebe said. 'That's a coup. Everyone will be there. Royalty, even. Queen Margathe, King David. I wonder if

135

Mrs McLean will wear the Hope diamond?'

'If she hasn't pawned it yet,' Henry said.

'I heard,' Ada said, 'that the Saltzes, who own that swank men's clothing store on "G" Street, go to the McLean home before every party to tie the men's ties for them.'

'For once I agree with Roosevelt,' Henry said. 'That crowd is a bunch of parasites if you ask me. All they do is party – parties every damn day in the paper – dinners, luncheons, teas, tea dances, receptions and cocktail parties. Dozens on one night. They ought to spend their money on war bonds instead.'

'I don't know,' Joe said. 'Think of the political intrigue that goes on. Wealthy, powerful people from all over the world live in Washington now. London, Paris, Moscow, Rome, Berlin, they're all occupied, or under siege. Parties give them the chance to get together and talk away from their offices and embassies. That's why American government people go.'

'Except for Congressmen and Senators,' Phoebe said. 'Can't afford to dress themselves, much less their wives.'

'What are you wearing?' Ada asked me.

'I don't know. I don't think it matters much,' I said. 'Don, my friend who invited me, says women wear anything to parties now.'

'You must dress appropriately,' Phoebe said. 'I don't care if there is a war on. There are certain standards women still must meet. Do you have a cocktail dress? Silk stockings? Jewelry?'

'I've got one pair of silk stockings I've been hoarding,' I said. 'But no party dresses. I have my pearls.'

'Pearls aren't correct for a cocktail party. I'll lend you some jewelry,' Phoebe said. 'I have some presentable pieces left.'

Ada put down her fork and wiped her mouth with her napkin.

'Come upstairs with me,' she said. Her tone of voice was more of a command than a request, and I obeyed.

We ran into Madeleine in the hall. Ada took her by the arm.

'Come with us,' she said. 'I've been meaning to see if some of my clothes fit you. Believe it or not, I was once as thin as you two are.'

Madeleine and I exchanged eager glances. Ada had beautiful clothes. Neither one of us was embarrassed at the prospect of wearing her reach-me-downs.

Ada's room was a mess, her bed unmade, face powder and perfume bottles spread across the dresser. Half the dresser doors stood open, overflowing with lingerie and nightdresses. The only tidy spot was the corner where her clarinet and music stand stood near a window, angled to catch the light.

The single narrow closet in my bedroom

137

sufficed to hold all my clothes with room to spare, but Ada had added a wardrobe to her room. She opened the doors and pulled out an armful of dresses.

'Here,' she said, 'this should work for the McLean party,' handing me an indigo-blue silk tea-length cocktail dress with lace cap sleeves and a sweetheart neckline. 'And you must have these,' she said, draping two smart suits, one a seersucker cotton and one black raw silk, both with fashionably squared shoulders, over my arm.

She gave Madeleine a topaz silk party dress with a flared skirt, a black knee-length skirt and two white blouses, and a khaki cotton suit with pink rickrack edging the jacket collar and sleeves.

'Try these on,' she said. 'I want to see you in them.'

Madeleine and I didn't have to be urged. We stripped to our cotton slips. The clothes fit us both, though mine were a bit large in the bust.

'Stuff some tissue in your brassiere,' Ada said to me. 'You could use some help in that area anyway.'

Madeleine and I thanked Ada profusely, and meant it.

In the hall, our arms laden with our loot, I cocked my head towards my bedroom.

'Come with me,' I said. 'We can do each other's hems.'

In my room we took turns standing on a

138

chair pinning our hems up. I had Madeline take in a quarter-inch from the bust darts of my dresses while we were at it.

'No tissue stuffing?' Madeleine asked.

'With my luck, it would slip down and fall out around my shoes,' I said.

'Do you ever wonder,' Madeleine said, through a mouthful of straight pins, 'about Miss Ada? Where she lived before the war, what she did?'

'What do you mean? I thought she was a music teacher in New York. When all the men enlisted, the bands starting hiring women musicians.'

Madeleine lowered her voice. 'Momma said that when she signed for her room, Miss Ada spelled her name with two "n's."'

Hermann, instead of Herman.

'Momma said that when Miss Ada noticed what she'd done she got real flustered and red in the face before she scratched the second "n" out.'

'Really,' I said. Sounded like Ada had anglicized her surname recently.

'I told Momma that Miss Ada's English was too good for her not to be a real American.'

'I think so, too.'

I'd wondered about Ada myself. She spoke even less about her life before the war than the rest of us. It was queer not to know more about the people I lived and worked with. I'd grown up in a town where everyone knew

139

everyone else and their families back years and years. Here we were all strangers, thrown together by a worldwide calamity. We could tell each other lies galore, invent life histories, and start over again more than once. Because of the war people found good jobs and had money to spend. Ada could play in a dance band, I escaped my parents' fish camp, and Madeleine daydreamed about moving to Europe and being free as a white woman. But all this freedom was unnerving, too. What did I know about the people I met except what they told me?

After Madeleine and I finished we hurried downstairs so as not to miss *Cavalcade of America*. I joined Phoebe and the other boarders in the lounge, while Madeleine went into the kitchen to sit at the kitchen table with her mother.

Phoebe hadn't redecorated since the twenties, the last time she had any money. The painted parlor set was chipped, its velvet upholstery worn in patches. Fussy fringed lampshades focused pools of light on the shabby cabbage-rose-patterned rug. A portrait of Phoebe in flapper spit curls and a beaded cloche hat hung over the fireplace mantel. I squeezed into the middle spot on the davenport, between Phoebe and Ada. I found I couldn't focus on the radio show because I kept looking at Joe. Surreptitiously, of course. Not that he was doing anything anyone else but me would find fascinating. There was Joe winding his watch, Joe stretching back in his chair while digging in his pockets for matches, Joe drawing on his pipe until red embers glowed in the bowl, Joe scanning the evening newspaper during a Lifebuoy commercial. Once our glances met, and we smiled at each other, him so sweetly I thought I would melt through the davenport and floor right into the basement.

Of all the people I'd met since coming to Washington, Joe was the one person I wished I knew better, but he was the only one who I was sure had lied to me, even if it was by omission. I should have been wary of him, but I was so taken with the man that I rationalized what I was coming to think of as his 'cover story'. After all, I didn't broadcast that before arriving here I'd spent most of my days elbow deep in fish guts wearing a hair net to keep stray hairs out of the coleslaw.

What I did know, with a shock that felt almost electrical, was that I was content to be a single woman with a good job, that my virtue was way past protecting and that Joe and I were going to a concert together Friday night.

The sitting room grew unbearably hot and stuffy, on account of the dim-out curtains, so soon as the show was over we all got up to go upstairs to our rooms, except Henry, who went outside onto the porch. Joe and I went up the stairs together, behind the others, and

141

at the second floor landing he took my hand.

'About Friday,' he said. 'How about going to the National Symphony Orchestra with me?' The orchestra played many Friday evenings on a barge out on the Potomac. I'd seen the photographs in the newspaper.

'I'd love to,' I said. 'Shall I fix us a picnic?'

'Don't,' he said. 'I want to take you to dinner.'

'That would be lovely,' I said.

Joe slid his hand around me, resting it in the small of my back, and pulled me to him. Then he kissed me. Tremors of pleasure cascaded down my back and settled at the base of my spine, still sparking. If we'd been alone in the house I would have headed for Joe's bed so fast I'm sure I wouldn't have touched the stair treads on the way up.

But Joe shared his bedroom with Henry, Mr Cold Water Bath himself. And Ada was next door to mine.

I pulled gently away.

'Did I do something wrong?' Joe asked. Hell, no, I thought, I just want to do more of it in private!

'No, no, not at all,' I said. 'I don't want anyone to see us.'

We heard Henry downstairs, slamming the porch door.

Joe grinned. 'I understand,' he said. 'Sleep tight.'

Joe released my hand and went on up the next flight of stairs to his attic, and I floated across the landing into my room, closed the door and flung myself across my bed. Way too overheated to think about sleeping, I dug out a Hershey's chocolate bar, unwrapped the foil and ate the whole thing.

Then I heard it, the sound of three sharp clangs echoing down the water pipe from Joe's bedroom. The sound was embarrassingly loud, but then I remembered Henry was still downstairs, so Joe had no reason to be quiet. I reached for my brass bookmark and tapped the pipe twice. Covering my head with my pillow in shame and anticipation both, I listened for a reply. It came – one quick ring. I guess that was our signal – three, two, one – our private good night. I wondered if Joe and I would ever find ourselves alone in this house, and what might happen if we did. It was some time before my heart rate slowed enough for me to go to sleep.

TWELVE

When I arrived at work the next morning I found Barbara at her desk in tears, with both Betty and Ruth comforting her.

'What's happened?' I asked.

'Eighteen- to twenty-year-olds register for the draft today,' Ruth said, tears welling in her own eyes.

'Barbara's younger brother,' Betty added. 'Richard.'

Barbara blew her nose into her handkerchief.

'I'm sorry, Mrs Pearlie,' Barbara said. 'I'm so worried about my brothers, and about my mother being left alone.'

I sat down next to her and took her hand.

'I believe,' I said, 'that if you applied for hardship leave you would get it. It would be better for the baby too, don't you think?'

'I suppose,' she said. 'But I want to do my part to win the war.'

I bit my lip. For heaven's sake, I thought, stop being a martyr and go home. Nothing you can do here will bring your husband back.

'Maybe you could get a defense job back

144

home,' I said instead. 'Is your mother able to take care of the baby?'

'Sure,' Barbara said.

'You should go, Barbara,' Betty said. 'Besides, you'll never meet a new man here, not with working and everything.'

'That's all you think about,' Ruth said to Betty. 'Men. You can get along without one, you know.'

'That's easy for you to say, Miss Mount Holyoke.'

'Enough,' I said. 'Back to work, everyone.'

Barbara dried her eyes and before long the office rang with the sound of clacking typewriter keys.

Don appeared at my door and crooked his finger at me.

I went into the hall. He glanced around, then took my hand.

'You ready for tonight?'

'I'm looking forward to it,' I said.

'Good,' he said. 'I'll pick you up at seven.'

'I'll be ready.'

Someone opened a door nearby, and Don dropped my hand.

'I'm calling a division meeting at ten this morning,' Don said, 'to get all of us up to speed after Mr Holman's death. Would you please attend? And could you take notes and type them up for me?'

'Certainly,' I said. 'I'll be there.'

Holding Don's hand didn't feel as good as holding Joe's.

★ ★ ★

Tall metal file cabinets, Re–Ru, to be precise, crowded the conference room. We had barely enough space to squeeze ourselves into the hard wooden chairs that surrounded a table that looked as if someone once butchered meat on it, it was so heavily scarred.

'Before you sit, Mrs Pearlie, would you mind bringing me a cup of coffee?' Don asked.

'I'd like one too, if you don't mind,' Guy Danielson said.

'Of course,' I said. 'I'll be right back.'

I noticed no one asked Dora to get coffee. But that didn't mean the men regarded her as an equal. I'd heard that General Donovan once said Dora would be a division head if she weren't a woman. Her doctorate only went so far.

On the way out of the cafeteria with two steaming cups of coffee, I paused at a table behind a pillar and set the cups down. How much would be too much, too obvious? After glancing around to make sure no one saw me, I sprinkled about a quarter teaspoon of salt in each cup, a little trick I'd learned from a veteran secretary at the Wilmington Ship Building Company back home. 'You don't want them to think you did anything on purpose,' she told me, 'you want them to associate you with bad coffee. They'll never send you for it again.'

146

Don slurped from his cup, and a disappointed expression crossed his face.

'Is it all right?' I asked.

'Sure,' Don said, 'it's fine.'

Guy sipped his coffee, then set the cup down with a gesture of finality.

'I'm so sorry,' I said, 'it must have been the dregs. I should have made a fresh pot.'

'Don't worry about it,' Don said, 'let's get down to business.'

Guy, Roger, Dora and Don's replacement, Alex Singer, another economist, rustled their papers. I noticed that we all wore eyeglasses. The Bad Eyes Brigade, the other branches of the OSS called us.

'So,' Don said, 'I need you to brief me on what you're working on. Only the most important projects. I know, Alex, that you've picked up my analysis of those international insurance files sent to us by the London office.'

'Yes,' Alex said, 'I've reviewed your work to date, and I'll be able to send a list of German industrial plants to the Joint Chiefs by the end of next week.'

'Good,' Don said. 'What's next for you?'

'Special Ops sent over a stack of seized tariff records. I'm to review them and identify new oil refineries.'

'Good. Dora?'

'I'm finishing a study of class conflict in France, requested by the State Department, so they can understand the backgrounds of

147

the various French Resistance groups.'

'All they need to know is that de Gaulle is a horse's tail,' Guy said.

'I agree,' Dora said mildly. 'But probably not for the same reason you do.'

Roger kept his temper, restricting his response to a clenched jaw.

'What's next for you, Dora?' Don asked.

'Vatican politics,' she said.

'That'll take a couple of years,' Roger said.

'Not at all,' Dora answered. 'I've got two students from the theological college at Catholic University researching the topic right now.' Good God, Dora had priests working with her! Talk about cats and dogs sleeping together!

I couldn't help thinking of my mother, who called the handful of people who attended Wilmington's tiny St Joseph's church 'Roaming Catholics'.

'Guy?' Don asked.

'The Foreign Nationalities Branch has sent me boxes of transcripts of interviews with Russian refugees, most of whom were living in Paris before they fled here. My directive is to analyze them for "items of interest". I've just started.'

'Roger?'

'As you know I've been reading French underground newspapers smuggled to Switzerland and forwarded on to us. The most important trend continues to be the German advance into Vichy.'

'Why is that?' Dora asked. 'Didn't we think the Nazis would occupy Vichy eventually?'

'The Nazi strategy has been to insist that a legitimate France does exist, that it has chosen freely to ally itself with Germany, that it is unoccupied. That's been a psychological advantage when dealing with the French people.'

'Vichy controls the French navy,' Don said. 'Where are they in port now?'

'Toulon. And we don't know which side the navy's on, frankly. We hear they might be convinced to join the Free French.'

'What makes you think that Germany will occupy Vichy soon?'

'Little things,' Roger said. 'Like—' and here he glanced at his notes. 'Theodor Dannecker will be welcomed to Marseille at a reception at the mayor's residence on July 7. That's next Tuesday.'

'Dannecker,' Dora said. 'The Gestapo's deportation expert in France.'

'And Eichmann himself is expected in Paris sometime in July,' Don said. 'That's common knowledge.'

I felt sick. The Gestapo would arrive in Marseille on Tuesday, less than a week away. For all practical purposes any chance of escape for Rachel and her family would be over soon, very soon. Bloch was certain to be on some SS watch list. He'd applied for a visa to leave the country. He'd made contact with the French Resistance. He spoke

English, and he'd traveled abroad at least once.

Dora asked the question I wanted to but couldn't.

'Is it too late for people to get out? What is being done?'

'Very little,' Don said. 'There are no visas available. Our own country won't issue an entry visa without a Vichy exit visa, which Vichy isn't granting.'

'That's appalling,' Dora said.

Guy shrugged. 'The State Department thinks that Jewish refugees are all Communists and Zionists.'

'Oh, for heaven's sake,' Dora said. 'Of course they are. You would be, too.'

'Ears only,' Don said.

I stopped taking notes.

'There's an official in our consulate in Marseille who is known to ignore orders and issue U.S. visas to Jews without Vichy letters of transit. And there's a female French clerk at the town hall that helps refugees obtain false papers. And someone in the prefecture of police. Then there're the Quakers and the Mennonites and the YMCA. They do what they can.'

'Can these people be contacted?' Dora asked.

'By us? Absolutely not,' Don said. 'We might attract attention to them, blow their operations.'

So it was still possible to escape, I thought.

I hoped Bloch knew whom to approach, since his overture to OSS had been stymied by the 'loss' of his file. Don nodded to me to start taking notes again.

'On a related topic, Mrs Pearlie tells me that a file she left in Bob Holman's office went missing after his death.'

I knew the file was stolen, but I had no proof, so I kept my mouth shut, as usual.

'An important one?' Guy asked.

'It concerned contact with a Frenchman, from Marseille as it happens, some kind of ... what, Mrs Pearlie?'

'A hydrographer,' I said. 'An expert on the Mediterranean coastline of North Africa.'

'Mr Bloch wanted us to get his family out of Marseille in exchange for helping the Allies. Mr Holman planned to refer the file to the Projects Committee. There's been no sign of it since his death,' I said.

None of us mentioned Torch, the planned Allied invasion of North Africa, by name.

'There are dozens of local marine pilots with practical knowledge of the North African coast,' Guy said. 'And I understand that our people are making good contacts with the French Resistance in North Africa. Do we need this man's help?'

'Probably not,' Don said. 'But if any of you come upon this file, please return it to Mrs Pearlie.' He nodded at me. 'Otherwise, don't concern yourself with searching for the Bloch file any longer, Mrs Pearlie,' he said.

'It's not high priority.'

'Yes, sir,' I said.

That file was important enough for someone to steal it and rip out its reference card in our index files. The remaining torn corner was evidence, plain as the Romanov nose on Guy Danielson's face. I couldn't prove any of it; I couldn't even prove the torn corner belonged to the Bloch index card. But I knew it. And no one could stop me from doing everything I could to find out what happened to Bloch's file.

The Gestapo would arrive in Marseille in just six days.

I made up my mind to speak to General Donovan in private and tell him the story of the missing Bloch file. He was the only person in OSS I could be absolutely sure I could trust. The McLean party tonight was my best chance to approach him, maybe my only chance, without alerting the person who'd stolen the file.

THIRTEEN

'I love these,' I said, drawing a string of faceted jet beads out of Phoebe's jewelry box.

'They are nice,' she said, 'but you can't wear black in the summer. Unless you're in mourning. Here, these are what I had in mind.'

She handed me a lavaliere with a blue center jewel surrounded by sparkling clear stones on a silver chain and matching ear clips. The art deco pieces were angular and bold, out of fashion now, but I liked them.

'These are lovely,' I said, 'but I'm afraid I might lose them.'

'Rhinestones and zircons,' Phoebe said, 'not worth anything. If they were, I would have sold them years ago.'

She helped me fasten the chain around my neck, and I clipped on the earrings. In the mirror it looked like I was wearing real diamonds and sapphires, at least to my unsophisticated eyes.

Phoebe hadn't noticed I wasn't wearing my hoarded silk stockings. It was too hot to encase my legs in silk. It might not be

153

ladylike, but leg make-up would have to suffice.

Out in the hall I bumped into Ada.

'You look swell, Louise, you really do,' she said. She pulled me into the light from the hall window and gave me the once over. 'Don't wear your glasses,' she said. 'You look so much younger without them. And you need more face powder and rouge.'

'Don't be silly,' I said. 'I'd rather be able to see than look younger. And I hate thick make-up. It feels like I'm wearing a mask.'

'I could quick tweeze and pencil your eyebrows...'

'No.'

Ada shrugged. 'It's your date,' she said. 'It seems to me you'd want to show this man you've got the goods.'

Joe was in the kitchen when I went back to display my finery to Dellaphine and Madeleine, as I'd promised.

'Mrs Pearlie, you do look grand,' Dellaphine said. 'This man coming, he must be your beau.'

'Not at all,' I said, glancing at Joe, who was filling a glass with water at the sink. 'Just a friend who needs an escort.'

'Think of all the famous people you're going to meet!' Madeleine said. 'Promise to tell us all about it?'

'I'll take notes,' I said.

A bit annoyed that Joe hadn't said anything to me, I went up the hall towards the sitting room to wait for Don. Joe followed me and we were alone for a minute.

'You do look nice,' he said, which meant more to me than all the grands and swells I'd accumulated so far.

The doorbell rang, and I went into the hall to answer it. But Madeleine pushed by me, and with her fingers to her lips, motioned me back into the sitting room. 'I'll get the door,' she whispered. 'You wait.'

I stood awkwardly inside the door of the sitting room and listened to Madeleine speaking to Don. Joe drew on his pipe to hide a smile.

'Let me see if Mrs Pearlie is ready,' Madeleine said to Don. She left the door and poked her head into the sitting room. 'Stay here for a minute,' she whispered. 'Keep him waiting.' She lingered in the hall before returning to the front door.

'Come in,' she said to Don. 'Mrs Pearlie is in the lounge.'

He'd brought me flowers, a big bunch of flamingo-pink dahlias. The only flowers I'd ever gotten before were the tiny daisies Bill had brought me, picked from his mother's garden, on our wedding day.

'These are beautiful, Don, thank you,' I said.

'You're more than welcome, and you look lovely,' Don said. Men had given up dinner jackets for the duration of the war, but Don was handsome in a dark double-breasted

155

suit.

'I'll put these in water, Mrs Pearlie,' Madeleine said, as she took the flowers from me. Don extended his arm, I took it, and we left. I had no chance to glance at Joe again.

Don's car was a black Cadillac coupe with big bullet-shaped front and rear fenders and a chrome egg-crate grill.

'What a beautiful car,' I said.

'Thanks,' Don said, 'it's one of the last ones that came off the line. My old bucket was running okay, but I figured I'd better get a new car now, Lord knows when they'll be available again.'

And spent around $4,000 for it, if I remembered the newspaper ads correctly.

Don opened the passenger door for me before getting in the driver's side. So he had good manners, too. Don would be a catch, like Betty said, so why wasn't I infatuated with him instead of Joe, the mysterious foreigner? It made no sense, but I postponed worrying about all that for another time. Instead I settled back to enjoy an evening I had never imagined experiencing, even in my wildest dreams.

Friendship House was way out on Wisconsin Avenue in the country. Built with Colorado gold money, the estate was as luxurious as any on the East Coast. I'd seen pictures of it in magazines, but I still wasn't prepared for the excess we saw as we drove up the approach to the mansion. How did this vast lawn stay green in this heat? Where did the McLeans find the staff to tend to the greenhouses, the golf course, stables, winding walks and a selection of wildlife that included, I swear, llamas!

We drove under a porte-cochere wider than the one at the White House. Much, much wider! Don gave the keys to his Cadillac to a Negro man in blue-and-gold livery who drove it off to some out-of-sight parking area.

Don offered me his arm as we walked up wide marble steps to the veranda, which ran the length of the house, already crowded with guests escaping the heat of indoors. The veranda was lit with torches, decorated with potted palms and masses of fresh flowers, noisy with social babble and the tinkle of ice in highball glasses. Music and light streamed out of five sets of French doors that opened from the veranda into the house.

We went through a short receiving line. Evalyn McLean was wearing the Hope diamond. It was big as an egg, and dangled down the cleavage of her Hattie Carnegie dress.

After pecking our famous hostess on the cheek and reminding her who he was, Don introduced me.

'And how is your dear mother?' Mrs McLean said to him.

'Fine, thank you,' Don answered, barely able to reply before she turned her attention to the person behind him, a red-faced man sweating through a foreign uniform I could not identify.

'Who's that?' I asked Don.

'Archduke Otto of Austria,' Don answered, moving me away. 'He never passes up free food and drink.'

A waiter balancing a tray of full champagne glasses stopped, and Don took two, handing one to me. I'd never had champagne. I took a sip. I liked it. Maybe not quite as much as a Martini, but I decided the flute was more elegant than a Martini glass. Holding it and watching the bubbles rise, I felt just plain refined.

'So,' I said to Don, 'who is your mother that she knows Mrs McLean?'

'Mother played bridge several times with her in Palm Beach last season,' Don said. 'When I came to Washington, Mother wrote Mrs McLean and asked her to invite me to one of her parties. Thought it would be good for my career. Give me a chance to make some connections, you know.'

Don scanned the veranda as we spoke, looking for important people. I saw my chance.

'Don't worry about me,' I said, 'if you need to mingle. I can entertain myself.'

'Are you sure?' he said. 'We'll meet up later, of course.'

'Absolutely.' I could think of nothing I'd like better. This gave me a chance to look for General Donovan.

So Don squeezed my arm and left my side to join a group of civil-service types talking earnestly in a corner. After setting my empty flute on a nearby table, I set out to explore.

The five sets of French doors opened into, respectively, a music room, a card room, a billiards room, a drawing room and a dining room. All those five rooms connected by way of more French doors to a ballroom, a vista of polished floor, where a tuxedoed swing band played sedate versions of 'A Tisket, A Tasket', 'Ain't She Sweet' and such. This room, too, was crowded with people, many of whom I recognized from their pictures in the newspapers. Alice Roosevelt Longworth in a dramatic scarlet ball gown, talking and gesturing a mile a minute, charmed a group of admirers at one end of the room, while another set of sycophants encircled Maxim Litvinov, the new Russian ambassador. I swear he was wearing a denim suit – how very proletarian of him.

Donovan wasn't on the terrace, in the ballroom or in any of the other party rooms. I was disappointed, but I knew he might arrive later, so I took a break from my search to find something to eat that didn't cluck or swim.

The buffet stretched the length of the banquet-sized table in the castle-sized dining

159

room. It was crowded with platters of food – beef tenderloin sliced thin, shrimp, tray after tray of canapés and mounds of sweets. The sugar must have been bought on the black market for a fortune. I loaded a plate with petits fours, sugared nuts, slices of tender beef, tiny sandwiches filled with ham paste, stuffed celery, caviar sandwiches and olives. I'd not eaten caviar before, and after tasting it I wasn't sure I would again.

'You need something to wash that down,' said a French-accented voice next to me. 'Let me get you some champagne.'

A handsome man standing next to me, with his own plate and champagne balanced expertly in one hand, bowed slightly. He snagged a bubbling flute from a nearby tray and handed it to me with a flourish. 'Lionel Barbier, at your service.' He glanced at my ring finger. 'Miss?'

'Mrs,' I said. 'I'm a widow.'

'Dear me,' he said, 'this terrible war. Leaving so many lovely women alone.'

And you're available to comfort us all, I thought.

'My husband died five years ago,' I said. 'Of pneumonia, after a bad case of measles. My name is Louise Pearlie.'

Lionel took my outstretched hand, turned it over and kissed it. I felt like I was in the middle of a silly Maurice Chevalier movie. Lionel even looked a bit like Chevalier, broad shoulders, dark hair slicked back and wide, toothy smile. He wore a perfect white flannel suit, not easy to keep pristine these days, and a green silk bow tie that matched his square breast-pocket handkerchief. He looked to be in his late forties.

'Your accent is *adorable*,' he said.

'I'm from North Carolina,' I said. 'And you?'

'Chatou,' he said. 'A suburb of Paris. I learned English at the British School there. The Nazis of course now occupy it.'

'I'm so sorry.'

'Thank you, it is a tragedy,' he said, dropping his voice and glancing around him, 'but the triumphant actors taking their curtain calls may discover a sequel is already being written, one in which their characters do not fare so well, *vous comprenez?*'

'I do. Are you a refugee?' I asked.

'No,' he said. 'I'm on the staff of the French embassy. I'm an assistant to the cultural attaché. These days I translate the American newspapers and magazines, mostly. Not so many cultural events to arrange, you understand?'

'I see.'

'And you?'

'I'm a file clerk.'

'Ah, a government girl. May I inquire, are you here tonight alone?'

'No, I came with a date. He's working the crowd. Man talk.'

'What an unromantic activity.'

161

I couldn't help but smile at him. He was flirting with me so obviously that it was comical, yet I was having fun.

'Can your date wait a bit longer?' Lionel said. 'Do you like jazz? I'd like to take you where, shall we say, the party is a bit livelier.'

I was instantly on guard.

'Don't be so wary,' he said, 'there's a house party at the estate behind this one, a party with a more colorful assortment of guests, but not at all disreputable, I assure you. I think you would enjoy it. The music is more modern. It's a short walk from here.'

If I hadn't had two glasses of champagne I would never have accepted.

'Why not,' I said. Lionel offered me his arm and off we went.

We followed a stone path lit by torches down a hill behind the McLean house. Where the torches ended the path became gravel, but I could see more lights glimmering ahead of us. We came to the end of the track behind another estate, not nearly as opulent as Friendship House, but grand nonetheless. The house was dark, but that wasn't where the party was.

A huge swimming pool designed like a grotto nestled in a natural hollow behind the house. Candles in glass bowls and magnolia blossoms big as dinner plates floated on the water. More torches lit a stone bar where colored bartenders mixed highballs and Martinis as fast as they could. A stone patio crammed with dancing couples circled the pool.

'You see,' Lionel said, 'the people who own this house, they are away in the Catskills. Their son has his own circle of friends. While his parents are gone he seizes the opportunity to entertain them.' He nodded toward a young man lounging on the bar, talking to a pretty girl in a flared skirt, and gesturing widely with his Martini glass. Our host was dressed in baggy white trousers, white shoes and a red-and-white-striped shirt, the cuffs unbuttoned and hanging from his wrists.

A dance band made up of six Negro hepcats played on a stage in one corner of the patio. Their leader, a big man wearing a porkpie hat and a zoot suit, dangling a cigar from his mouth, pounded on a piano.

An acrid smoke, not cigarette, not cigar, hung in the air.

'Do you smell that funny odor,' I whispered to Lionel. 'Do you think something's on fire?'

'My dear,' Lionel said, smiling at me. 'That's hashish!'

'Really!' I said. I sniffed expectantly. I felt nothing, and none of the other guests displayed the symptoms of reefer madness, described so colorfully in *Crime Detective Magazine*. I was a bit disappointed.

I was a world away from the veranda and Mrs McLean's upper-crust guests. These people were having more fun.

163

It was a sophisticated crowd that I was sure wouldn't be welcome at Mrs McLean's, or at any of Washington's established restaurants and clubs. I noticed several couples where one of the pair wasn't exactly white. I'd never seen a mixed-race couple before, but I reminded myself that I was a modern girl and I didn't stare.

Then, as the band played the sultry sound of Duke Ellington's 'Mood Indigo', I saw two men dancing together, arms around each other's waists. I drew my breath in so quickly I choked on my champagne. Lionel handed me a cocktail napkin.

'Americans,' he said, 'you are so, what should I say? Naive?'

I hastened to assert my sophistication. 'Not at all,' I said. 'I had a catch in my throat.'

'Those two,' he said, nodding toward the male couple, 'one of them is Sir Julian Porter, personal secretary to the British ambassador, the other is a trade attaché for the Portuguese. The homosexual, he is many important people in the European foreign services, they are the most efficient underground network in Europe. If you want to get anything done quickly and efficiently, you ask a three-letter man to do it.'

'Really,' I said. 'You seem to know everyone. How long have you been at the embassy?'

'Since 1938.'

So Lionel was working in the French

embassy when France fell. It must have been an excruciating experience for him, watching his country conquered by Germany. The embassy staffers 'welcomed' the new Vichy ambassador, Henry-Haye, when he arrived in Washington to take control of the French embassy. He must have sworn allegiance to Vichy and Marshal Pétain through gritted teeth. Most of those loyal embassy staffers, even the janitors, proceeded to feed Vichy secrets to the Allies as fast as they could smuggle them out. I suspected Lionel was of the Gaullist persuasion, and wondered what kind of secrets he had access to. Lionel might be a useful person to know. I caught myself in mid-thought. What was wrong with me? I was a file clerk obsessed with a folder of missing papers. I didn't require a contact at the Vichy French embassy.

Lionel pulled me onto the dance floor, and I soon found myself happily jitterbugging away to 'C Jam Blues', followed by 'All That Meat and No Potatoes'.

I bumped into one of the mixed couples I'd noticed earlier, but retained my poise, even after I recognized Roger Austine.

'Mrs Pearlie,' Roger said, 'let me introduce you to my fiancée, Marie Lebron.' Marie was a stunning light-skinned Negress who wore her saffron silk dress with poise and style. She held out her hand to me.

'Mrs Pearlie,' she said, with a Caribbean accent, 'I think you work with Roger?'

My worldliness knew no bounds. I squeezed her hand in return. 'I do. I'm a file clerk.'

Marie rolled her eyes. 'I expect you are more than that. I have three languages, and the men I work for speak only one, yet I am a secretary.' She tucked a jet-black lock of hair under her turban. 'And when we go to a party, Roger and me, we must stay, what is the English expression? Below stairs. If it weren't for these awful Nazis, I would not live in this place.'

'It's not for ever, darling,' Roger said, kissing her on the cheek. 'Wait until the war's over, then we'll get married and live wherever you like, Havana, or Kingston. Maybe Paris. Someplace civilized.'

Roger and Marie went looking for a cold drink, and we continued to dance. Lionel behaved like a gentleman. He kept his hands where they belonged.

Finally, hot and tired, I broke away and pulled Lionel out of the crowd. 'I have to go,' I said, 'to freshen up and find my date.' More importantly, I needed to find General Donovan.

Lionel rolled his eyes. 'Why? Is there a law in America, that you must leave a party with the man you came with?'

'Sort of,' I said. 'But he's my boss, too.'

'I see.'

'We're just friends.'

'Mrs Pearlie, would you be so kind as to

give me your telephone number?'

I hesitated. I knew nothing about this man. He could be a spy, or an arms dealer. I only had his word that he worked for the French embassy.

'I don't think so,' I said.

'I understand,' he said, shrugging, and pressing a calling card into my hand. 'But if you want me for anything, you may find me at this number. I live at the Wardman Hotel apartments.'

He gripped my hand with both of his, and looked at me with sober eyes. 'Anything at all you need, government girl, you telephone me.'

I hurried away back up the path to the McLean estate. What was that all about, I wondered. I stopped for a minute to catch my breath, and glanced at Lionel's card. It looked authentic, but I expected that I should throw it away. I'd enjoyed being the target of attempted seduction, especially by a gentleman with a French accent, but I doubted it would be so amusing a second time. Nonetheless I tucked the tiny cardboard rectangle into my pocketbook.

Inside the mansion I refreshed myself in an opulent ladies' restroom stocked with embroidered hand towels and perfumed soap. I didn't look too disheveled, considering I'd jitterbugged in this heat. All the corn-starch I'd dusted all over myself before dressing must have kept perspiration at bay.

167

I went looking for a cold drink and found myself in a large alcove off the ballroom. It contained a table with a punchbowl full of lemonade. I drank a cup straight down, then dipped out another. When I looked up I almost knocked over the whole table, punchbowl, cups and all. Clark Gable stood across the way, alone, gazing out a window. The man was impossibly handsome in an immaculate suit, but I was taken by how dreadfully unhappy he seemed. He turned to catch me staring at him, then donned his celebrity face and smiled at me. He had the whitest teeth I'd ever seen.

'Ma'am,' he said, bowing ever so slightly.

'Hello,' I said, stupidly holding out a cup. 'Would you like some lemonade?'

'No thank you,' he said, 'I favor something a bit stronger.' He retrieved a highball glass half full of amber liquid from the windowsill.

My hand trembled as I dipped lemonade into my own glass, sloshing it onto the tablecloth. As I wiped at it with a napkin I bumped the table, sending the punchbowl sliding towards Gable. He stopped the slide with one hand, and held tightly to the bowl while I cleaned up the mess.

'You must be used to rescuing yourself from star-struck fans,' I said.

Gable gulped from his highball.

'Oh, I suppose so,' he said, 'but it's a good problem for an actor to have.' He smiled at me again, more authentically this time.

168

Crinkly laugh lines spread over his face. I felt myself relax.

'And what is your name?' he asked.

'I'm Louise Pearlie. I work for the government.' I was tired of using the words 'file clerk'.

'As do we all, these days,' Gable said. 'I'm here to persuade all these rich people –' waving his glass at the crowds in the ballroom – 'to buy war bonds instead of giving expensive parties.'

'Is that why you're hiding out in this alcove?' I asked.

'I admit to being a bit tired of being on display,' he said. 'I'd like to contribute more substantially to the war effort. I'm joining the Army Air Corps, but I doubt anyone will let me fly real missions. I'm too old, for one thing. But boot camp and training will keep me busy.'

We both ran out of small talk. Gable contemplated his glass for a few seconds and his shoulders slumped. Then he straightened up and seemed to rouse himself.

'Must go make the rounds now,' he said. 'Duty calls.'

'Of course,' I said.

He squared his shoulders and made his entrance into the ballroom, attracting all eyes instantly, and left me remembering that his wife, Carole Lombard, had died a few months ago in a plane crash while touring the country promoting war bonds. I'd read that Gable had to be restrained by rescue crews from trying to reach the crash site himself.

My brief encounter with Mr Gable that night reminded me that no one, no matter how rich, how famous, how insulated from everyday life, was exempt from loss during this horrible war. Phoebe could lose one of her sons any day, as could the Roosevelts and countless others. Gerald, Rachel and little Claude might be loaded onto a filthy cattle car and shipped east to a labor camp next week, and here I was acting the merry widow, jitterbugging and drinking champagne.

I went looking for General Donovan. I scouted every room, cased the veranda, hunted among the dancing couples in the ballroom and even staked out the men's room.

Just when I was about to give up, I heard the General's voice. I found the OSS director, a kindly, chubby, pink-faced man, why they called him 'Wild Bill' I had no idea, in the billiards room drinking with a group of serious, dark-suited men.

One of the men was Don. That instantly squelched my plan. How naive could I be? Of course General Donovan wouldn't ever be alone at a party like this, or anywhere else I might run into him, for that matter. I couldn't possibly have a private conversation with him. My spirits sank, and with them my

170

hopes for helping Rachel. Suddenly I had no patience for this pretentious party, the politicians and refugees jockeying for advantage, and society women weighed down by their jewels. I just wanted to go home and nurse my sick heart.

Don saw me standing in the doorway, and inclined his head toward the door to the ballroom. I nodded, slipped out, and waited for him, listening to 'The "A" Train', so mellow and melodic compared to the earthy music at the party next door.

'Did you see?' Don said, taking my arm. 'I was talking to General Donovan. Holding my own, too.'

'That's great,' I said. 'I'm sure you made a good impression.' I couldn't have cared less, actually.

'I hope so.' Don glanced at his watch. 'Are you about ready to leave? I know we haven't spent much time together this evening, but I want to be in the office early tomorrow. Have you had any dinner?'

'Oh, I've danced, and eaten,' I said. 'I don't mind going now.'

On the drive home I created a wonderful fantasy to put my mind at ease. Rachel and her family had already escaped France and were living happily in Switzerland. I hadn't received any of her letters yet because of the war. Rachel didn't need me to help her escape; she was fine, and Claude too. I grasped on to this fictional straw and held on for dear life. What else could I do? I was out of ideas.

We necked for a while in Don's car outside my boarding house. I was curious how I would feel about, well, you know. What a dud! I felt not a single spark, not one! I got a better tingle from hearing Joe knock on a pipe in the bedroom above me, not to mention the seismic activity I felt during his kiss on the staircase! So much for Don. I couldn't marry him, no matter how much money he had.

Apparently I wasn't in the market for a husband, despite my parents' instructions. What was I in the market for, I wondered. I needed to think about that before I went out Friday night with Joe.

Once inside and upstairs I slipped into Ada's room.

'Ada, Ada,' I said, shaking her awake.

'What!' she said. 'Did you have a good time? Tell me everything!'

'I met Clark Gable!'

'You did not!'

'I did so!'

'Oh, my God! Did you talk to him?'

'A little, but not before I almost tipped a punchbowl of lemonade all over him.'

'What was he like?'

'A hunk of heartbreak, just like in the movies.'

She jiggled my arm. 'Tell me more.'

'Mrs McLean did wear the Hope diamond. But I've got to go to sleep. Work tomorrow. I'll tell you everything else at breakfast.'

Back in my room I hung my new dress, new for me anyway, carefully in my closet and drew my nightdress over my head. I was terribly hot, but I couldn't run the bath or I'd wake Phoebe. I tiptoed across the hall and soaked a washcloth, lifting my nightdress to sponge myself. After brushing my teeth I slipped back into my bedroom.

Someone had placed the vase of dahlias Don brought me on my dresser. And a letter from my mother. I'd seen it when I'd gotten home from work but had been too busy to read it. I was wide awake, so I sat on my bed cross-legged and slit open the envelope. My mother's letters didn't vary much from week to week. The fish camp and marina, church, my brother's children, how crowded with soldiers Wilmington had gotten. But when I opened the envelope, a rectangle of cardboard fell out.

It was a postcard from Rachel.

She was still in Marseille.

FOURTEEN

My heart filled my chest and my lungs seemed to stop working, like the time I fell out of a pecan tree in the back yard of my home in Wilmington, landed flat on my back and had the breath knocked out of me. After what seemed like many minutes I gasped, drew in air, light-headed with relief to know Rachel was alive, disappointed that she was still in Vichy France.

Headed 'Marseille, June 3', the card was postmarked in Lisbon three weeks ago. Rachel must have given it to some lucky friend with an exit visa to mail for her in Portugal.

'Dearest Louise,' Rachel wrote, her familiar handwriting cramped into the tiny message space. 'No time to write a letter. Can you help us get out of Vichy? It's very bad here now, we can't get a visa. Love, *au revoir*, Rachel.'

'Can you help us?' I've been trying, I telegraphed my thoughts toward France, I've been trying.

I turned the postcard over. It was a simple tourist card, with a view of the Château d'If,

174

the island prison off Marseille where Edmond Dantes, the hero of *The Count of Monte Cristo*, languished for so many years. I'd told Rachel that if I ever got to visit her, I wanted to see that famous island first thing. She'd laughed and teased me about being a bookworm.

I went to bed, but couldn't sleep. My mind wandered from the McLean party – where I'd ogled the Hope diamond, been seduced by a Frenchman, eaten caviar and drunk champagne, seen two men dancing together, chatted with a colored woman who was better dressed than I and met Clark Gable – to my fears for Rachel and her family. Terrible, awful fears.

Since I'd failed to speak to General Donovan at the party I was at a loss to know what to do for Rachel next. 'Can you help us?' she'd written. I felt hopeless and helpless.

Finally I fell asleep. It's not surprising that a haunting dream disturbed my rest. In the dream I searched a frozen landscape strewn with corpses, inspired I'm sure by the pictures I'd seen in *Life* magazine. Of course I was looking for the remains of Rachel and Claude, turning over the bodies of every woman and child I saw. There were so many of them. And I wasn't alone. Phoebe and Eleanor Roosevelt, holding hands and accompanied by Fala, sought their sons. I saw Clark Gable, in an Army Air Corps uniform, carrying a shovel, hunting for his wife's grave. None of us found what we were looking for, and at last the dream dissolved into a new day.

It was a little after ten o'clock Thursday morning when Barbara snapped. I was longing for my coffee break, since I'd gotten so little sleep the night before. Ruth was loading files onto her file cart. Betty was typing yet another report, single-spaced, with nine sheets of carbon paper squeezed between ten sheets of typing paper.

Barbara rose from her chair, lifted her typewriter and flung it with all her strength across the room. It crashed against a wall and thudded to the floor, loose keys scattering everywhere. Betty held up her arms to fend off the airborne bail, and Ruth flinched. I got up from my seat to go to Barbara, but her expression stopped me.

'It's no use,' she said. With both fists she slammed the two-foot stack of newspapers in her in-box, it teetered, then collapsed, pages slithering along the office floor.

'There's nothing we can do here,' she said. 'We can't stop them.' She gathered up a neat pile of newly typed and alphabetized index cards and flung them in a wide arc about the room.

Ruth spoke first.

'Dearie,' she began.

'What dimwit thought all this could help win the war?' Barbara interrupted, gesturing around the room. 'It's just paper. I wish I were a man. Then at least I could enlist and kill Nazis.'

'Barbara,' I said. 'We are all doing everything...'

Cold-eyed, fists clenched, she glared at me. 'There's not one American over there yet, and people are dying every day. Every day! When in God's name are we going to invade Europe?'

Betty tried next. 'It takes time,' she said, 'we've got to train soldiers, build airplanes and ships...'

'Do you know what's on page one of this worthless excuse for a newspaper?' she said, gathering up the morning edition of the *New York Times* and shaking it at us. 'Not starvation, not the refugee crisis, not cold-blooded murder, it's all about Governor Lehman donating his tennis shoes to the war effort! With everything that's going on in the world! The Governor's tennis shoes! And if I have to hear one more time about how Fala sacrificed his chew toys to the scrap-rubber drive I'll strangle the spoiled little beast with my bare hands!'

I wondered if Barbara was having a nervous breakdown. I'd never witnessed one before, but this appeared to fit the bill. I didn't know what to do. Should I call the security guard? Don? If I did that, what would happen to Barbara? And her child?

Barbara opened her pocketbook and removed her powder compact and lipstick. She calmly repaired her face. Then she replaced her cosmetics, snapped shut the pocketbook, slung it over her shoulder like a rifle and strode out of the room.

'Aren't you going to do something?' Betty asked me.

'No,' I said. 'I'm not. Let's see if she comes back today. Or tomorrow. I'll put her down as sick. If she doesn't show up on Monday, I'll report it.'

'By then she might have left town with the baby,' Ruth said.

We were civilians, but OSS reported to the Joint Chiefs, so we were disciplined like soldiers. Leaving OSS without permission was tantamount to going AWOL.

'I know, I know.' I said. 'I'm still going to wait. For now let's get this mess cleaned up, before somebody comes in and sees it.'

The three of us stacked and sorted until Barbara's desk looked normal, like she'd be back from the ladies' room any minute. I wondered how soon we could replace her if she didn't return, there was an awful shortage of clerical workers. I didn't want to think about dividing her work up among the three of us.

'Well,' I said. 'I need coffee. Hold the fort for me for fifteen minutes, then I'll come back and you two can go.'

I joined Roger Austine at a table in the cafeteria. He was alone, so I got right to the

178

point.

'Roger,' I said. 'What's happening in Vichy?'

'Good morning to you, too! Why do you want to know?'

'One of my girls had an attack of nerves after reading the *New York Times* this morning.'

'Oh. I'm so sorry. Well, the news is bad, of course. I expect by fall Vichy won't exist, the Germans'll occupy it. With all that entails.'

'What are we doing about it?'

Roger shrugged. 'We sit on our fannies and research and write newsletters and circulate reports and memos and issue recommendations. What General Donovan and General Marshall and the Big Chief do with all that, they decide, not us.'

He lowered his voice. 'Have you heard?' he asked.

'What?' I said.

'Dora's lost her Top Secret clearance.'

I was stunned. 'You're joking.'

'I wish I was. I think Guy had something to do with it, that fascist. Not only that, I think Don, with Guy's connivance, didn't protest.'

'Why? She's brilliant! Everyone says so!'

'Dear girl, she's Red and sleeps with women. So much more important than the quality of her work. Remember, our beloved nation was founded by Puritans, and they still move among us!'

'She's not Red.'

179

Roger shrugged. 'I wouldn't be surprised if she did favor a very deep pink. The question is, is she untrustworthy? I don't think so.'

'Donovan admires Dora, so maybe he's trying to protect her.'

Roger raised an eyebrow. 'You thought of that, too? If she doesn't have access to secrets, she can't be suspected of passing them. At any rate, she was quite calm about it. Packed up her books and notes and toted it all over to the Library of Congress. She commandeered a table in the reading room and got right back to work.'

'Her Catholic University students are working there already.' I tried to picture Dora spending every day with a couple of seminarians. Would they be wearing monks' robes? Or black cassocks? I stifled a giggle brought on by nerves as much as amusement.

One thing you had to credit to the Nazis, they'd united a lot of very different sorts of people in opposition to them. I wondered if that camaraderie would last after the war.

Roger left and Joan joined me. She looked stricken.

'You heard about Dora?' she asked.

I said I had. 'Roger implied that Guy might have had something to do with it.'

'I wouldn't be surprised.' She stirred her coffee compulsively. 'The thing is,' she said, 'looking around, I wonder how that lost file of yours figures into all this.'

I felt my heart rate pick up speed.

'What do you mean?'

'General Donovan asked me today if the file had been found. Very unusual for him. He's too busy to worry about such things. It wasn't but ten minutes later that I heard Dora had lost her clearance.'

'It could be a coincidence. If you think about it, it's not surprising she lost her clearance,' and I stopped without finishing my sentence, wondering if I should.

'Why?'

'She's not most people's idea of a regular American.'

Alone in the office for the few minutes that Ruth and Betty were at their coffee break, I laid my head on my desk and permitted myself to feel overwhelmed; by Barbara's despair, by Dora's demotion, by my ambiguous feelings for Joe, and my fears with Rachel's safety.

I alone knew that Bloch's file had been stolen, not lost. Someone had taken advantage of Holman's death to swipe that file and to steal Bloch's index card, wiping him off OSS radar. Why? And who? A mole, or a sleeper, here at OSS, who wanted to neutralize Gerald Bloch's usefulness to the Allies? I didn't much care about Gerald, truthfully, I just wanted Rachel and Claude to escape France, find safety somewhere until the war was over.

What more could I do? Without documents to forward to the OSS Projects Committee there was no hope that any attempt would be made to rescue the Bloch family.

Receiving Rachel's postcard had reconnected us after years of silence, in a cascade of emotion that reminded me of our friendship so poignantly, and made me more determined than ever to help her if I could.

In a single flash of inspiration, it came to me, the entire preposterous scheme. This city was one gigantic file cabinet. If we had a file on Gerald Bloch because he was a prominent hydrographer who might be useful to the Allies, some other government office might have one too.

I would reconstruct the Bloch file from paperwork I located elsewhere, pretend I had found the missing file and present it to Don to forward to General Donovan and the Projects Committee.

I was congratulating myself on the genius of my plan when Don appeared at my door.

'Hi there,' he said, smiling at me.

'Hi.'

He sat on a corner of my desk.

'I had a very nice time last night,' he said.

'Yes,' I said. I was in a tough position here. This man was my boss. I wished to be polite, but not encouraging. I couldn't directly say I didn't want to date him again.

'I was wondering if you were busy on the Fourth?' he asked. 'I thought we could go sailing on the river, take a picnic.'

'I'm so sorry,' I said. 'I've already made plans.'

'You can't break them?' he said, clearly disappointed.

'No, I'm afraid not.'

'Perhaps the following weekend?'

'Perhaps,' I said.

My coolness made Don frown, but thank God, Ruth and Betty came into the office before he could speak. Betty's face lit up with speculation.

'Thank you, Mrs Pearlie,' Don said, politely, on his way out of the office.

'You're welcome, Mr Murray.'

I should never have necked with the man. I should have parted from him yesterday evening with a handshake, a convenient widow accompanying her boss to an important party.

'Oh, calm down,' I said to my girls, as they erupted in giggles after Don was out of earshot. 'I am not interested in Don. Don't you dare spread it around that we're an item.'

Betty felt my forehead.

'No fever,' she said. 'So you're not delirious. You must be bucking for a goofy discharge instead.'

'Stop it,' I said.

'We heard in the cafeteria, from some of the other girls, that Mr Murray told Roger Austine that you'd be a perfect wife for a

183

man with ambition. That you knew how to dress and when to join in a conversation and when to be quiet, and that you were a real sport when he left you alone so he could hobnob with the big shots.'

That reminded me of a recent Dorothy Dix witticism – I read her newspaper column without fail – that a man likes a woman with a brain as long as she only brings it out in an emergency.

'He does have money, too. I checked the social register. His mother is a Gibbs, they own People's Drug,' Ruth said.

'I'm not attracted to him,' I said, 'at all.'

'Don't you want to have a home and children?' Betty said. 'Belong to a country club? Do you want to work in an office for the rest of your life?'

I thought of Joan's lovely apartment, her car and her clothes. Did I long for the same comforts enough to marry someone for his money? Marriage was difficult enough when you loved your husband. But who knew if I'd be able to work after the war, after the men came home to their old jobs. And if I could work, would I have to live in a boarding house for the rest of my life?

'Enough of this,' I said. 'We need to get busy. If Barbara doesn't come back, we'll have to do her job too.'

Still clucking like a couple of matchmaking hens, Ruth and Betty went back to their desks. I retreated behind my partition to think, putting Don out of my mind. Where could I find more information about Gerald Bloch?

The original scribbled note about Bloch came to us from an operative in France through the OSS London office by way of a locked OSS diplomatic pouch, so there'd be no copies in Codes and Cables. No one had the keys to those pouches except David Bruce in London and General Donovan. General Donovan's files were unavailable to me, Joan had made that clear.

When I received the memo and original request for information from Donovan's office and added it to our subject file on Bloch I created the only OSS file on the man, and it was gone. I did find one document in another file, the program from the 1936 Edinburgh conference where Charles Burns and Marvin Metcalfe had first met Gerald Bloch. Metcalfe gave me a second copy of that program and reprints of three of Bloch's obscure journal articles when I visited him. That was a start, but it wasn't enough.

It was possible that the State Department had a dossier on Bloch, especially as he had applied for a visa, but I certainly couldn't attempt to penetrate the State Department. Security was much tighter than at OSS. If I got past the squads of military guards, I'd never get out the building with any official papers. Even if I had one of those nifty

matchbox cameras Eastman Kodak develop-
ed for photographing documents, which I
didn't, I needed original materials to make
the file look authentic.

I needed to acquire actual documents, and
the best place to find them? The embassy of
Vichy France. It leaked like a sieve already.
With Nazi record-keeping as obsessive as it
was, it seemed likely to me that the Vichy
embassy would have information on Gerald
Bloch. He was a prominent scientist, a Jew
who'd applied for a visa to leave France on
more than one occasion; perhaps the Gestapo already knew he'd approached the
Resistance. And I had a contact there, Lionel
Barbier, who'd told me to call him if I
needed anything, anything at all.

I prayed I was right when I sensed that he
was anti-Vichy.

Joan and I had arranged to meet for lunch at
the drugstore on the corner, but I arrived
early, sliding onto a stool at the soda counter. I ordered a Coke and a grilled-cheese
sandwich from the soda jerk.

Joan joined me. She looked uncharacter-
istically tired. Black circles rimmed her eyes.

'I'm not all that hungry,' she told the soda
jerk, ordering vegetable soup. That was odd,
too. She usually ate a cheeseburger, French
fries and a vanilla milkshake, with gusto.

'Look, Louise,' she said, then stopped.
'What?' I said.

'Nothing.'

'What's wrong, Joan? Are you okay?'

'Why is it I'm always attracted to the wrong men?' she said.

'Like who?' I asked, knowing what she would answer.

'Charles Burns,' she said. 'The creep.'

I thought he was a creep, too, but I wondered how she'd come to that conclusion.

'I ran into him outside my hotel last night and suggested we have dinner together. He accepted, we had a good time I thought – hell, I even picked up the check, since I'd asked him. You know what? He didn't even walk me upstairs to my room! Much less kiss me goodnight.'

'I'm so sorry,' I said. 'How rude.'

I didn't tell her that Charles had made a pass at me minutes after he'd turned her down after that afternoon we'd spent at her apartment.

'If you were a man, and some girl was making a fool out of herself over you, wouldn't you be a gentleman and tell her you weren't interested, instead of accepting bridge and dinner invitations?'

'Yes,' I said, 'I would.' Perhaps Burns thought a connection to General Donovan's secretary might be useful to him, I thought, but I kept that to myself.

'I think he's interested in you,' Joan said.

'What?'

'He asked me lots of questions about you.

Don't be surprised if he calls.'

'I wouldn't go out with him if he were the last man on earth,' I said. I suspected that Burns was after sexual adventure, not marriage. He couldn't seduce Joan, she was wealthy, from a prominent family who could damage his career, and besides, Joan would expect an engagement before Charles got her in bed. Me, on the other hand, I was an insignificant widow; who would care if he lured me into an affair? No one would expect him to marry me, and having already surrendered my virginity, I was past ruination.

Joan stirred her drink with a straw.

'All the girls from my sorority pledge class are married. Most of them have had babies. Some of them have two babies. I know I'm not pretty, but I'm not ugly, am I?'

'Stop that,' I said. 'You're one of the best people I know. You've got a million friends. You'll meet the right man, I know you will.'

'Sure. Let's not talk about it any more.' Joan looked around. The soda jerk was at the other end of the counter building a banana split.

'I brought you these,' she said, slipping several sheets of paper out of her handbag and passing them to me under the counter. 'Much against my better judgment. Don't look at them now. Just put them in your pocketbook.'

'What are they?' I asked.

188

'Carbons of the documents we have about Gerald Bloch from General Donovan's files.'

I was horrified.

'Joan, you can't! If he discovers they're missing...'

'No,' she interrupted me. 'The originals are still in his files. What I did was type new documents, copying what we had, with carbons. Then I destroyed my typed originals.'

'I can't thank you enough,' I said.

'I couldn't stop thinking about your friend. But don't tell me what you're going to do with these, I don't want to know.'

'Okay,' I said. 'I won't.'

'I've got to get back to the office,' she said. 'Take care.'

I went to the restroom and assessed the pages Joan had given me. What luck! Just as I'd decided to reassemble Bloch's file, Joan delivered crucial documents to me! Two carbons each of the translation of the French Resistance fighter's note and the memo from General Donovan requesting information. I wondered if these papers, added to the copy of the 1936 hydrology conference program given to me by Marvin Metcalfe, were enough to create a replacement file on Gerald Bloch. Would such sparse information compel OSS to act? What other documents might be neatly tucked away in the file cabinets of the Vichy French embassy that could bolster Bloch's chances?

With the Gestapo arriving in Marseille next week, there was no time to lose.

'I can't believe I'm abandoning you and the children,' Gerald said.

Rachel buried her head on Gerald's shoulder, but she'd given up crying weeks ago. Crying took too much energy, energy she needed to cope and to survive.

'We'll be safer if you're gone,' she said.

Gerald knew she was right. If the Nazis came here to arrest him, they would likely take Rachel and the children too. If he left them behind, the Gestapo might not bother with his family.

So much for his pitiful attempt to barter his family's freedom for his expertise. He'd failed, and now he had to abandon them in hopes the Nazis would forget them. He'd join the Resistance anyway, of course.

Gerald's arm circled Rachel's newly slender waist, and he kissed her gently on the cheek. Yesterday, on his way home from work, four Vichy French police stopped him, inspected his identity papers, searched his pockets and his briefcase and interrogated him for an hour, right out in the street. Rachel watched from their doorway, sure he was about to be arrested. They'd let him go, but not for long. He was an authority on the North African coast, so he was destined for prison or execution. It was just a matter of time.

A heavy vehicle rumbled to a stop outside their house, brakes squealing. They both froze. Rachel cracked the front door and peered out. The truck bore the Vichy government seal, but the four soldiers in the truck bed, guarding more than a dozen civilian Frenchmen, wore German uniforms and carried machine guns. The truck idled while its driver consulted a map before driving away, down the street and around the corner.

Gerald hoisted his bag over his shoulder.

'Don't worry about us,' Rachel said. 'We'll get extra rations because of the baby.'

She watched Gerald edge his way down the dark street, hugging the boarded-up buildings, pausing before turning the corner where the *pâtisserie* once stood. She had no idea where he was going or if she'd ever see him again. Tears coursed down her cheeks. She and her children were on their own.

I ducked into a drugstore phone booth, slipped a nickel into the slot and dialed the number Lionel had given me.

''Allo,' Lionel answered.

'Lionel, it's me, Louise, from the party, remember?'

'Of course. How could I forget? We had such a nice evening.'

'I was wondering whether, well, I've got to run an errand for my boss, up on embassy row this afternoon, and I wondered if we could have a drink?'

'*Absolument*. I would love to see you again. Shall we meet at Harry's Pub, in the Wardman Hotel? What time?'

'Six o'clock?'

'*A ce soir.*'

I hung up the telephone. That was done. Now what? Marvin Metcalfe had sent the original 1936 conference program to OSS. Perhaps he had more material than he'd already given me.

I picked up the phone again and called my office. Pleading renewed toothache, I said I was on my way to my dentist's office and wouldn't be back until tomorrow.

I found Metcalfe in his office grading a stack of blue books. The room was stifling. A floor fan on its highest setting whirled air around the room, to little effect. The windows were closed.

Metcalfe caught me looking at them.

'Bloody things are painted shut,' he said, offering me a chair. 'What is it now?'

'I wanted to ask you some more questions about Gerald Bloch,' I said. 'OSS is interested in compiling a more complete folder on him.' For appearances' sake I took a notepad and pen from my pocketbook and waited expectantly.

'Anything I can tell you would be based on our conversation at dinner back in 1936,' Metcalfe said. 'Let's see, he was a surveyor for a salvage company in Algiers for several years. I believe his family owned the company. Then he went back to France and studied at the University of Aix. He focused his studies on the French North African coast, which is why I passed on his name to OSS. He worked at the Marseille Hydrographic Office.'

'What exactly is a hydrographic survey?'

'A preliminary marine chart.'

My skin prickled. The Allies were searching for harbor pilots who knew their way around North Africa. Wouldn't navigation charts our own people could use be even more useful?

And Algiers was a strategically critical city in French North Africa. It was of crucial importance for Operation Torch. Perhaps this was the key to why Bloch's file had been stolen.

'So,' I said brightly, 'that's most useful. Do you have any more documents that we can add to Gerald Bloch's file?'

Metcalfe sighed heavily, shook his head and got to his feet, swinging his braced leg under him.

'If paper could win this war,' he said, 'we'd be in sight of Berlin by now.'

He dug into an old wooden file cabinet squeezed between his cluttered bookcase and the stuck-closed window.

'Tomorrow I'm going to bring a hammer and chisel and open this goddamned window. I'm going to buy a window-mount fan and prop it in there. I'll have to chain it to the radiator to keep someone from stealing it but I don't care.'

As he spoke Metcalfe riffled through the file-cabinet drawers and drew out a folder, a cluttered, thick, beautiful folder. He sat down at his desk and began to remove papers and hand them to me.

'Here,' he said, 'yet another copy of the 1936 conference program. And here's one of the 1939 program, held here in DC. Bloch wasn't there, do you still want it?'

'Sure,' I said. Why not? What was one more piece of paper?

'Oh,' he said, 'and this. Taken when we were in Edinburgh in 1936.'

He handed me an unremarkable photograph of a half-dozen people in a Scottish pub. An old one, from what I could see of the plaster and half-timbered walls behind the group gathered around a table.

'We got the bartender to take it. That's me, Bloch and his wife, Burns, some Scottish girl he picked up and two German fellows whose names I can't remember.'

Rachel looked very happy. She held a wine glass in her hand, and leaned her head against her husband's shoulder. His arm encircled her. They were both smiling for the photographer.

I took off my glasses and rubbed my eyes.

'Are you all right?' Metcalfe asked.

'I'm fine,' I said, picking up the papers he'd given me from the corner of his desk. 'Why didn't you send all this to OSS earlier?' I asked.

'OSS asked for names. I sent you a name.'

'Can I keep these?' I asked.

'Of course.'

I didn't offer Metcalfe a receipt and he didn't ask for one. He was bent over his blue books again before I got through his office door.

I stuffed the papers into my pocketbook and headed back outside into the heat.

While preoccupied with my thoughts I almost ran Joe down. He strode ahead of me down Twenty-Third Street toward Washington Circle. On his way home, perhaps? For some reason I didn't try to catch up to him. Instead I dropped back and followed him, curiosity overwhelming any sense of propriety. When he got to Washington Circle, instead of taking Pennsylvania toward our neighborhood, he went north on New Hampshire. Then he ducked into a grocery store, a classic espionage evasive tactic. What was going on here? Why would Joe be doing this?

Heart pounding, I followed him down the frosted-foods aisle, through swinging doors into a storeroom, past stacked boxes of cereal. He turned, scanning the storeroom, and I ducked behind an open door into a janitor's closet. What in God's name would I say to him if he spotted me? A few seconds later I heard him go out the back door. I rushed after him, cracked the door open and peered out. He was walking, more quickly now, down the alley. I followed behind. We came out, a minute apart, into a narrow, pretty street marred by a mound of scrap metal at the alley entrance. I ducked behind it, then cautiously edged around the corner. I watched as Joe climbed a flight of brick steps to the black front door of a small row house, inserted a key into the door and went inside. I heard the door catch behind him. The street was still empty. I ambled, at least I hoped it looked like ambling, my hat tilted over my eyes, down the street and passed the house while trying not to stare at it. The one street-level window was curtained and the blinds drawn. So I turned at the corner and went back to inspect the house more carefully. There was no sign identifying the building and no house number. A flight of steps led from the sidewalk down to a basement level with another locked door flanked by a barred and curtained window.

There was no indication at all of the purpose of the house. Surely if it was a language school there'd be a sign identifying it and advertising its purpose? Why did Joe try to conceal where he was going? And why didn't the building have a street number? In DC that meant only one thing. Secrets.

FIFTEEN

The street remained empty. I put my ear to the door. I heard the distant sound of typing and a telephone ringing. I considered knocking, but if someone came to the door, what would I say? What if it was Joe?

I went further down the street and discovered a tiny cafe occupying the street floor of another row house. Inside the cafe was refreshing, window shades drawn, the breeze from a ceiling fan cooling it. The dining room was empty except for an elderly colored waiter reading a newspaper at one table who rose to show me to a seat.

'We're done cooking lunch,' he said, 'and we ain't open for dinner until four-thirty, but we've got some real good cherry pie and coffee I could bring you.'

I ordered pie and coffee and drank two glasses of iced water from the metal pitcher the waiter set on the table. He brought me my order and sat down again with his newspaper. The pie was delicious. I ate dessert so seldom now that pie seemed decadent, an indulgence I should feel guilty about enjoying.

I felt the adrenalin draining from me. Now I knew for sure that Joe had been lying about his job, if only by omission, and I didn't know what to make of it. I still liked him so much I couldn't believe that he was engaged in anything nefarious.

'Excuse me,' I said.

The waiter lifted his head from his newspaper. 'Yes, ma'am?' he answered. 'More coffee?'

'No thank you, but I'm wondering if you could help me. My employment agency sent me to an address on this street, but I think it must be incorrect. There's no number three-twenty-one on this block. Do you think it's that house with the black door down at the end? The one with no house number?'

'I doubt it,' he said. 'That's not a public place of business. I ain't ever seen anyone go in who didn't have a key. But the people who work there, they come in here for lunch sometimes. Some of them are mighty queer.'

'What do you mean?'

'Some of them have long beards and foreign accents. A couple wear hats even indoors, or what I could call beanies.'

'Skull caps?'

'I guess. And the ones with the hats and beanies won't eat nothing we cook. They order black coffee and bring a paper bag of their own food. But some of them are regular Americans, they seem just like you and me, eating hamburgers and milkshakes.'

'You don't know what kind of work they do?'

'Nope.'

'Well,' I said. 'I best call my employment agency and tell them they gave me the wrong address. Do you have a telephone?'

'Nope. There's one at the Esso filling station two blocks up on the corner.'

I thanked him and headed off toward the Esso station. Once out of sight of the cafe I turned back toward my boarding house. I forced thoughts of Joe ruthlessly out of my mind. I had to concentrate on my plan for the evening.

I took a bath and washed my hair, enjoying the feel of my body as my skin cooled in the breeze from my fan. I considered what to wear, which required less thought since Ada gave me that armful of clothes. I chose the black raw-silk suit, which I wore without a blouse, and fastened my pearls around my neck. Those pearls reminded me of Rachel again, as if I needed reminding.

'Can you help us?' Remembering Rachel's plea summoned up the awful, terrible pictures I'd seen in *Life* magazine. Anxiety clutched at my bowels and stomach. I felt tears forming, but crying would ruin my face, so I squeezed back my tears and forced myself to focus on the evening ahead.

It was blazing hot outside, and the Wardman

199

Hotel was many blocks north on Connecticut Avenue on the other side of the Taft Bridge. I hoped to God I'd find a bus or a taxi, or I'd arrive late and in a state.

Downstairs I ran into Phoebe in the hall. She drifted up tome, eyes dilated from the laudanum she took for her headaches.

'Going out, dearie?' she asked.

'Yes,' I said. 'I'm meeting a friend for a drink at the Wardham.' Never lie more than you absolutely must, was one cardinal rule I'd absorbed at OSS.

'Your beau?'

'I don't have a beau, Phoebe,' I said. 'This is just a friend.'

'It's a long way to the Wardham.'

'I know. It makes me hot to think about it. I hope I can find a cab.'

'Why don't you take my car?'

I caught my breath. Drive, actually drive, myself? I longed to.

'I couldn't,' I said.

'Don't be silly. It's got a full tank of gas, and just sits in the garage. It needs to be driven, or I'll lose my ration.'

I carefully backed Phoebe's stubby two-door coupe out of the narrow garage, engaged the clutch, shifted gears, and headed west on 'K' Street. I drove twice around Washington Circle for the fun of it, admiring the vast George Washington University Hospital, pitying the poor souls queuing at bus stops and slug lines. I drove north on New

200

Hampshire, circled Dupont, and north again on Connecticut, passing a score of handsome buildings, most of them foreign embassies. Just before I crossed the Taft Bridge I saw the Vichy French embassy, a stone mansion shrouded in ivy surrounded by a vast lawn.

I motored slowly over the bridge to take in the view. Houseboats with laundry draped over deck chairs to dry lined both banks of the Potomac. Colorful sailboats, with their masts lowered, drifted gently at anchor in the soft breeze. I wanted to keep driving for ever. Out into the green, shady countryside, where waging this war was simple and uncomplicated, only a matter of buying war bonds and eschewing sugar.

The Wardman Hotel in all its Beaux Arts splendor rose before me. Red-brick edged with bright-white painted trim and balconies, the Wardman was the best temporary wartime address in Washington. Diplomats, movie stars and businessmen leased more permanent residences at the Wardham Apartments, which spread out behind the hotel.

After parking the car I walked past manicured gardens to the front door of the hotel. I passed the huge swimming pool, surrounded by umbrellas, lounge chairs and men and women in revealing bathing suits. Phoebe often complained that once the war started people began going about half naked.

201

The cool water looked so inviting I would have loved to jump right in.

The Wardman lobby was two stories high, the ornate ceiling supported by thick marble columns. Lionel waved to me from a table in the lobby bar. I slid into a chair next to him.

'I took the liberty of ordering us some champagne,' Lionel said. 'I hope you approve?'

'Absolutely,' I answered. A bartender appeared with a bar towel draped over one arm and, with a flourish, showed the bottle to Lionel, who nodded, uncorked it with a pop and a fizz and poured bubbly liquid into flutes. Then he plunged the bottle into a silver champagne bucket full of ice next to the table.

'Caviar?' Lionel asked.

'I'm afraid I haven't acquired that taste.'

'Canapés, then,' Lionel said to the waiter, who nodded and slipped away.

'You look *charmante*,' Lionel said.

'And you are very handsome.' He was, too, elegant in his expensive gray lounge suit in a way that American men rarely managed.

I suffered a minute of self-doubt. Who was I, where was I, and what in God's name was I doing? Dressed in a chic suit, flirting with a French diplomat, in an exclusive hotel bar? A day after meeting Clark Gable at Friendship House, and a day before going out on a date with a Czech refugee?

I'd arrived in this town a widow who'd

never left North Carolina and had been with the same man since we were children until he died, and now I was about to ask Lionel to help me steal files from the French embassy.

I calmed my nerves by swallowing the rest of my champagne. Lionel poured me another flute. My tolerance for alcohol was remarkable, too, considering I'd arrived in Washington having never partaken of anything except the occasional sherry glass of blackberry wine.

'So, my dear,' Lionel said, 'what can I do for you?'

'Is it that obvious?'

'A bit. When we parted I got the distinct feeling that you were not interested in seeing me again, then I receive your phone call, and here you are, radiating purpose.' He smiled. 'I do not mind,' he said. 'This is the reason one socializes in Washington, to meet people who might be useful to one, is it not?'

'I suppose,' I said, 'but this is the first time for me.'

'Always the nerves with one's first time.'

He was flirting with me again. I guessed that no matter how useful we might be to each other, the romantic possibilities would never be far from Lionel's mind.

'You know where I work; where do you?' Lionel asked.

'I work for the government. I'm a file clerk.'

'Where?'

'I can't say.'

'Is this official business?'

'No.'

'Why don't you tell me what you want from me, *chérie*.'

I lowered my voice and leaned forward.

'I need you to steal a file from your embassy for me.'

Lionel laughed. 'My dear, you are, what is your word, loony.'

'So you won't do it?'

'Not alone. For me to agree, you must take the same risks as I do. And I could not cooperate with any plan which, say, endangered French nationals.'

'No.' I gained some time by munching on a smoked-salmon canapé. Lionel waited patiently.

'Where I work,' I ventured, 'I came upon a file.'

'As a file clerk must often do.'

'Yes. Well, it concerned a French family, Jewish, who need help escaping from Marseille.'

Lionel frowned. 'Marseille is about to become a very dangerous place for *les juifs*.'

'I know. The Gestapo...'

Lionel placed his hand over my mouth.

'Do not say that word. Curse them all, they will rot in hell. Our job is to speed them on their way.'

'This family, the husband is an expert in a

subject that could be helpful to the Allies.'

'I see. He wishes to trade his knowledge for his family's safety.'

'My agency was scheduled to consider his offer. But the file vanished during a ... disruptive event. Everyone believes it was lost. I am sure it was stolen.'

'Someone does not want this man to assist the Allies?'

'I don't know. This is difficult to explain –' and I took a gulp of champagne – 'but I want to help his family. His wife is a dear friend of mine. We went to school together. I can't bear the thought of what might happen to them.' My voice broke, and I swallowed another gulp of champagne.

Lionel shook his head. 'Women,' he said, 'you think with your hearts.'

'If you, we, can get into the French embassy files, I might be able to find documents on this man, reconstruct a file and continue the process...'

'To free him and your friend's family.'

'Yes.'

'You do this on your own, because you have no idea who in your office might be involved in the theft of the file?'

'Yes. Of course, I do think this man has valuable knowledge.'

'Otherwise there would be no chance that your, ah, agency would accept his offer.'

'Exactly.'

Lionel leaned back in his seat and pulled a

cigarette case out of his pocket. He extracted a cigarette and offered it to me.

'I can't,' I said. 'It makes my throat sore.'

Lionel put the cigarette into his mouth and lit it with an embossed lighter. He focused on smoking it while contemplating a tall potted palm across the lobby.

'I don't buy your story, my dear,' he said.

I was taken aback.

'What do you mean?'

'There is more than friendship here, I think. To undertake such a difficult task, such a dangerous mission, on your own, for a school friend you haven't seen in years?'

I didn't answer him for a long time.

'Rachel was, is, the best friend I've ever had,' I said. 'But you're right, there is more. I am deeply indebted to her for more than her friendship.'

'How?'

'I'd rather not say. It embarrasses me. And we promised each other never to mention it.'

He stubbed the cigarette out into the ashtray. 'I loathe Vichy,' he said. 'If Pétain and Laval were here with us I would strangle them both with my bare hands and happily hang for it. I detest the Nazis even more. They have seized my family home for officers' quarters. My mother is living in the maid's room off the scullery. She is forced to cook their meals.'

'I'm so sorry.'

'We are all sorry. But sorrow without

206

action is worthless. I will help you, government girl, but what can you do for me in return?'

Seeing the shock on my face, he laughed. 'I am not talking about *relations sexuelles*. I am not that vulgar. Not in public, at any rate. What I must know is, do you have any useful information you can give me in return for my help?'

'No.' And I didn't. What could I do for Lionel that wouldn't compromise me at OSS?

'I do not wish to endanger you,' he said, 'but one day you might come across some tidbit of information, perhaps even outside your office, during your daily life, that might seem inconsequential, but could be very useful to me. You could share it with me.'

'Yes,' I said, 'perhaps I could do that.' In your dreams, I thought.

'Let me think about the details. May I call you about nine on Saturday morning, with my plan?'

'Of course,' I said. 'I'll be waiting.' I gave him my phone number.

I'd just agreed to penetrate a foreign embassy without cover or back-up. The spooks called that going naked, and I felt exposed, all right.

'So you do think you can get me into the embassy?'

'*Ma chérie*,' he said, 'it will be simple. I will arrange the details. Saturday is your July

207

Fourth. The embassy staff, including the ambassador, the pig, will be gone for the weekend, leaving only the watchman and his dog. The dog, by the way, is fond of me. I have given him many treats. You have seen the Vichy embassy? It's *un grand château*, what you would call a mansion. You and I will simply walk in, I will explain to the guard that you are my mistress and we require *un endroit tranquille*. The French are always susceptible to the entreaties of lovers.'

'Does that make sense? Why couldn't we go to your apartment?'

'That would be most insensitive of us. My wife lives there.'

'We have company,' Joe said.

He stood on the porch, his morning cup of coffee in hand, staring across the street. I looked, and felt my heart jerk. Two FBI agents leaned on a lamppost, scanning our street. They were unmistakable. And one had a yellow feather in his hatband.

'What have you done?' Joe asked, lightly.

'Me? Nothing. You?' I said.

'I'm pure as the driven snow. Maybe Dellaphine's been selling her hooch on the black market.'

'Dellaphine makes hooch?'

'Didn't you know? Small batches, in the laundry room. Peach brandy mostly. It's not bad.'

Despite our banter, I was worried. If the

agents were watching Joe I might find him packed and gone when I got back from work today. I might never see him again, much less know what he did with himself behind that black door.

'They're moving down the street now,' Joe said, 'taking up position at another street lamp.'

'Maybe it's not Dellaphine they're after,' I said.

'Hope not, for their sake. I expect she'd put up a fight.'

'You know you're not anybody in Washington unless you've got a file at the FBI.' I'd heard that General Donovan's was two inches thick and that Hoover kept it on his desk.

Ada came onto the porch, still wearing her dressing gown.

'Hey, Ada,' I said. 'Come look. There are two FBI agents across the street.'

Every drop of blood drained from Ada's face, her eyes rolled up into the back of her head and she slumped to the ground.

SIXTEEN

Neither Joe nor I moved fast enough to break Ada's fall. She landed hard on the carpet but missed hitting any furniture.

'Help me sit her up,' Joe said. 'Put her head between her knees.'

I did. Joe pressed one hand on the back of Ada's neck. She slowly gained consciousness.

'Dearie, what's wrong?' I slid an arm around her to support her. Joe fetched one of the fans that lay around the house and waved it vigorously. Color slowly came back into Ada's face.

'I'm all right,' she said. 'Really, I am.'

'I'm sorry we startled you like that,' I said.

'Those agents,' Joe said, 'they're wandering up and down this whole block. Who knows what they're doing here.'

'Oh, it wasn't that,' Ada said, too quickly. 'I didn't feel well anyway. I don't think I had enough supper last night before I went out, and I drank one too many Martinis.' Her voice trembled as she spoke, and she gripped my hand so tightly it hurt.

Joe and I glanced at each other. I could tell

he didn't believe her either.

'Let me get you upstairs,' I said.

'Can I help?' Joe asked.

'We'll manage,' I said.

I guided Ada up the staircase. She dragged herself along, clinging to the banister like an old woman.

I got Ada into her bed, then went to the bathroom for a damp washrag soaked in camphor. When I returned she was trembling uncontrollably, clutching the bedclothes around her, clearly terrified. I climbed onto her bed, put one arm around her and pressed the cool cloth against her forehead with the other.

'Why do you think the FBI is watching this house?' she asked.

You tell me, dearie. You're the one who fainted. And you said it had nothing to do with the agents.

'Joe and I were wondering if they were after Dellaphine for making peach brandy,' I said instead.

'She makes peach brandy? Why hasn't she offered us some?' We both giggled, but then Ada stiffened with fear again.

'I think they're watching me,' she said, her voice timorous with anxiety.

I didn't say anything, just patted her hand.

'Don't you want to know why?' she asked.

'It's not any of my business,' I said.

'If I tell you, you've got to swear not to tell anyone else.'

'As long as you're not a German saboteur or something,' I said.

She paled again, and tears filled her eyes.

'It's terrible,' she said, 'so terrible.' Ada squeezed my hand even harder, so hard I had to pry her fingers loose.

'I am married,' she said, 'to a German officer in the Luftwaffe.'

'Oh, my God, Ada!'

'He was an airline pilot for Lufthansa. Friends of my parents introduced us. His English was very good, he was handsome. We were happy together until the Nazis came to power. Rein – my husband – became an admirer of Hitler. We fought constantly. One day he didn't return with his scheduled flight from Berlin. I remember it so clearly, it was a few days before Christmas in 1938. I got a telegram from him instead, telling me that he'd accepted a commission, asking me to join him in Germany. I refused. He still occasionally writes me letters, but of course I don't answer them.'

I instantly recognized the enormity of Ada's predicament.

'I was born here, my parents immigrated as a young couple to open a bakery. I never learned German, my parents refused to speak it in my presence. I am an American. I hate the Nazis. I never want to see Rein again. Sometimes I dream he's been shot down, that he's dead, that I'm free of him.'

'Can't you divorce him?'

212

'Not now – that will draw attention to me. I have to wait until after the war.'

'Oh, Ada.'

'The government will intern me if I'm discovered.'

I didn't try to reassure her on that point. She was right to be worried sick. All over the country people with close relatives in Germany were being sent to detention camps, whether they were American citizens or not. Until this minute I had thought it was a good idea myself.

I heard Joe's voice, calling up the stairs to us.

'They're gone,' he said.

Ada buried her head in my shoulder.

'Don't tell,' she said. For a second I wondered if it was my duty to inform the OSS that I knew the whereabouts of the wife of a Luftwaffe officer. I decided it wasn't. I was just a file clerk.

'I won't,' I said. 'I promise.'

Barbara didn't come into work Friday morning. Ruth and Betty pestered me until I called her boarding house, but she refused to come to the telephone. Her landlady told me that she was sure Barbara was planning to leave Washington and go home.

I could kick myself. If I'd assumed, or pretended to assume, that Barbara was ill, I could have waited until Monday, but now I had to report that she'd left the agency. If I

213

didn't I might face disciplinary action myself.

I went to Don's door and knocked.

'Mrs Pearlie?' he said. I couldn't tell from Don's demeanor whether he still thought I had wife potential. I hoped not.

'Mr Murray, I'm sorry to say that Barbara Rollins has left OSS and plans to return home without permission or notice.' I explained what had happened.

'Oh, hell,' Don said, taking off his glasses and rubbing his temples.

'She had a breakdown and left the office yesterday. I didn't say anything to you because I wanted to give her a chance to return to work today.'

'You did the right thing. You're sure she's not coming back to work?'

'I got that impression from her landlady when I called this morning. And Don, she has a child, and she's a war widow. What would OSS do about this, do you know?'

'Hell. Do you think you could catch up with her?'

'I'm willing to try.'

'Here,' Don said, pulling a form out of a drawer. 'This is a request for emergency leave. If you can find her and get her to sign it I'll approve it.'

Don rubbed the bridge of his nose before replacing his glasses. He'd acquired dark circles under his eyes since assuming Bob Holman's job. He already looked years older.

'Thank you,' I said. I turned to go.

'One more thing, Mrs Pearlie...'

'Yes,' I said, turning back to face him.

'About that missing file...'

'Yes?'

'I trust you're not spending any more of your time searching for it.'

'No, sir.' Not today, that is.

'Please don't. There is too much other work to be done.'

'I understand.'

That was interesting, I thought, on my way back down the hall towards my office. Now why did Don think it was necessary to mention the Bloch file? He'd already told me once before, during the meeting, to forget it. Had someone seen me while I was out of the office, supposedly at the dentist? What about Metcalfe? Had he called Don to ask if I had the authority to question him?

Once I allowed fear to insinuate itself into my mind, suspicions galore rushed in. Had Joe seen me following him? Had the waiter at the cafe mentioned the curious woman who'd asked him questions about Joe's building? Had someone notified the FBI, who staked out our boarding house this morning to watch not Ada, not Joe, but me? Most worrisome of all, could I trust Lionel? Wouldn't it be reasonable to abandon my plan to pull a black-bag job at the Vichy French embassy before it became an international incident?

I went into the ladies' restroom to compose myself. I splashed cool water onto my hot face, and I tried to set aside my fears for Rachel and consider my position rationally. I reminded myself that Gerald Bloch's file had been deliberately stolen and that someone, possibly a mole within OSS, had destroyed all evidence that it had ever existed. I had to assume that meant Bloch was an important person, perhaps more important than I realized based on what information I had managed to collect about him. I couldn't talk to anyone at OSS about this because I didn't have conclusive evidence that the file had been stolen, and I didn't want to drive the mole further underground. Surely it was my duty to free Bloch to do whatever it was he was qualified to do for the Allies, for Torch, and so spare Rachel and little Claude from a future spent in a Nazi labor camp.

I didn't trust Lionel as far as I could throw him, but I had to behave as if I did to get inside the Vichy embassy.

And I had to trust Joe, and this was where my feelings became complicated. I was going on a date tonight with a man who was undercover. There was no way to deny that despite my attraction to him, I knew nothing about him, and might even be in danger from him.

I was going to do it anyway. First, because I wanted to, and second, because breaking our date might make him suspect me. The spy business was a game, I'd often been told, and I intended to play this one to its conclusion.

But first I had to find Barbara if I could and get her to sign that emergency leave form.

I knocked on the door of a run-down row house on Virginia Avenue. A woman wearing a faded housecoat and a dirty apron opened it.

'I called earlier,' I said. 'I work with Barbara. Is she here?'

The woman raised her index finger to her mouth and shushed me, cocking her head towards the downstairs front room comparable to the one that we used as a lounge at Two Trees. I could see beds lining the wall, all occupied by sleeping women.

The landlady shooed me outside and closed the door behind her.

'The night-shift workers are asleep,' she said.

The day shift must sleep in the same beds at night. Same sheets too, no doubt. Barbara's wages were better than many, but she needed most of it to pay her baby's boarding expenses.

'Has Barbara gone?' I asked.

'I'm afraid so,' the woman said, shaking her head. 'I tried to talk her out of it, afraid she'd get in trouble. But she packed this morning and went off to pick up her baby.'

'Do you know how she's leaving town?'

'From Union Station, where else? First train she can catch to Newark.'

It would take Barbara some time to pick up her baby and get to the train station, especially taking the bus. I might be able to catch her.

The traffic on New York Avenue wasn't heavy, but it intensified once my bus turned onto Massachusetts Avenue and approached Union Station. I hadn't been to the giant railroad station since I arrived here in December, on a Southern Railway train. I'd never been north of Richmond before.

For much of the trip I'd perched on my suitcase in the aisle of the train packed with GIs who spent their journey sleeping, playing cards, or writing letters, letters they tossed out of the train windows at every stop, knowing someone would stamp and mail them.

Although I'd read, heck, practically memorized the Esso tourist map and guide Daddy gave me before I got on the train in Wilmington, nothing prepared me for the sight of Union Station. The white granite Beaux Arts building was monumental, covering more ground than any other building in Washington. Its vast gold-leafed barrel-vaulted ceiling soared almost a hundred feet overhead. During the war fully two hundred thousand people a day scurried beneath it, bound for hundreds of destinations.

For many it was the starting point for adventures that would take them to distant parts of the world.

The waiting room, over twenty-six thousand square feet, was designed to look like the central hall of the Baths of Diocletian. Five vast arches and Ionian columns and sculptured allegorical figures, not Roman gods of course, but modern ones, Fire, Electricity, Freedom, Knowledge, Agriculture and Mechanics, towered overhead. A secure Presidential suite and platform, included in the building design because President Garfield was assassinated while waiting for a train on a public railway platform, ran underneath the building.

I'd seen a lot of great public buildings and monuments since coming to Washington, but frankly none of them held a candle to Union Station.

I went in the entrance loggia, momentarily quailing at the sight of thousands of people jamming the waiting room. They crammed themselves onto rows of high-backed benches or slept on the floor, queued at restaurants, the barbershop, drugstores, newsstands and the ornate wood-carved information counter that jutted out onto the vast marble floor of the lobby. I'd never find Barbara here. But I pulled myself together, plunged into the crowd and elbowed my way to the Trains and Tickets entrance. I couldn't get onto the concourse without a ticket, so I purchased one to Newark – the next one left in twenty minutes – and passed through the wrought-iron gate onto the Baltimore and Ohio platform. She would have to leave for Newark from there. A train marked for Pittsburgh idled on the tracks. I searched the platform for Barbara. She wasn't there. I sat on a bench to wait. She might be in a bathroom, or at one of the restaurants or shops. The Pittsburgh train whistle blew, steam poured from its smokestack and it lunged forward like a racehorse leaving its gate, gathering speed as it chugged out of the station. Passengers hung, shouting, out of the windows, touching the hands of their loved ones running alongside the train. Soldiers stood on the railroad-car porches, smoking, trying to look nonchalant, as the train carried them to some northern port to be shipped out, probably to Britain to prepare for Torch, although none of them knew that.

The Pittsburgh train was barely out of the station when the train bound for Newark arrived from Norfolk, its old-fashioned engine bell clanging like a church bell on Sunday morning. Passengers swarmed off the train, shoving each other and shouting for redcaps. I watched the gateway from the waiting room onto the platform and finally spotted Barbara. She carried her baby over one shoulder and a suitcase in the other hand. Behind her trudged a colored redcap hauling two more overstuffed suitcases, one tied shut with rope.

I called out to her.

She saw me and stopped, the redcap almost running into her. She put down the suitcase and shifted the sleeping baby, a barefoot little girl wearing a faded pink-checked dress and sunbonnet, to her other shoulder.

'What are you doing here?' she asked.

'Let's talk, you have a few minutes before the train leaves,' I said.

Barbara turned to the redcap and gave him her seat number and a dime. He manhandled all three of her suitcases into the train.

'Don't try to talk me out of leaving,' she said.

'I'm not, I'm the one who suggested you apply for leave, remember? Which you neglected to do.'

She shrugged, but followed me to a bench.

'Let me take her,' I said, reaching out for the baby.

She handed the little girl to me and I cuddled her on my lap. She was about a year and a half old, I guessed, though I was no expert, with dark curly hair and a heart-shaped mouth. Barbara straightened her dress, tucked tendrils of damp hair under her straw hat and wiped her face and neck with a handkerchief.

'Why are you here?' she asked again.

To save your hide, I thought. 'There's a

form and a pen in my pocketbook,' I said, my hands full of baby girl. 'It's an emergency leave request. Sign it and Mr Murray will approve it. That way you won't get into trouble.'

Impatiently she removed the form, scanned it, signed it and stuffed it back into my pocketbook.

'Okay,' she said. 'You've done your good deed for the day.' She reached for the baby.

Remember what she's been through, I thought to myself. 'She's sweet,' I said, handing the little girl back to her.

'I'm glad she's a girl,' Barbara said. 'It'll be easier to raise a girl by myself.'

At the steps to the train she turned to me.

'For people like you,' she said, 'this war is mostly an adventure, the chance to live in a big city, make lots of money, feel important. After the war is over you can pat yourselves on the back. For me, my husband is dead, and I've got two brothers in uniform who might be next. Nothing could replace them. You've heard the rumors about what's going on in Europe. If only some of them are true, it's a calamity, a disaster, for the Jewish people.'

She turned and climbed on her train before I had a chance to respond.

Rachel opened her door. She was ready. She'd been packed for days. She knew she could take one suitcase for herself and one for the children, and she'd sorted their clothing and blankets carefully. She added a few pictures removed from their frames, one of her parents, one of Gerald, and one of herself and Louise one weekend in New York that felt like a thousand years ago. She found room for a pad of paper and some pencils and a couple of children's books. She'd sewn two silver spoons into Claude's teddy bear and the last three links from her gold bracelet into the waistband of her dress.

The man who came to fetch them was a Vichy policeman.

'*Madame*,' he said, 'you understand, it is time to go?'

'Yes,' she said.

'It will not be so bad,' he said, taking the suitcases while Rachel grasped Claude's hand and hoisted the baby to her shoulder. 'There are children for your son to play with, and extra milk for the baby.'

He loaded the suitcases into the police van and helped Rachel and the children into the back.

'It's not safe for you here any more,' he said.

The Nazis had ordered the Vichy French authorities to clear out the Old Port neighborhoods that lined the Marseille harbor. The Nazis feared the residents would assist any Allied invasion that might come from the Mediterranean, and planned to destroy

the medieval buildings and build new forti-
fications.

Rachel found she didn't mind leaving so
much. Prison was prison.

SEVENTEEN

I didn't blame Barbara for her rudeness or
her cynicism. She was right about everything
she said, except one. It wasn't too late to save
countless lives in Europe, not only Jews, but
soldiers, Resistance fighters, refugees and
millions of civilians, by winning this war as
quickly as possible.

Outside Union Station I joined a queue for
the next bus. It was still morning, already so
hot the sticky asphalt pavement sucked at
my shoes. I was awfully tired, and longed to
go home to 'Two Trees' and nap on the wicker couch out on the porch under the ceiling
fan. Instead I had to get back to the office,
with Barbara's signed leave request for Don
to approve and a mountain of papers and
memos on my desk to sift through. I felt a
headache coming on at the thought of it.

A faded blue Ford coupe pulled up and a
familiar voice called out to me.

'Louise,' Charles Burns said. 'I was just
driving by. Can I give you a lift?'

'Oh, yes, thank you,' I said, clambering into the front seat of the car. 'It's so hot, I can hardly bear the thought of the bus.'

'Glad to be of service,' Charles said, shifting gears and edging out onto Louisiana Avenue. 'What are you doing here, if you don't mind me asking?'

'One of my girls up and left work,' I said. 'She was on her way home. I brought a leave form for her to sign so that she wouldn't get in trouble.'

'That was good of you.'

'I suppose. What are you doing out and around this morning?'

Charles cocked his head towards the back seat of the car, which was piled with documents and books. 'A retired geography professor wrote me and said he had a collection of African maps we could have, so I went out to Chevy Chase to get them.'

'Anything useful?'

'Haven't really looked yet, but I sure hope so,' he said.

He shifted to a lower gear as traffic slowed. 'Look,' he said. 'In lunchtime traffic this will take us forever. How about we stop and get something to eat?'

'I appreciate the offer,' I said. 'But I need to get back to work. Don's expecting me. If you like, I'll get out and take the bus anyway, you don't have to drive me.'

'No, no,' he said, 'it was just an idea.'

I lost myself in thought until I realized we

were headed north instead of west.

'What are you doing?' I asked.

'There's a great cafe a bit farther on,' he said. 'I ate there last weekend. It's refrigerated. You'll like it.'

Fury boiled up inside me. The gall of the man, ignoring my wishes. I longed to tell Charles that I was on to him, the slug, but I bit my tongue. He was the head of a division of my OSS branch and one of my bosses. I had to be polite and deferential to him.

'I need to get back to work,' I said instead of what I wanted to say. 'Please stop and let me out, and I'll find a bus or a taxi.'

'Come on,' he said, 'you know you want to go. I'll clear it with Don. I'll say we had a flat tire or something.'

I gripped the car door handle.

'Let me out right now,' I said. 'Now.' Forget tact, I wasn't putting up with this.

Charles ignored me. While I boiled with anger he kept driving.

'Listen,' he said, 'I need to talk to you. About some stuff at work. Consider this a business lunch.'

'You know damn well we can't talk about work in a public place.'

'This isn't very public. It'll just be the two of us.'

With both hands I struggled to open my door, but it was locked. There must have been a master lock on the driver's side of the car. As I rattled the handle Charles leaned over and grabbed at me with his right hand and dragged at my arm, tearing my hand away from the door handle. His thumb and fingers dug deep into my flesh. 'Let go,' he said, 'you can't get out. Don't be so stuffy. We'll have fun. I'll cover for you with Don.'

The way he said the word 'fun' frightened me. The ugly word 'rape' crossed my mind. Surely he didn't intend to force himself on me?

Oh God, had Charles been waiting for me at Union Station? Found out from one of my girls where I might be and loitered on the curb, with a pile of old maps in the back seat of the car as an alibi, to pick me up?

We passed the Columbia Institute for the Deaf and turned north. Brentwood Park. Tree-filled, quiet and empty on this hot day.

Charles pulled into a shady spot and stopped.

I tried again to open my door.

'Louise,' he said, 'I just want to talk to you about something important. Please.'

I hauled off and slapped him with the flat of my hand. 'You bastard,' I said. Charles flinched, whether from the slap or my unladylike language I didn't know.

'Who do you think you are?' he asked, rubbing his cheek. 'I could get you fired in a heartbeat.'

'Just try,' I said. 'By the time I get done with you, you'll regret treating me this way. So help me!'

'All right, all right, don't blow your top. Christ, you can be a nasty, foul-mouthed broad. I'll drive you back to the office.'

'Only if you unlock this car door. Otherwise I'll scream bloody murder as soon as I see a cop.'

'Okay, okay. Whatever you say.'

I was still livid, and when Charles stopped for a red light a few blocks away, I flung open my door and got out, slamming it shut after me.

Charles leaned over the passenger seat.

'Oh, for Pete's sake!' he said. 'Get back in. I didn't mean anything, honest. I just wanted to have a quiet chat with you.'

'When I say no, I mean no,' I said, and turned to find a bus stop.

The light changed, Charles shrugged and drove on by me.

I walked, fists clenched, past the nearest bus stop, a full three blocks, until I calmed down. By that time I was so hot and footsore I hailed a taxi. The cost of the taxi and the unused ticket to Newark would cripple my budget for the rest of the month, but it was worth it.

When I returned to OSS I stopped at the cafeteria for a fast lunch of milk and crackers. Joan was on her way out, in a hurry, smiling at me and waving as she passed by. It was ironic, she was rich and eligible, and desperately wanted a boyfriend, but had so much trouble finding one, and I, a drone in eyeglasses, seemed to be fending off men. It made no sense to me.

I noticed a knot of people gathered around the bulletin board where Administrative posted notices.

A sign lettered in red and blue announced an afternoon reception commemorating 'a British–American controversy of the mid-eighteenth century. All OSS personnel will participate.'

'If there's free food, everyone will turn up, no worries there,' said a clerk from Morale Ops.

I stood holding my plate and watched Don chat up a blonde secretary from the Foreign Nationalities branch. I was relieved. Much better for my career for him to move on than for me to dump him.

The OSS cafeteria bulged with staff, all of us with small paper American flags pinned to our clothing. Patriotic-themed food crowded three cafeteria tables – celery stuffed with cream cheese dyed red, vanilla-iced cookies shaped like stars, blue swizzle sticks to stir the ginger-ale punch.

Despite the President's ban on fireworks and public gatherings, most everyone had big plans for the weekend of the Fourth, swim parties, barbecues, picnics and trips to the beach. Betty and Ruth were bound to the coast on a YWCA bus excursion, and had bought new two-piece bathing suits for the trip. They anticipated that most of the servicemen from Fort Myers would be waiting for them.

The USO was hosting parties and cookouts for all the servicemen who wouldn't be at the beach picking up government girls. Ada's band was playing at one.

Me, I planned to celebrate Independence Day by breaking into a foreign embassy.

To my surprise Dora appeared at my side. I must have appeared flustered, because she reacted quickly.

'Fortunately,' she said, 'one doesn't need a top-secret clearance to attend a party in the cafeteria.'

'I'm sorry,' I said.

'Don't be. I'm fine. At least in the Library of Congress reading room I don't have to listen to Guy and Roger bicker.'

She caught sight of Don chatting up the blonde girl.

'I see you're out of the running for wife,' Dora said, nodding at them.

'Thank goodness,' I answered. 'Has he been looking long? Where was I in the queue?'

'Since he arrived, and second. Men are odd creatures. If they don't marry the first girl they're stupidly smitten with, they begin to search for a mate in a most cynical fashion. Don doesn't need money, so other qualities appealed to him. It's odd, men seem to need a wife in order to succeed in a career, but women can't marry and have a career both.'

'I heard through the grapevine that Don thought I was perfect for him, what with being so reliable and all. Until I hedged when he asked me out a second time.'

'You're not interested in remarrying?'

'I don't know, I'm confused about that. My parents are pushing me to find a husband, that's for sure. And I was happy when I was married. But I'm content now, too. Why jeopardize that? Besides, I've found I enjoy making my own money and my own decisions. I don't know if I could give that up. I doubt that Don would make a modern husband.'

'Wise of you. Tell me, dear, if you don't think I'm being impertinent, how much education do you have?'

'I finished junior college, a business course,' I said, surprised.

Dora nodded, almost to herself. 'Have you thought of getting a full college degree?'

'No, not really. I don't know how I would pay for it.'

'Think about it,' she said. 'I'll return to Smith after the war. If you want to go to college, come and see me. We'll work it out.'

'Thank you so much, I will.' College! Me! My brain buzzed with the possibilities.

'Louise,' she said, interrupting my day-dreams, 'did you ever find that file you were looking for? What was the man's name?'

'Gerald Bloch,' I said. 'No, I think it's lost for good.'

'If you do ever locate it, would you route it to me? I'd be interested in seeing it,' she said. 'Just curiosity,' she added. 'And after I get my clearance back, of course.'

'Of course.'

Dora was the second person in my branch today to mention Bloch's file. I longed to ask her why, but thought it wiser to drop the subject.

A group of Dora's friends beckoned her over to join them, and I was left munching a sugar cookie, thinking of joining Joan, who was across the room with her crowd, when the sound of men arguing rose above the background noise of the reception. As a circle around the two squabbling men gathered, I saw that Guy Danielson and Roger Austine were at its center. Guy was flushed with anger, and Roger gripped the back of a chair as if he intended to fling it at Guy any second. Don and a couple of others pulled the two men away from each other and into opposite corners of the cafeteria. I couldn't hear Don chewing out Roger, but I could see the grim expression on his face. Good thing General Donovan and the branch directors hadn't arrived at the party yet.

The last person I wanted to see, Charles Burns, materialized at my elbow, holding a paper cup in ink-stained fingers. He wobbled a bit, leading me to suspect he'd added something alcoholic to his punch. I tensed, but he behaved as if nothing had happened earlier in the day, when he shanghaied me after I'd refused his 'lunch' invitation. I didn't refer to it. Much as I despised the thought, much as I wanted to dump my punch over Charles's head or kick him in the shins right there in public, I knew it was best to forget, well, pretend to forget, the whole nasty incident. Charles had an important job at OSS and I was just a file clerk.

'Did you see that?' Charles asked.

'I did, what set them off?'

'Danielson made a comment about Austine's fiancée – about how he must prefer dark meat. She's colored, did you know that?'

'Barely. She's lovely.'

'I'm sure she is. They can't live in this country, though.'

'I'm sure they don't care to.'

'It's politics, too. When Bob died and Don got his spot, Roger and Guy realized that Don's a brown-noser and will go whichever way he thinks Donovan is already leaning. That will leave Guy and Roger both without much influence. At least Holman used to listen to both of them. But what do I know. I just catalog maps.'

Lieutenant-Colonel Huntington slid onto the chair and dropped a stack of folders onto the table. He realized that FBI Assistant

233

Director Tolson had been waiting for some time, since his ashtray contained two cigarettes smoked down to their filters.

'I apologize for being late,' Huntington said. 'The traffic.'

'I understand,' Tolson said. He dug a handful of papers out of his briefcase and stacked them opposite Huntington's pile.

They met alone in a small stifling room on the third floor of the Post Office, off Pennsylvania Avenue. Neutral territory. Neither agency would consent to meet at the other's offices.

'So,' Tolson said, 'what have you got?'

'We can exclude some of our suspects,' Huntington said. 'Mrs Louise Pearlie left the building before the coroner estimates Mr Holman died. Private Cooper, the front-door guard, saw her leave.'

Tolson put a check mark next to her name on a list.

'Also Joan Adams, General Donovan's secretary. She came down the back stairs and left immediately through the side door.'

'Are you sure?' Tolson asked. 'The guard at the side door can't see directly into the building.'

'He heard her. She walked right down the stairs and out the door.'

Tolson checked off Adams's name.

'Danielson, Murray, Austine and Dora Bertrand were together in a meeting that didn't break up until Mrs Holman's wife

234

started screaming,' Huntington said.

Tolson looked up, smirking.

'But Miss Bertrand did leave once. To use the ladies' room down the hall in Mrs Pearlie's office. Which was after Mrs Pearlie left. She would have the time and opportunity to slip into Holman's office and kill him.'

Huntington rolled his eyes. 'Just barely,' he said, 'I know she's a favorite suspect of Director Hoover's.'

'Charles Burns saw her too. He was delivering maps around the building.'

'To Holman,' Huntington said.

'Among others. At any rate, Holman was alive when Burns saw him. And then Miss Bertrand passed Burns in the hall.'

'All the more reason to eliminate Miss Bertrand as a suspect.'

'Why?'

'Do you really think Miss Bertrand would murder Bob Holman during OSS business hours, immediately after being seen in the vicinity of his office? It's absurd.'

'These socialists are fanatics.'

Sometimes Huntington wondered if the FBI understood that the country was at war with Nazi Germany, not left-wing Americans.

'Look,' Huntington said. 'Charles Burns and Holman's wife had the same opportunity that Bertrand had. Private Cooper said that Mrs Holman didn't scream for some minutes after she entered Holman's office.'

235

'She was in shock. And why would Charles Burns kill Holman? His background is flawless. He's from an old American family, good schools.'

Huntington let that one go by without comment.

'Look, I have no evidence that any OSS staffer killed Holman. A person's politics and sexual orientation don't constitute evidence. We have to start all over, sift through the facts,' Huntington said.

Tolson shrugged. 'If you insist.'

'Holman's window was wide open. Anyone could have gotten into his office. I suggest that we widen our investigation to include the soldiers bivouacked outside and other OSS staff who left the building from other exits. And talk to the Negro messengers who came into the building shortly before the end of the day. Someone may have seen something we've missed.'

'Then you risk word getting out that Holman was murdered. Do you want all of Washington to know how inept OSS security is? Does General Donovan want the President to learn that one of his men was killed in his own office?'

'General Donovan wants to find Holman's killer.'

'No,' I said.

'Just a dab,' Ada said.

I consented to two drops of Evening in

Paris, one behind each ear.

'You should be wearing shorts,' she said. 'Or a playsuit.'

'We're having dinner before the concert, and besides I'm too old to expose my thighs,' I said. My petticoat skirt and embroidered blouse were clearly pre-war so no one would begrudge me the fabric.

'You'd look so much prettier with a little more make-up,' Ada said.

'I think I look nice.'

Ada threw up her hands in resignation, and I went downstairs to meet Joe. Joe, the bearded refugee with a foreign accent, little money and plenty of secrets. Who made my heart pound and blood rise into my cheeks. I didn't understand my attraction to him. Here I'd blown off Don, a real catch according to the girls in my office, only to be drawn to a man of mystery, like a heroine in a Gothic novel. Perhaps I liked him because he was such poor marriage material, because liking him was an adventure, an adventure that wouldn't leave me tied to him for the rest of my life.

My family would be shocked at the way my mind worked these days.

Joe met me at the foot of the stairs, looking less threadbare than usual in pressed slacks and a crisp sports shirt. He dangled a set of keys in his right hand.

'Mrs Knox insisted we take her automobile. I've not driven on the right side of the road, ever, want to navigate?'

'Sure.'

Joe backed cautiously out of Phoebe's garage, turned onto New Hampshire and headed west toward the Potomac River.

'You're doing fine,' I said.

'Thanks,' Joe said.

'You've never driven anywhere else other than in England?'

'No,' he said. 'I've lived most of my life there, but when I was a child I spent holidays with my grandparents outside Prague.'

I managed to contain my curiosity and didn't ask him any more questions.

'Whoa,' I said, 'that's the exit!'

Joe stopped turning into the wrong end of a one-way driveway and went on into the entrance, parking in the tiny lot of a restaurant close enough to the Potomac that I could catch a whiff of river air. Inside the restaurant was quiet and cool. White tablecloths and napkins dressed the eight tables, most of which were already occupied.

The owner greeted Joe in a Slavic language heavy with gutturals. Joe introduced us. The owner's first name was Karel, but I didn't catch his surname. Karel led us to an empty table in the back of the dining room, removed the 'reserved' sign from it and seated us. The table, set with heavy silver and a cut-crystal vase containing a single flower, overlooked a tiny back garden.

'I hope you like this place,' Joe said. 'It's

the only restaurant around where you can get Czech food. Although they make their living from Hungarian goulash.'

'It's lovely,' I said. 'It feels a thousand miles away from Washington.'

'That's the idea,' he said.

'I have no idea what any of these dishes are.'

'If you don't mind, let me order,' he said. When the waiter came Joe ordered in Czech, at least I assumed it was Czech, then translated for me. 'Garlic soup, veal roast with wine sauce, potato dumplings and beer.'

The waiter brought us tall steins of Pilsner, so cool and refreshing I drank mine halfway down immediately. It was mealy, tart and golden, unlike any American beer I'd tasted.

'This is wonderful,' I said.

'Pilsner is the national beer of Czechoslovakia. It's aged in oak barrels. Karel saves what he has for his Czech customers. He won't be able to import more until after the war.'

The waiter set bowls of steaming garlic soup before us. Garlic was a new experience for me. Stoically I sipped some from my spoon. I followed with a slurp.

'This is delicious. What's in it?'

'I used to watch my grandmother make it. You crush salt and garlic together in a mortar and pestle and boil it with the potatoes and spices. I remember having it poured over fried bread in the bottom of a soup

239

bowl for supper.'

I tilted my bowl to scoop up the dregs.

The veal roast with wine and potato dumplings and more beer followed.

'Dessert?' Joe asked.

'I couldn't possibly,' I said.

'How about if we walk to the Water Gate and back? We can leave the car here. Maybe we'll have room for dessert when we get back.'

Joe took my hand as we walked along the Potomac to the concert site. I felt content and happy, although mental warnings about Joe, like little cartoon balloons hovering over my head, kept popping up, reminding me the man was a stranger. Where I grew up, everyone knew everyone else's business, and I was used to feeling secure. I had to remind myself to be cautious.

'Louise,' Joe said, 'I need to tell you something.'

My heart rate surged.

'Okay.'

'I hope that the word "deceive" is a bit strong for what I've done. I've encouraged you and everyone else at the boarding house to think I'm a poor refugee college instructor.'

I didn't answer him.

'I'm not. Well, I am poor, but I've got a British passport. I have dual British and Czech citizenship. But I'm not a language teacher.'

240

'And?'

'You don't seem surprised.'

I shrugged. 'It's wartime. Half the people in this town are undercover.'

He chuckled. 'Undercover. I guess that is as good a word for it as any.'

We walked along silently for a bit.

'At least you haven't walked off in a huff,' he said.

'Why should I? But can you tell me what it is you do?'

'No,' he said, 'but I swear, it's nothing subversive, or even dangerous, certainly not in opposition to your country. I work for a humanitarian organization, not a government.'

'You're not a spy?'

He laughed. 'Absolutely not. I have changed my appearance a bit, in case I run into someone I'd rather not know I'm here. I've grown a beard, wear European clothes and carry that briefcase filled with Czech literature. I still have family in Czechoslovakia, and they don't have British passports.'

Wearing glasses with clear lenses qualifies for more than 'a bit', I thought. I called that a disguise.

'Do you mind if I ask if you're Jewish?'

'Not at all. I am. But I'm not religious.'

What an interesting idea. Where I came from no one could call himself a Baptist without attending church. And not just on Sunday morning either. It was almost another full-time job – Sunday School before services, Tuesday evening supper and choir practice, women's service group lunch and sewing for our soldiers on Wednesday, men's breakfast and Bible study Thursday morning, the youth group on Friday night – some people I knew in Wilmington spent part of every day at church. I hadn't been to church once since arriving in Washington, and I didn't miss it one bit.

'I don't understand,' I said. 'How can you be Jewish without being religious?'

'It's more like being a member of a tribe,' he said. 'Like the Apache Indians, or a Scottish clan.'

'Oh,' I said. 'How do you bear it?'

'What?'

'Everything that's happened to your country, to England.'

'I can't afford to worry about anything I can't do something about. I'm focused on what I can do.'

I still didn't know what that was, or even if what he told me was the truth.

As we walked along Rock Creek Parkway and down Riverside, we joined a throng of people moving in the same direction. It was a happy crowd, dressed in gaily-colored shorts, polo shirts, play clothes and even some swimming suits, ready to start their holiday weekend.

The wide stone steps of the Water Gate that led down to the Potomac River formed a kind of amphitheater. For years the National Symphony Orchestra's barge, which carried an orchestra shell, moored there for summer concerts. The lucky ones, like us, had tickets and could sit on the stone steps directly in front of the barge. The rest had to set up lawn chairs on the greenway.

We threaded our way through a crowd so dense that at one point I walked directly behind Joe, clinging to his shirt, as he elbowed his way towards the stone stairs and our seats.

As dusk fell a squadron of canoes, emerging from under the arches of the Arlington Bridge, glided down the river to float near the barge. A lantern gleamed from every bow. They looked like fireflies hovering over the water.

'So,' I said, 'what are we hearing tonight?'

'Jerome Kern and Victor Herbert, directed by a guest conductor, Charles O'Connell. He supervises the symphony's recordings for RCA Victor.'

'I thought they wrote musicals and operettas.'

'The Kern selection is an instrumental arrangement – "Scenario for Orchestra: Themes from Show Boat". The Herbert is his "Cello Concerto No. 2". But I wouldn't be surprised if we heard some show tunes.'

'I hope one of them is "The Last Time I Saw Paris". Did you see *Lady Be Good*?'

'No, I don't go to the movies. I think I

243

should, though. Moving pictures seem to be so important to Americans.'

Then I surprised myself.

'Let me choose one and we'll go soon,' I said.

'I'd like that,' Joe said. 'Maybe next weekend?'

I'd asked a man out on a date. Ada would be proud. If I wasn't arrested tomorrow breaking into the French embassy. My insides clenched at the thought and bile rose into my throat, before I remembered that I'd be safe with Lionel.

The orchestra filed out on stage, followed by the conductor, and the music began, wafting across the tidal basin.

Once an airplane, with red and green lights blinking at its wingtips, passed overhead, muting the orchestra's sound.

Occasionally Joe whispered in my ear, explaining something about the music to me, but he wasn't at all condescending. We held hands most of the evening and I loved feeling the intimacy of his body pressed close to mine.

After the program ended the orchestra played some show tunes for an encore, and I did get to hear 'The Last Time I Saw Paris', and couldn't help thinking of Lionel again.

After the concert was over, as we walked back towards our car, Joe asked me if I'd like to finish our meal and have dessert. I wasn't hungry, but I wanted to spend more time with him, so I said yes.

Inside we sat at the same table. The waiter brought us coffee and a menu.

'Why don't you order for me again?' I asked.

'Two apple strudels,' Joe said to the waiter. We sipped our coffee.

'I have something I've been wanting to ask you for a long time,' Joe said. 'Promise not to laugh.'

'Sure,' I said, 'ask away.'

'What's a fish camp?'

'Oh,' I said. 'Well, it's kind of a, well, how shall I describe it? My parents' place is on the Cape Fear River. It's got a bait and tackle shop, a fishing dock and a marina, and a seafood restaurant. We can cook whatever the customers catch themselves, or what the commercial fishermen sell to us. And we have our own crab pots. We always have cole slaw and hush puppies and a dessert, usually banana pudding or strawberry pie.'

'Sounds rustic and delightful.'

'Squalid and smelly is more like it.'

'You didn't like working there?'

'Not at all. My parents and brother adore it, though. They'd open on Sunday if the law allowed it.'

'If you hated working there, why did you do it?'

'Because after my husband died I had nowhere to go and no way to make a living, that's why.'

'I'm sorry, I didn't mean to dredge up anything unpleasant. You've mentioned working at a fish camp several times and I didn't know what that was.'

'No, I'm the one being impolite. I hated being dependent on my family and don't want to be reminded of it.'

Our strudel came. It was delicious, all sweet warm apple filling and crisp pastry. Joe ordered more coffee, and before I knew it I blurted out just the question I was embarrassed to ask him.

'It is you, isn't it, knocking on the pipe sometimes in the evenings? Not Henry?'

'Yes, and thank goodness it's you, too! I've been afraid I might be on top of Ada.'

The double entendre sent waves of scarlet up Joe's face and I couldn't help but laugh.

'I meant, oh you know!' he said.

'Of course,' I said.

'We'd better go,' Joe said, covering his embarrassment by sliding back his chair and helping me out of mine. 'Karel's blowing out all the candles.'

The nightwatchman encountered Lionel Barbier smoking on the wide stone veranda of the Vichy French embassy.

'You're here late tonight,' he said. His guard dog, a black Alsatian, sniffed Barbier's hand, then wagged his tail in recognition.

Barbier dropped his cigarette on the stone floor and crushed it with his foot.

246

'Working,' Barbier said. He dug into a pocket and brought out a peppermint candy, unwrapped it and presented it to the dog, which crunched it happily.

'You're the only person here,' the night-watchman said. 'The weekend has begun for everyone else.'

'Actually, *mon ami*, I wished to speak with you.'

'Yes?'

'I have an American girlfriend.'

'You are fortunate.'

'I believe my wife is becoming suspicious. I can no longer rent a hotel room for fear someone from the embassy might see us. Tomorrow is our anniversary.'

'You and your wife's?'

'No, *imbécile*, me and my girlfriend's! We met a year ago tomorrow. We wish to celebrate, of course. My office, as you know, has a very comfortable sofa.'

The nightwatchman groaned.

'I cannot...'

'Of course you can,' Barbier said. He drew a thin wad of American dollars from his suit pocket.

'There's no harm in it, I suppose,' the nightwatchman said, taking the money and tucking it into his pocket. 'This girlfriend of yours, is she pretty?'

'Of course! You'll see for yourself tomorrow night,' Barbier said.

'Use your key,' the nightwatchman said. 'It

will be less conspicuous.' Barbier unwrapped another peppermint and fed it to the dog.

On the way home Joe focused on driving on the correct side of the road in the dark, challenging since the street lights weren't lit because of the dim-out rules. Me, I concentrated on kissing him.

Or rather, intending to kiss him.

I had it all worked out.

Once we got back to the boarding house, I'd offer to make us coffee. We'd go into the lounge, sip our coffee and talk about our evening. The house would be dark and quiet, of course, since everyone would be upstairs asleep. Joe would put his coffee cup aside, turn to me, put his arm around my waist and draw me to him. We'd neck for as long as we could before losing control. Well, I expected Joe to ask, I'd be disappointed if he didn't, but tonight wasn't the night for that. I wasn't ready, and I wanted to be alone with him, without any chance of interruption.

How did a girl carry on a romance in a boarding house, anyway?

I couldn't take my eyes off Joe, his gaze fixed on the road ahead, his capable hands gripping the steering wheel, his arm muscles flexing as he changed gears. We were almost home.

'That's odd,' Joe said, breaking into my romantic reverie.

'What?' I answered.

'All the lights are on downstairs.'

He was right. Bright lights edged the blackout curtains of the lounge, hallway and kitchen of 'Two Trees'. At nearly midnight. Something terrible must have happened.

EIGHTEEN

My first reaction was fear for one of Phoebe's sons.

Joe quickly parked the car and we hurried up the drive to the front door, instinctively holding hands.

Phoebe met us in the hall. She looked a little weary, but nothing like she would have if one of her sons had been killed or injured.

'There's a young foreign woman here to see you, Louise,' Phoebe said. 'A refugee.'

Rachel!

'She wants to speak to you, only you, but her English isn't very good.'

So it wasn't Rachel.

'She insisted on waiting for you,' Phoebe said. 'She's in the lounge.'

I hastened past Joe and Phoebe into the lounge. A woman who I guessed was in her mid-thirties sat primly on the davenport. A threadbare cotton dress hung on her thin frame. A cardboard suitcase tied up with rope sat next to her on the floor. She wore scuffed brogues and thick socks on her feet, a beret tipped back on dirty blonde hair that hung to her shoulders and a blue much-darned cardigan sweater, clothing too warm for Washington in the summer, but not for an ocean crossing.

Ada sat across from her. Either she or Phoebe had brought the woman something to eat and drink, because a tray with an empty glass and crumby plate rested on the coffee table in front of her.

When the woman saw me, she stood up and reached out her hand. 'Louise Pearlie?' she asked, in a thick German accent. Her grip was firm and her face was strong and composed.

'Yes,' I said.

'Bad English,' she said.

'That's all right,' I answered.

'Henrietta Falk,' she said, patting her chest with the palm of her hand. 'Rachel's friend.'

I sank heavily onto the davenport. My vision darkened, bright spots drifted in the air and I was afraid I would faint. Ada quickly took my hand, and Phoebe brought me a glass of water.

'Are you all right?' Ada asked.

'I think so,' I said.

'It's terribly hot in here,' Joe said. 'With your permission, Phoebe, let's dispense with the dim-out rules tonight.'

'Certainly,' Phoebe said.

Joe drew back the curtains and flung open the front windows. Cool air, or what cool passed for on a July night, breezed into the room. I pulled myself together.

'Who's Rachel?' Phoebe asked.

'A dear friend of mine from college,' I said. 'She's French, and Jewish. I haven't heard from her in a couple of years, except for one postcard. I'm terribly worried about her.'

Henrietta, who'd moved onto a chair next to Ada, began to nod vigorously.

'Is Rachel still in Marseille?' I asked. 'In her home?'

'Home, no. Not home. Oh, what is the word!' Henrietta bit her lip.

'Let me help,' Joe said. He turned to Henrietta and began speaking in German. His words unleashed a torrent of more German from Henrietta. When she stopped to catch her breath, Joe turned back to me.

'Your friend Rachel is in an internment center in Marseille,' Joe said. 'She had to leave her apartment building in the Old Port. The Nazis evacuated the buildings that overlooked the harbor.'

Rachel and her family had been evicted from their home. Was this a preliminary step to sending them east? I was devastated.

Henrietta tugged on Joe's sleeve, and spoke again.

'She says,' Joe said to me, 'that Rachel's husband had to flee Marseille, he's with the

251

Resistance now, but Rachel and the children are together at a place just for women and children, a converted hotel. Henrietta met Rachel there.'

'Children?' I said. 'There's just Claude.'

Henrietta understood me, because she cradled an imaginary baby in her arms, and said, 'Louisa.' A little girl named after me.

Only Ada's firm grip on my arm kept me under control.

'How did you find me?'

Joe repeated my question in German, she answered, and he translated. 'She had your parents' address, she telegraphed them as soon as she arrived, and they replied with your address here,' he said.

'Ask her what I can do to help Rachel,' I said to Joe.

Henrietta started to shake her head before he finished speaking.

'Very little, she cannot get a visa,' Henrietta said. 'The authorities suspect her husband is with the Resistance. But you can send packages, through the Red Cross, or the Quakers.'

Henrietta handed me a paper, just half a lined page torn from a cheap pad, folded in two. Scrawled on the page in Rachel's hurried handwriting were the words 'Hôtel Bompard' and a Marseille address, signed with an 'R', and a tiny heart.

I looked at Henrietta questioningly.

'That is the address for the packages.

There was no time for Rachel to write more. I had to go.'

'Is there any talk of the Germans sending them east?' I asked. 'To a labor camp?'

'There are many rumors,' Henrietta said.

Ada squeezed my hand again. 'I'm sure that won't happen, dear,' she said.

Joe and Henrietta continued their conversation in German.

'Henrietta is from Breslau,' Joe said. 'She is going to live with her cousin in Cincinnati. He sponsored her for a visa. She's going to work in his restaurant.'

Henrietta put her palm to her chest again.

'My cousin Adam Falk,' she said. 'Two Oh Five Forest Street, Cincinnati, Ohio. My train leaves at eight fifteen tomorrow morning. I must go now.'

'Please ask her to stay the night,' Phoebe said. 'She looks like she could use a bed and a good breakfast.'

Joe repeated Phoebe's invitation, but Henrietta shook her head. 'I must go to *Bahnhof* now,' she said. 'The train leaves at eight fifteen tomorrow morning.' She finished in German.

'Her cousin sent her a ticket and a little money. She's scared to death she'll miss the train,' Joe said.

Henrietta picked up her suitcase and headed for the door, clearly intending to walk all the way to Union Station in the middle of the night.

'Can I drive her in your car, Phoebe?' Joe asked.

'Of course,' Phoebe answered.

'But she can't stay at the station until morning,' I said.

'It's safe enough,' Joe said. 'It's open all night, there are people everywhere, and she can get something to eat, sleep on a bench. We've all done it.' He grabbed his hat and followed Henrietta, who was already on the porch, took her suitcase from her and led her down to the garage.

In the lounge Ada, Phoebe and I sat, silent, listening to Joe drive away with Henrietta.

'I'm very sorry about your friend,' Phoebe said to me.

'Me, too,' Ada said. She shivered. 'I hated hearing them speak German. It's such an ugly language.'

And until now none of us had any idea that Joe knew German.

All my plans for a romantic tryst with Joe vanished. Instead I went upstairs and locked myself into the bathroom. Then I sat on the cool tile floor and fell apart, sobbing, terrified for Rachel and her family. This feeling of security Rachel had, she and her father, since I'd known her at college, because she was a French citizen, because her family had been more French than Jewish for generations, had been pure delusion. Europe wasn't civilized any more, and wouldn't be as long as the Nazis were in power. The Gestapo were due to arrive in Marseille in a few days, and they wouldn't care what passport any Jew carried.

Tomorrow I had planned to break and enter the Vichy French embassy and steal foreign government documents with the help of an embassy attaché I barely knew.

Cold fear gripped me. What if I got caught inside the embassy? I would be on French soil and subject to French law. A French prison! The Devil's Island penal colony outside French Guiana was the closest. Maybe Lionel had already informed on me. Maybe gendarmes would be waiting to arrest me once I set foot on the embassy grounds.

And if I escaped the Vichy embassy but the OSS found out about my activities? What if Charles was pestering me, not because he had designs on my virtue, but because he was suspicious of my preoccupation with Gerald Bloch's missing file? What if Marvin Metcalfe had called Don to check up on me? What if the FBI agents outside 'Two Trees' yesterday morning were watching me, not Joe or Ada?

The US federal woman's prison was in Clarkson, West Virginia.

At the very least I'd lose my job and find myself back in Wilmington, deep-frying hush puppies, at my parents' fish camp.

I must have been out of my mind to think that I could do anything to help Rachel. I was just a file clerk. I wasn't trained, not to mention authorized, to pull off an operation like this.

I'd had way too much confidence in my abilities and let my imagination run away with me.

The obvious, sensible thing to do was to destroy the documents I'd collected, cancel my lunatic plan for tomorrow, go into work on Monday and brief Don about the tiny torn corner of the index card that convinced me Bloch's file was stolen. He would listen patiently, and when I could offer no evidence for my suspicions, placate me, and I would have done everything I could. Rachel's fate, along with Claude's and the baby's, was out of my hands. Always had been. There was simply nothing I could do.

Except arrange to send Rachel and the children a Red Cross package. I'd read about the contents of the standard relief food package. Raisins, a can of corned beef, crackers, a chocolate bar and two packs of cigarettes. Rachel didn't smoke. Maybe she could barter the cigarettes for food.

I couldn't bear it.

Was there a remote chance that the wild plan I'd concocted, of planting a new Bloch file at OSS, could work?

If there was, I had to try. Or I wouldn't be able to live with myself.

I heard the grandfather clock in the downstairs hall strike midnight. It was Independence Day, 1942. Today I was going to pull a black-bag job at the Vichy French embassy.

'This hamburger is, without a doubt, the best thing I have ever eaten in my life,' Joe said. 'No wonder you Americans live on them. Look at everything on it, minced beef, cheese, lettuce, tomatoes, mayonnaise...'

'When you have cheese on it, we call it a cheeseburger,' I said. 'Haven't you had one yet?'

'No, I wanted to try one, but it always looked so messy. I'm not used to eating with my hands.'

Henry, wrapped in one of Dellaphine's aprons, the red-and-blue-checked one with white lace trim, in honor of the occasion, appeared at the door of the porch with a plate of hot dogs. Joe gingerly took one.

'Don't tell me you haven't had a hot dog either?' Ada asked.

'This is my first. Henry, what is this flavor? It's sort of woodsy.'

'I always barbecue over hickory.'

'You absolutely must have mustard and onions on a hotdog,' Phoebe said, passing Joe the condiments tray, as Henry loaded up his own plate with Dellaphine's potato salad and baked beans. Patriotic songs from the radio floated out onto the porch, while the fan circled overhead.

No one mentioned the drama of the night before, but Joe, Ada and Phoebe were being

257

excessively cheerful this morning. Even Henry was kind to me, asking me how I wanted my hamburger cooked, whether I wanted my bun toasted and if I'd prefer my cheese melted on the burger or the bun.

'It doesn't seem like the Fourth without fireworks,' Ada said, 'or a parade.'

'I've got sparklers,' Henry said. 'We can fool around with those.'

'Dellaphine's going to make ice cream,' Phoebe said. 'But we all have to take a turn cranking.'

'Aren't you going out later?' Joe asked me.

My mouth went dry. 'I was supposed to go to a pool party at the Wardman,' I said, 'but I haven't heard from my friend.'

Nine o'clock had come and gone several hours ago and Lionel hadn't called. At first I was nervous, then I became terribly distressed. Something must have happened to discourage him from our hare-brained scheme. I didn't blame him. It was an awful risk, and as the hours passed until we were supposed to undertake it, it seemed more and more risky.

There wasn't anything I could do without Lionel's help, no way to get the documents I wanted without access to the Vichy French embassy files. Maybe I had to accept that there was nothing I could do for Rachel and her children.

If only I could get the sight of those frozen corpses strewn across the pages of *Life*

258

magazine out of my mind.

Out in the hall the telephone rang, and I heard Dellaphine leaving the kitchen to answer it.

She stuck her head out onto the porch and looked right at me. 'Mrs Pearlie, it's for you,' she said.

'Maybe that's your friend,' Ada said.

I went out into the hall and picked up the telephone receiver, waiting for Dellaphine to get back to the kitchen, where she and Madeleine were eating their lunch, until I spoke.

Lionel answered me.

'I am sorry to be so late calling,' he said. 'Listen carefully.'

Later that afternoon I went up to my room to get ready. I selected the same black suit I'd worn to the Wardham, but beneath the jacket I added a low-cut cornflower-blue silk blouse with the art deco necklace that Phoebe had lent me and then insisted I keep. I planned to clip on the matching earrings later. I stowed my compact, a red lipstick, a pair of black high-heeled pumps, and a hairbrush in a black handbag, the roomiest one I owned. The irony of it didn't escape me – a black bag for a 'black bag job'.

I tied a silk scarf that matched my blouse around my head and slipped on my sunglasses. I was ready to go. And I was truly scared.

I went downstairs into the front hall. My hands were shaking and I thought I might lose my lunch.

Then I heard the President speaking on the radio, which was turned up loud so we could listen to music on the porch. It was Roosevelt's July Fourth address to the nation, and you could hear a pin drop in the house. 'Not to waste one hour,' he said, 'not to stop one shot, not to hold back one blow – that is the way to mark our great national holiday in this year of 1942.'

'Where's your swimsuit?' Ada asked me, coming out into the hall, after the President stopped speaking and the strains of 'God Bless America' filled the air. I could hear the grinding noise of the ice-cream maker resume from the porch. More than I could say I wished I were waiting to take my turn cranking.

'Right here,' I said, holding up my bag.

'I hope it's a two-piece,' she said.

'It's not.'

'Have fun,' Phoebe said, passing by with a tray full of dirty dishes.

'I may be getting home late tonight,' I said.

I walked two blocks to the corner of 23rd and 'I'. A dusty black Citroën pulled up next to me. Lionel leaned over from the driver's seat to open the door. I slid in.

'Ready for our little adventure?' he asked.

'I am,' I said. Misadventure was more like it.

We arrived at the Sheraton, a hotel that overlooked the French embassy, parked, went in a back door and walked three flights up to the safe room Lionel had booked under an assumed name.

'Okay,' Lionel said. 'Now we begin the performance.'

We'd already decided that if we were caught in any other state than in possession of stolen documents, we'd pretend that we were really having an affair. Who was to say we weren't?

I took off my jacket, put on my earrings and heels and layered on thick red lipstick, blotting it with tissue. I stuffed the blue scarf and my sunglasses into my pocketbook, brushed out my hair, and the two of us went down the back stairs to the street. There was no one in sight, so we sauntered around to the front door of the hotel, and went inside to the bar. I did my best to look and act like a floozie.

We had a drink, ordered all the canapés on the bar menu, talked and laughed, and generally attracted attention to ourselves. Once Lionel put his hand far up my skirt and rested it on my thigh. I pushed it away.

He leaned over to whisper to me, 'You must act the part, my dear, *sophistiquée*. This is not your small town.'

He was right, of course, we needed to be

convincing. I let him replace his hand.

After we had performed the roles of reck-less lovers as long as we could without getting arrested for drunk and disorderly, Lionel took out his wallet and gestured to the waiter.

'Two bottles of cold champagne to take with us, please,' Lionel said. 'It's our anni-versary.'

We left the hotel carrying the champagne, still laughing. Lionel took my elbow and steered me around back of the hotel.

'This way.'

We walked through the dimly lit grounds of the Sheraton until we arrived at a service gate that opened onto Kalorama Road. It was unlocked. We slipped through and cross-ed the street, still in character, holding hands and talking. We paused outside the stone gates of the embassy.

'Ready?' Lionel said.

'I'm ready,' I said.

Together we staggered up the driveway to the stone mansion. Lionel inserted a key in the front door that looked like it should open a dungeon in a medieval castle, and the door swung open.

He led me through the handsome foyer floored with marble deep into the building and down a narrow corridor and up two flights of stairs.

'*Et voilà*,' he said, flinging open a door.

Lionel's office was quite large, once a

dressing room, I thought, because of the cupboard and closet inset into the interior walls. A long mullioned window overlooked the back entrance and service area of the embassy. Papers, books, newspapers and a few framed photographs jammed the cupboard. A desk and office chair stood in front of a row of file cabinets, and a sofa, covered in a rich but worn red brocade, sat under the window. Lionel promptly drew heavy curtains across the window before he turned on his desk lamp.

'We wouldn't want anyone to witness our love-making, would we?' he asked.

A rap sounded at the door. I sat down on the sofa, crossed my legs – negligently allowing my skirt to ride up quite a bit – and unbuttoned my blouse to reveal the swell of my breasts, augmented by tissue paper stuffed into my bra, as Ada had once recommended.

Lionel opened the door.

'My dear friend,' he said, pulling the guard inside the room. 'Have some champagne, celebrate with us!'

The guard's dog, a huge Alsatian straining at his leash, his ears flat against the back of his head, followed him in. The guard kept the dog close, but he still made me nervous. But once Lionel gave him a peppermint he wagged his tail like any household mutt.

'This is Nancy,' Lionel said, introducing me to the guard. 'Nancy, meet Carobert.'

'Nice to meet you,' I said, reaching my

hand out to him languidly, an adverb I'd read often in romance novels, and he took it, bowing.

Lionel popped the cork of the first bottle of champagne and toasted us. Carobert drained his glass, and Lionel offered him another. At first he declined, but then reconsidered, draining that glass, too.

'I must go,' he said. 'My duties, you understand.'

He and the dog left, and Lionel dropped back down on the sofa next to me. He put his arm around me, and his hand on my thigh again.

'My dear, you were splendid,' he said to me.

'Of course,' I answered. 'The role of sexy mistress is second nature to me. What now?'

'We wait for a few minutes. Until the guard is on the other side of the building. Then we go on to the file room.'

In the meantime Lionel popped the cork on the second bottle of champagne and poured the contents into a potted philodendron.

'What a waste,' he said, 'but we must look as if we have enjoyed ourselves without clouding our wits.'

Lionel opened the office door slowly and peered out into the hall, listening quietly. I kicked off my heels.

'Come,' he said, reaching for my hand. I grasped it, he pulled me into the hall. It was quite dark, even embassies were subject to the dim-out regulations, and we were pursued by long shadows as we crept down the hall, through a door, and down another hall, this one so narrow I could reach out my arms and touch the walls, deep into the building.

We stopped in front of an anonymous door and waited, listening. My heart pounded and there was a harsh roaring in my ears. Lionel opened the door with another ornate key, we slipped inside and closed the door behind us.

The vast room was once a ballroom, I suspected, two stories tall, with stained-glass windows and parquet floors. We'd come in a back way, probably a service entrance. I saw the main double doors on the other side of the space, secured with a bar and a lock the size of my hand. The space now stored documents.

Shelves of outsized folders lined two walls. Legions of wooden file cabinets stood at attention in rows, with barely enough room between the aisles to move. Lionel led me into the thicket, past the Hs, Is, Js, across an aisle, and to yet another bank, the Cs, and finally to the Bs. 'Bloch,' I said, 'Gerald.' Lionel opened a file door and rummaged through it. He shook his head.

'I am sorry, my dear, there is nothing here.'

'No,' I said. I pushed him aside and went through the files myself. No Gerald Bloch.

'No,' I said again. 'It can't be.'

Lionel shrugged.

Since I'd conceived of this little amateur caper of mine, I hadn't let myself consider the chance that the Vichy French embassy had no record of Monsieur Bloch, hydrographer, resident of Marseille. I wanted those documents, without them I could do nothing for Rachel's family. I was deeply disappointed.

'Louise,' Lionel said. 'Come. We are supposed to be making passionate love in my office. If the guard returns and we are not there, he will sound the alarm.'

Tears welling, I gazed out over the ballroom, at row upon row of file cabinets.

'Not yet,' I said. 'We must keep looking.' As I pulled away from him I knocked over a floor lamp. It landed on the floor with a crash. We both flinched, and Lionel dragged me behind a file cabinet, where we sank to the ground and hid. We waited, but no one came.

'We've got time,' I said. 'I'm not leaving without searching through as many files as I can.'

'Are you demented?' Lionel said. I got up, pulling my hand out of his grip.

I ran over to an 'M' catalog and looked up Marseille Hydrography Office. Nothing. I ran down an aisle to the 'I's. Nothing on the International Hydrological Association. Where else could I look?

Lionel had followed me, but now he gripped my arm, hard.

'Let's go,' he insisted.

'Not yet, let me think,' I said.

'The time for thinking is done,' he said. 'Now is the time for leaving.'

I still resisted him. 'Surely we have a few more minutes,' I said.

This time he twisted my arm, hurting me so much I gasped.

'Now,' he said, his eyes narrowing. I didn't argue with him.

Lionel guided me out of the room and locked the heavy door behind us. We crept back the way we came until we got to his office. Inside I dropped onto the sofa, cradling my arm.

'I'm sorry, Louise,' he said, looking again like the friendly, kind Lionel I knew. 'It was necessary for us to go.'

'It's all right,' I said. 'Of course we needed to leave.' I didn't mean it. I no longer liked him much.

We heard a sound at the end of the hall, the slam of a door followed by human footsteps and the four-legged pattering of a dog.

'It's the guard!' Lionel whispered.

We both looked at our watches. Only twenty minutes had passed since we'd left. I remembered the guard's Karabiner slung over one shoulder and the handie talkie that dangled from the other.

'He's back much too soon,' Lionel hissed.

'Do you think he suspects?' I asked.

'If he did surely he wouldn't return alone.'

'Maybe he wants more champagne.'

We both hesitated, thinking the same thing. We hardly looked like lovers who'd been alone for twenty minutes.

'Quickly,' I said.

The steps came closer and closer, the dog whined, perhaps anticipating peppermints, and the door opened, without a preliminary knock.

I squealed and jumped up from the sofa, stark naked except for Phoebe's necklace glittering between my breasts. I covered my most private body parts with my hands. The guard shined his flashlight directly on me, and shrieked himself.

'Idiot!' Lionel shouted, rising beside me, as naked as the day he was born. *'Imbécile! What are you doing?'*

Gallantly he wrapped his crumpled shirt around me. I tried to cry, but couldn't pull it off, instead burying my face in Lionel's shoulder.

The guard fell back and dropped his flashlight from my body.

'I am so sorry!' he said. 'I thought, I was just checking!'

'On what? How far we had gotten! Get out of here!' Lionel said.

The guard and the dog, still whining for a treat, left the room, leaving Lionel and me scared out of our wits.

'My dear,' he said, 'you have so much courage!' He laid a hand on my shoulder, but I shook it off.

'Get dressed quickly,' I said. 'He must be suspicious of us, or he wouldn't have come back so soon!'

'Perhaps we should linger,' Lionel said, 'won't it seem odd if we don't conclude our assignation?' I couldn't help but notice that Lionel was aroused. I'd never seen an uncircumcised man before, and was not inspired to prolong the experience.

'Come on!' I said, reaching for my clothes.

Lionel grasped my arm again.

'My darling Louise,' he said, 'you do not look sufficiently *satisfaite*. This is not acceptable. I have my reputation to consider.'

'Your reputation will survive,' I said.

He pulled me toward him, wrapping his arms around me, pinning mine to my side, his intentions obvious. Lionel was much stronger than his foppish appearance suggested. I was as angry as I was frightened. If I resisted, fighting and screaming, it might bring the guard back. If I didn't it wouldn't be rape.

'Let me go, Lionel, please,' I said. 'I don't want to do this.'

'Ah, but I do,' he said. 'And I've risked my life to bring you here. I expect some reward. One instant of ecstasy in this terrible world that is almost intolerable for me to live in otherwise. Is that too much to ask?' He

269

pinned my arms behind my back with one hand, and with the other began to caress my flank.

'I'll scream,' I said, 'I will.'

'Why? You're not a virgin,' he said. 'An act of reluctant love would be much more bearable than arrest, would it not?'

He was correct, of course. He knew that when he brought me here. That I would submit in order to escape exposure, a cheap price for a chance to rescue Rachel's family.

Then I knew.

'You have it,' I said.

Lionel raised an eyebrow at me. 'Of course,' he said. 'I fetched it as soon as you told me of it.' He released me, knowing I could hardly escape while still naked. He opened a desk drawer and drew out an envelope file secured with a thin red ribbon. 'Monsieur Gerald Bloch, hydrographer of Marseille, husband of Rachel? That's him, is it not?'

'Yes,' I said. 'Give it to me.'

'I have been through it many times,' he said. 'With a fine-toothed comb, as you say, and I find nothing remarkable.'

'Why the charade?' I asked. 'Why bring me here, pretend to search, when you had the file all along? Why put yourself in danger of being caught with me?'

Lionel shrugged. 'I hoped you might have some good intelligence to share with me, some nugget I could relay to my superiors, that you would give up at the last minute to help your friend.'

'I thought you loathed Vichy.'

'I do. More than you can imagine. So much I do not want to set foot in France until the war is over. So I wish to ingratiate myself with the ambassador to preserve my own position here. As for your precious file, I might still give it to you, if...' and he gestured to the sofa.

Well, why not? Women all over the world were sleeping with men they despised for scraps of information that might help defeat Nazism. Honey traps, they called them. What made me so special, my body so precious? Lionel was right, I wasn't a virgin, and although I loathed being intimidated, sleeping with Lionel wasn't the worst thing that could happen to me. If I was discovered, arrested or lost my job, that would be unbearable.

He smiled at me, kind Lionel again. 'Who knows, you may not regret it.' He reached for me.

A bell sounded, three times. It echoed in the hall outside Lionel's office door.

'*Merde!*' Lionel said. He drew aside the window curtains. I caught a glimpse of three black Cadillacs motoring up the drive.

'It's the ambassador, the *collaborateur*,' Lionel said. 'Why is he here, on a Saturday? Get dressed, quickly!'

He didn't have to suggest it twice. We both

threw on our clothes.

'This is a catastrophe,' he said, with an ear to the door. 'He never arrives without an entourage, deputies, bodyguards. They will guard all the doors.'

'How will we get out?' I asked.

'It's you, not us,' he said. 'No one will care if I am here, the guard will never report that I entertained a guest.'

Simultaneously we looked toward the window. Lionel's office was on the third floor, but I remembered the thick ivy that shrouded the embassy.

Lionel shoved the sofa aside, and the two of us struggled to raise the sash. It creaked and shuddered, but finally rose. Lionel held it open.

'Out,' he said, 'quickly, quickly!'

'Please, Lionel, give me the file!'

'No,' he said, 'I can't risk it, if they capture you with it, they'll know I helped you steal it! Without it we could still pretend we were lovers looking for a quiet spot to spend the evening.'

'Please!'

'No! Get out!'

I swung myself onto the ledge of the window. I'd climbed enough trees and vines during my childhood that I figured the ivy could hold my weight. And it did, mostly. I edged my way down the wall, grasping thick ropes of ivy, feeling with my feet for footholds, and easing my way down. Once a vine did give way, tearing free of the stone wall, but I only slid a few inches before I caught hold of another.

I reached earth safely. The rear grounds of the embassy were empty. I looked up at Lionel's window, overwhelmed with anger and frustration. I picked up a rock and threw it towards the window, imagining it crashing through glass and cracking Lionel's skull.

'God damn you!' I screamed at him, uselessly.

I was livid with Lionel and furious at my own naiveté. If I'd had a gun I swear I would have shot him dead.

The rock I threw bounced off a mullion, and to my surprise the window opened. Lionel leaned out and dropped a file envelope towards me. It fell, drifting a bit, at my feet. I retrieved it, ripped off the ribbon that tied it closed and drew out a handful of papers. I saw Gerald Bloch's name, stuffed the papers back into the file and looked for a way out of the still empty back grounds of the embassy.

Lionel leaned out the window and screamed at me.

'Run, idiot!' he shouted. 'Run!'

As I turned the guard's huge Alsatian, dragging his leash, careened around the corner, not barking, but running flat out straight at me. His intensity was terrifying.

NINETEEN

The dog bounded toward me, his ears flat back and teeth bared, his handler nowhere to be seen. I searched the ground and selected the largest rock I could find. If I could stun the dog, I could still escape. I wondered how close I should let him get before I struck. Then he was just a few yards away from me, and I could feel my bowels lurch and blood rush to my heart.

Then I heard Lionel screaming.

'*Couché! Couché!*' he shouted. The dog skidded to a halt, confused, and looked up at Lionel, who leaned out of his window. '*Viens ici!*'

A shower of peppermints dropped from the window. The dog considered his choice, looking at me, then at the peppermints scattered under Lionel's window. If I hadn't been terrified, his confusion would have been amusing. The Alsatian decided in Lionel's favor, trotting over to the treats.

'*Bon garçon!*' Lionel screamed to the dog. '*Au pied!* For Christ's sake, Louise, run!'

I ran pell-mell across the rear grounds of the embassy, so fast my lungs burned. I tore across the dry brown lawn, past an empty garden shed and wood house, and through a back service gate onto Kalorama Road.

Once outside I forced myself to walk. Casually I went down the street and crossed into the Sheraton grounds. I had the key to the hotel room Lionel had rented, and I saw no reason why I shouldn't go there to collect myself. Besides, I'd left my jacket and head-scarf there and I badly wanted to cover myself.

Once inside the hotel room my nerve abandoned me. I sat on the bed and began to sob. I couldn't stop trembling. My arm hurt. A deep black bruise was forming where Lionel had twisted my elbow.

After a few minutes I ran out of tears. In the bathroom I soaked two towels and wash-ed the sweat of fear and heat and exertion from myself as best I could.

I remained in the hotel room in case the embassy guard raised an alarm, but from the window I saw that the embassy was dark and quiet. I'm embarrassed to say that instead of instantly examining the documents I'd stolen, or rather 'liberated', as real spooks said, I fell sound asleep.

When I awoke it was pitch black. I could just detect a murmur of voices from the hotel lobby. I washed what was left of my make-up off my face, put my jacket on over my blouse and wrapped the scarf around my head. I slipped out of the room, went down

275

the back stairs and out into the street. By God, I'd gotten away with it.

I unlocked the door of my boarding house and tiptoed into the dark hall. I'd been lucky to find a taxi at this late hour. Otherwise I would still be walking, fending off sailors and soldiers on weekend leave looking for a bed for the night.

I was starving, so I felt my way back to the kitchen, where I hoped I could find something in the refrigerator to hold me until breakfast. I didn't want to turn on any more lights than I had to. I wasn't in the mood to make up any stories about the Fourth of July party I had supposedly attended.

A dark shape that rustled when it moved rose up in front of me and we collided. Madeleine and I both managed to stifle our exclamations. She reached for the light switch on the stove, which cast the dimmest of glows.

She looked beautiful. Her chocolate skin gleamed against the topaz of the party dress Ada had given her. Whatever you called the color of her lipstick, it was perfect with her complexion.

'Where have you been?' I asked. 'It's very late.'

'I could ask you the same thing!'

'At my pool party.'

'You don't look like you've been swimming.'

'No, I guess I don't.'

'I've been to a jazz club on "U" Street. Cab Calloway was playing. He was jumpin' tonight.'

'By yourself?'

'No. My man drove me. He has a car.'

'Does your mother know about this?'

'I'm eighteen. Besides, she got a Nembutal from Mrs Knox on account of she hasn't slept well for the last few nights. She doesn't even know I'm gone.'

I let it go. Madeleine was a grown-up working girl, and smart, and looking out for her was not my job. I started to root around in the refrigerator, but the pickings were slim. Pickles and leftover hotdog rolls didn't sound appetizing to me.

'There's peach ice cream in the freezer,' Madeleine said. 'Mr Joe insisted we save some for you.'

I reached into the freezer compartment and pulled out a bowl of ice cream covered with a dish towel, way more than I could eat.

'Have some with me,' I said.

'Sure,' Madeleine said.

We found spoons and sat at the kitchen table and ate out of the bowl together. The ice cream was sweet, creamy and cold. Every now and then I'd bite into a frozen chunk of fresh peach. Between us we finished the entire bowl.

'Well,' Madeleine said, stretching her arms. 'To bed.'

I yawned in reply.

I didn't even think of looking at the documents I'd stolen. I was too exhausted. I stripped, tossing my clothes into a pile on a chair, threw on a nightdress and dropped onto the bed, falling into a sound sleep.

When I awoke the next morning sunlight blazed into my room. I glanced at my alarm clock. It was ten o'clock! I couldn't remember when I'd last slept this late. I had so much to do. I got out of bed and dressed quickly, in trousers, a red-checked shirt and rope sandals. I slipped down the stairs, starving and thirsty. I heard voices on the porch, but thankfully no one noticed me. I didn't want to deal with anyone yet today.

A pan of biscuits and a pot of hot coffee sat on the stove. I poured a cup of coffee, grabbed a biscuit and crept back upstairs. I could hardly wait to see what I'd brought back from the Vichy French embassy.

After I returned to my bedroom, for a minute I thought my pocketbook, with the purloined documents inside, was missing. My heart thudded, and my imagination instantly pictured either Ada or Joe as foreign spies. Then I caught sight of a corner of my bag sticking out from under the pile of clothes I'd tossed onto a chair last night before going to sleep. I took a huge, deep breath of relief, and reached for the bag.

I sat on my bed with my handbag's contents spread out neatly before me. One paper I recognized was a photostat of Bloch's request for an American visa in 1940, thank God. I couldn't reconstruct the file without it. There was another photostat of a single-spaced memo in German, with the SS crest on the letterhead. The predatory eagle perched on top of a swastika gave me the creeps. Since I couldn't read German I had no idea what it said.

The only document in French was a short typewritten note on Vichy French letterhead. I fetched Milt Jr.'s French dictionary.

The gist of the note was that Gerald Bloch was a valuable resource on the hydrography of the North African coast, and that by no means was he to be issued an exit visa.

I added the documents Joan and Metcalfe gave me to the papers I'd stolen from the embassy. I now had two copies of Donovan's memo and the translation of the Resistance contact's note, reprints of Bloch's scholarly articles I'd gotten from Metcalfe, the ones whose titles I'd translated at the public library, Metcalfe's photograph of himself, Bloch, Rachel, Burns and others in a pub in Edinburgh in 1936, two programs from the 1936 hydrographic conference in Edinburgh, one of the 1939 conference in DC, which Bloch did not attend, a photostat of Bloch's visa request in 1940 identical to the one in my original file, the Vichy French letter and the SS memo.

I had all the documents I needed to reconstruct a file, an even more complete file than the original, in fact, for me to 'find' at work tomorrow, a thought that made the hair on my neck prickle and sweat bead on my upper lip.

I had no intention of telling OSS that Gerald was no longer with his family. Gerald's original request was to rescue his family, not him, and free him to help the Allies. If OSS knew Gerald had already joined the Resistance, there'd be no need to help his family escape.

Then I realized I couldn't include the Gestapo document in Bloch's new file. If the original file had contained it, I would certainly have mentioned it to Don after its loss. Besides, I didn't know what it said, although I could guess, and if I got caught smuggling it into OSS, I could never explain how I came into possession of it.

I decided to recreate the original file with a set of Joan's carbons, the journal reprints, the Edinburgh photograph, the visa request and copies of both the 1936 and 1939 conference programs. If this didn't convince the Project Committee to extract Bloch's family from Marseille I didn't know what would. Would they even have time? I knew the Gestapo would arrive in Marseille on Tuesday – God, that was only two days away!

What to do with the extra documents? Burn them? I chewed on a pencil. What else could I do to improve Rachel's chances of escape? Again I tried to convince myself this quest of mine wasn't just personal. Bloch appeared to be an important person who could play a critical role in the coming invasion of North Africa. If he knew that his family was safe, he would be free to help the allies. I didn't know who in the office took advantage of Bob Holman's death to steal the file, and I didn't know whom to trust. That left me with the responsibility to do something, anything.

A knock on my door startled me.

'Honey,' Ada said. 'You awake? Dinner's ready.'

Sunday dinner was important to our little jerry-rigged family. Phoebe insisted on preserving this bit of pre-war civilization, even though she and Dellaphine were the only ones in the house who attended church regularly. Dellaphine always cooked us a hot meal, although we'd have been happy with much less. Most boarding houses didn't offer Sunday meals, so all over the city folks were making Spam sandwiches for themselves.

When Phoebe and Dellaphine brought in platters of fried chicken and sliced tomatoes, bowls of mashed potatoes and butter beans, and pitchers of iced tea and lemonade, I realized I was hungry. I hadn't had a full meal since lunch the day before.

'How was the pool party?' Ada asked me.

'Oh,' I said, lying extravagantly, 'it was swell. The Wardman pool is in the shade, so the water was cool. We had cocktails and my friend who lives there barbecued steaks and corn on the cob.'

'I didn't hear you come in,' Ada said. 'You must have stayed late.'

She wasn't pumping me, I didn't think, but her questioning made me apprehensive.

'After the pool closed we went to my friend's apartment and listened to the radio,' I said.

'What program?' Joe asked.

Was he pumping me, too? He wasn't looking at me, instead regarding his forkful of butter beans quizzically, as he often did American food, before eating it.

'There was a Gershwin program on, then *American Hit Parade*,' I said. Thank goodness I'd looked at the newspaper before leaving yesterday. 'And thanks, everyone, for leaving me some ice cream. It was delicious.'

'You're more than welcome,' Phoebe said. 'I'm glad you enjoyed it.'

'You'll have to take an extra turn cranking the next time we make it,' Henry said.

'Done,' I said.

Joe pushed his plate away.

'Don't get up yet,' Phoebe said. 'Dellaphine has a surprise for you all.'

Phoebe and Ada took our plates back to the kitchen and came back with dessert plates and forks, followed closely by Dellaphine, beaming, with a peach pie.

'I had all these peaches left over from the ice cream,' she said, slicing the pie carefully into equal slices and placing them on plates. Henry finished his before she was through dishing up the rest. Joe ate slowly and deliberately, and I followed suit.

'Will there be any sugar left for the rest of this month?' Ada asked.

'Peach pie don't take much sugar,' Dellaphine said. 'Besides, we already used most of our ration in the ice cream.'

'Worth every grain,' I said.

'I hope you and Madeleine saved some of this for yourselves,' Joe said, rounding up crumbs from the piecrust with his fork for a final tiny mouthful.

'We made us a little tart from the extra fruit and pastry,' Dellaphine said. 'We're going to have it with our coffee after we clean the kitchen.'

'I'll help you,' I said.

The words slipped out of my mouth. I wasn't sure who looked the most shocked, Phoebe, Henry, Ada or Dellaphine. Joe smiled behind his hand, like he always did when amused by American customs. For a minute I was astonished, too. Had I just offered to help the colored cook clean up the kitchen?

I folded my napkin and left it at my place.

'Since I didn't crank,' I said, 'and you saved me ice cream, it's the least I can do.'

283

I helped Phoebe and Dellaphine clear the table, and went back into the kitchen. Phoebe gave me a perplexed look before she left and went to join the others in the sitting room. Madeleine, who was scraping food scraps from our plates into a bowl to take out to the chickens, stopped to watch me put on an apron and pick up a dish towel.

'I'll dry,' I said, as Dellaphine plunged her hands into a sink full of suds and dirty dishes. We worked quickly, talking about the weather and war news, and not how I was helping them with the dishes. When we were done I hung up my apron and went upstairs, ostensibly to take a nap.

When I got to my room I met Ada coming out of it.

TWENTY

'Hi, dearie,' she said, 'I borrowed some face cream, hope you don't mind.' She had my blue jar of Pond's in her hand. I was surprised that she would go into my room alone, and it must have shown on my face, because she quickly apologized.

'You were busy downstairs, and I just ducked in,' she said. 'I want a bath, and I couldn't find my own cream.'

That seemed unlikely to me. The woman had enough creams and lotions scattered around her room to moisturize a battalion of WACS. I put on an unconcerned face.

'Of course, Ada, you can borrow anything you like.'

She crossed the hall to the bathroom. Ada did have a towel and robe with her, I noted, but if she were a German spy, she would be prepared to back up her bath story.

Ada a German spy, what nonsense. My imagination was working overtime.

I went into my room and closed the door, leaning against it. What an idiot I had been not to lock my room when I went down to dinner, with all those papers spread out over the bed. We usually did lock our rooms, Phoebe insisted, but on the weekends, when we were all in the house together, it didn't seem so necessary.

I sat down on my bed and crossed my legs. The papers seemed undisturbed, thank God. And the German memo was face down, so the Nazi letterhead wasn't visible. If Ada had caught sight of that while crossing the room she would surely have stopped and looked at it, anybody would. I couldn't remember turning the memo on its face, but I must have done, mustn't I?

I put Ada out of my mind and concentrated on the task at hand. I began by leafing through the programs for the 1936 and 1939 hydrological conferences. I'm not sure why I took the 1939 program from Metcalfe, since Bloch didn't attend, but maybe I could use it to illustrate the importance of hydrography to the war effort. I scanned the 1939 document. Our own Charles Burns had made quite a bit of academic progress in the years between the two conferences. In 1936 he and Metcalfe together had presented 'An Analysis of Recent African Atlases'. Three years later, in 1939, Burns alone offered 'Mediterranean Sea Circulation and the Algerian Gyres'. No wonder he'd been recruited to the OSS Map Division. But something about that title rang a distant bell in my head.

I turned to Bloch's journal reprints. I'd roughly translated their titles in the library after getting them from Metcalfe, on the same day that I saw those awful pictures in *Life*.

For a few minutes I could hardly breathe, much less think. At last I understood exactly what had happened to the original Bloch file. The implications of the discovery stunned me. Gerald Bloch might well be a valuable Resistance recruit, but his file wasn't stolen for political reasons. The thief who capitalized on Bob Holman's death to steal Bloch's file had a purely personal motive.

If I had looked closely at the 1939 conference program, as soon as I'd got it from Marvin Metcalfe at our second meeting, I would have known who stole Bloch's file before I even thought of breaking into the Vichy embassy.

I still had to figure out how to help Rachel. I hadn't risked my career, maybe my freedom, involved Joan and Dora, to stop plotting now.

I decided what to do with the 'extra' documents. I folded a carbon of the Resistance note, the SS memo and one of the 1936 conference programs into an envelope, tucked it into my pocket book and went downstairs to find Joe.

Thank God he was alone in the lounge. 'I can't sleep,' I said to him. 'It's too hot. I think I'll walk down to the park and sit under the trees in the shade for a while. Maybe get a Coke on the way. Want to come?'

Joe looked up from the Sunday newspaper. 'Sure,' he said.

We stopped at the filling station on the corner and got two ice-cold Cokes out of the red chest refrigerator.

The first shady park bench we passed was occupied by a sleeping GI who must have missed the last Saturday night bus to Fort Myers. He clutched an empty bourbon bottle and a paper lunch bag with a USO label to his chest, snoring. We didn't disturb him. He was already AWOL and another couple of hours wouldn't make a difference to his sergeant.

We picked a bench under a cherry tree, its

blossoms long gone, leaves limp with thirst, and watched the traffic go by on Pennsylvania Avenue.

'Before the war this city would be quiet on a Sunday,' I said. 'No traffic, no restaurants open, that filling station where we got our drinks would be closed. Doing anything except going to church was sacrilege.'

'I wasn't living here then,' Joe said. 'This has been my only experience with the States. It's like a beehive. Even London is quieter.'

'I wonder what life will be like after the war,' I said. 'It can't return to the way it was.'

'You have more hope of that here than we do in Europe,' Joe said.

'Joe,' I said, summoning all the courage I had, 'I need to talk to you about something. Or rather, someone.'

Joe pulled out his pipe and began the ritual of loading, lighting and smoking it by knocking it on the corner of the bench to loosen the ash.

'All right,' he said.

I withdrew the precious envelope from my purse, turning it around and around in my hands while I talked.

'I saw you on Friday,' I said, 'when you went into that house with the black door.'

'What are you talking about?' he answered, drawing on his pipe, very calmly, I thought, under the circumstances.

'I was on my way home from an errand at George Washington University. You went

288

into an unmarked house. I believe that's where you work.'

'Oh, you do,' he said. 'And what do you think it is that I do?'

'I don't know exactly,' I said, 'and I don't care. What I'm asking you is to help a Jewish family escape from Marseille. Rachel's family. Time is very short.'

Joe took his pipe out of his mouth and looked at me incredulously.

'If you think I can manage something like that you are sadly mistaken,' he said. 'I'm only a soldier, a private in my organization,' he said.

I hooted.

'What does that mean?'

'I don't believe it, that's what it means,' I said.

He put his pipe back into his mouth and puffed on it. Pipe-smoking, I thought, was an excellent way to gather one's thoughts before speaking.

'So, who are you,' he asked, 'that you can be asking such favors?'

'I can't say, you know that. And my request isn't official. I came across a file. My people can't take action on it.'

I handed him the papers. He frowned when he saw the Gestapo crest, and by the way his eyes traveled back and forth across the page, I knew he was reading the German document.

He looked up at me. 'I can't imagine what

you must have done to get this,' he said.

I didn't answer him.

'Tell me.'

'I can't.'

'Louise, there must be more to this than a schoolgirl friendship, for you to take such risks. If you want me to help you have to tell me the truth.'

I had never told anyone. It was too shameful.

'All right,' I said. I took a deep breath. 'I let Rachel pay for my last year at junior college. My parents couldn't. She insisted. I let her. I told my parents I'd gotten a scholarship.'

Joe looked perplexed.

'Rachel had a small inheritance from her mother – a bond maturing in an American bank account. She said it didn't matter if she cashed it in because her father was so rich anyway. She said she didn't want to finish St Martha's if I couldn't be there with her, that I was her only friend in the world. She withdrew the money and I let her pay my tuition and room and board. I was desperate to stay in college.'

'Okay,' Joe said.

'Don't you understand?' I said. 'The Nazis seized all Rachel's father's money. If she still had that bond in an American bank, who knows what it might be worth now, it might have qualified her for a visa.'

Joe tapped his pipe on the bench.

'If I hadn't finished my junior college

course, I wouldn't have gotten my job at the Wilmington Shipbuilding Company, or my job here,' I went on. 'I'm free and safe and employed, and Rachel and her children...' I stopped, unable to continue, and buried my face in my hands. When I recovered my poise I turned to him. 'Do you know what she asked me for in the letter Henrietta brought?' I said. 'A Red Cross package!'

'Listen to me, Louise. You could not have known Rachel would need that money. There's no reason for you to feel guilty.'

'Wouldn't you?'

'Maybe so.' Joe folded the papers in half and handed them back to me.

'Please,' I said, holding his hand back with my own.

'I told you I work for a humanitarian organization,' he said. 'What influence we have we must use sparingly. Do you know how many people want to get out of Europe? So many more than we can help. We've booked every berth in every ship that will dock in Lisbon in the next year, and it's not enough.'

'If you knew what I've been through to get those papers,' I said, then stopped. 'Well, you'd help me. I know you would.'

'Louise, for heaven's sake!'

'Please.'

'All right. But all I can do is see that this information gets to our office in Lisbon. The decision won't be up to me.'

291

'Thank you,' I said.

'Can we go home now?' he asked. 'It's hot as Hades out here.'

Once back in my room I drew on the white cotton gloves I wore to church in the summer. I located an eraser and rubbed it over as much of the surface of one set of Joan's carbons as I could without smearing the words. Then I did the same with the Vichy memo. I carefully folded the two sheets and placed them in a fresh envelope, licked a stamp and affixed it. I addressed the envelope, in block letters with my left hand, to 'Sir Julian Porter, Personal Secretary to the Ambassador, Embassy of Great Britain, Massachusetts Avenue, Washington DC.' Porter was one of the two men I'd seen dancing together at that unconventional party behind Friendship House.

I placed the envelope in my pocketbook to mail on the way to work. Here's hoping the European Foreign Service homosexual underground was as effective as Lionel said it was.

I did my best to erase fingerprints from the other documents, a task made more difficult by my trembling hands. That's how I realized I was scared to death. I placed the documents in my pocketbook to take to the office.

I went downstairs and found Dellaphine in the kitchen, knitting. I sat down next to her and watched for a few minutes.

She looked up at me. 'You jiggling the table with your knees, baby,' she said. 'You okay?'

'I'm a little nervous,' I said. 'Big day at work tomorrow.'

'Want a shot of bourbon? That should settle you down some.'

'Yes, please,' I said.

Dellaphine rose and took a ring of keys from her pocket and went into the pantry, where I heard her unlock a cabinet. She came back out with a tumbler holding an inch of gold liquid.

'Don't let the others see this,' she said. 'There are only a few bottles of Mr Knox's stash of Jack Daniels left.'

'Thanks,' I said. I sipped and watched Dellaphine knit, her needles flashing, and thought of the unfinished socks in my own knitting bag.

'I wish I could knit like you,' I said.

'You could, baby, you just not interested,' Dellaphine said. 'You're a career girl. Like my Madeleine. Why should you knit when you can work at a good job and buy war bonds?'

I didn't close my eyes that night. Not once. I lay in the dark and thought about what I intended to do the next day. I believe I was more frightened of trying to slip documents into OSS than I'd been of breaking into the Vichy embassy. Cold and clammy with fear, I turned off my fan and curled up under a sheet for the first time in weeks.

I kept picturing being searched as I went into my building. If the FBI suspected me of anything at all they could arrange it. What would happen to me if I were caught? What crime could I be charged with? Treason? Surely not that. Breaking countless OSS regulations? I heard about a woman once who'd been caught slipping documents into her briefcase at the end of the day. She was a Communist, it turned out, but her husband was a big-shot New Dealer so she only got fired. I couldn't even think about losing my job. I'd almost rather spend years at the federal prison for women in Alderson, West Virginia, than find myself back at my parents' fish camp. Finally dawn allowed me to get out of bed. I dressed and went downstairs to the kitchen. Dellaphine, still in her dressing gown and bare feet, looked up at me, surprised.

'You up early,' she said.

'I couldn't sleep,' I said. 'Give me something to do.'

She didn't question me, handing me an apron. By the time Phoebe came into the kitchen we were nearly finished. The bacon was crisp, the toast buttered and the juice poured. Dellaphine finished whisking the eggs and poured them into her favorite cast-iron skillet. Phoebe and I carried the bacon, toast, juice and pot of coffee into the dining room where the others were gathering. If Joe and Ada and Henry were surprised to see me in an apron helping Phoebe they didn't show it.

Phoebe picked up the tray of warm plates heaped with scrambled eggs and hurried into the dining room so the eggs wouldn't get cold. I poured everyone's cups full of coffee before I sat down, still in an apron.

I couldn't eat. My stomach had shrunk into a tiny painful ball in my abdomen, while a sharp pain jabbed me in the base of my neck. When I was done pushing my food around the plate and the others had finished I helped Phoebe take the plates into the kitchen and stack them on the sink.

I removed my apron and hung it on a pantry hook.

'Why, Mrs Pearlie,' Dellaphine said, with a gleam in her eye, 'ain't you going to stay and help me scrub the floors and change the sheets?'

'You don't have any idea how good that sounds to me right now,' I said.

The government car idled outside the old apartment building on 23rd and 'E' that housed OSS. Two G-men peered out of the side window.

'Do you see our girl?' the first agent asked.

'Not yet,' the second agent, who had a tiny yellow feather stuck in his hatband, said, lowering his binoculars.

'I guess we have to wait. How long, that's what I want to know. It's blazing hot already.'

'It's early yet,' the other agent said. He riffled through a sheaf of papers in his lap. 'Let's get this other stuff out of the way and come back later. She's not going anywhere. She doesn't suspect anything.'

TWENTY-ONE

I stepped off the bus on the corner and stopped cold, frozen with dread by the sight of my office building. I was almost knocked down by the press of other departing passengers getting off behind me.

'For God's sake, lady, get out of the way,' one of them said.

I forced my reluctant legs to move and found myself standing on the patch of withered lawn that fronted the building. I wasn't sure I could go any further. My mind was supremely conscious of the danger posed by the folded papers in my pocketbook. Hadn't I taken enough risks, hadn't I done enough? I could tear up the documents into tiny pieces and discard them in the trash barrel over by the lamppost. For a second that seemed like an excellent plan, but I noticed all my fellow office workers entering the building carrying pocketbooks and briefcases just like always.

I moved up the sidewalk. Was I imagining things, or did there seem to be more soldiers about than usual? And weren't they all looking at me? My God, they were! Every head was turned in my direction, every single one! Sweat broke out all over my body and I heard a deep ringing in my ears.

Then I realized the soldiers were ogling the peroxide blonde beside me, the one with long legs and high heels, swaying her hips in a fanny-hugging polka-dot frock.

My heart was pounding and I feared my red face would attract attention, so I detoured over to the shade of a nearby tree to compose myself. Vice-President Wallace's dog, a Great Dane, woke from his nap and lifted his head. He accompanied Wallace's daughter Jean to her job at OSS every day and walked her home in the evening. I scratched his head behind his ears.

'Hey, sweet boy,' I said. 'If I get arrested, will you protect me?'

The big dog leaned happily into my shoulder and slobbered. I scratched him some more and babbled nonsense to him until I'd composed myself, and joined the throng of co-workers heading into the building.

'Whatcha got in there?' Private Cooper asked, gesturing toward my black handbag. He shifted the rifle on his shoulder.

'What?' I said.

'In your bag,' he said. 'What's in it?'

My tongue froze in my mouth.

'You women and your knitting, and your magazines, and your lunches,' he said. 'You could supply a squadron with the stuff you carry to work every day.'

He squinted at my badge and nodded me into the building. Once over the threshold I felt such relief I could have melted onto the floor. I leaned against the wall for support for a minute before I headed down the hall.

Once in my office I set down my handbag on my desk. I was safe. Never even think of doing something like this again, I chided myself. Never. Ever.

Betty and Ruth were already at work. A few minutes later a new girl, who introduced herself as Brenda Bonner, arrived, standing timidly at the door, a stack of paperwork in her arms. She looked about twelve. I explained to her the procedure for typing up index cards, and the office settled down into its usual routine. Ruth pushed her cart stacked with files into the hall while Betty forced multiple pages of typing paper and carbon paper behind the bail of her typewriter.

I sat at my desk concealed behind the partition that separated me from the rest of the room and assembled a new and improved Bloch file. I included every document I had – the hydrology conference programs, the carbons Joan had given me, the reprints of Bloch's journal articles, the photostat of the Vichy memo and the photograph of Metcalfe, Burns, and the Blochs in Edinburgh in 1936.

I collected a few random files and left the office, radiating a businesslike sense of purpose. After filing all the other folders I knocked on Don's door.

'Look what I found,' I said, without introduction, and shoved the Bloch file at Don. 'Gerald Bloch's file.'

'Really,' Don said, taking it from me.

'It was in the "P" file room, on top of a file cabinet.'

Don frowned.

'I think that Mr Holman must have stuck it there, you know, confused because he was feeling ill, since it's clearly marked to go to the Projects Committee.'

I turned to leave, eager to escape. But Don gestured to me to wait, so I sat and watched him while he carefully read through the file. I knew he could read French. And he was a bright man, and would want to be credited with this. Please let him notice. It would be too suspicious for me to show it to him. I might have to explain everything I'd done, I'd be in pure trouble, and the Projects Committee might be less inclined to help Rachel.

Don shook his head, minutely, and his brow furrowed. 'Well,' he said, 'it might not be too late to help. We'll see what the Projects Committee recommends.'

He hadn't noticed, damn it!

'I skimmed the file myself, Don,' I said. 'I was curious, you know, it disappeared right out of Mr Holman's office when he died. So odd.'

'Like you said, Bob must have been feeling ill before his attack and left it in the main file room.'

'Did you notice,' I said, as evenly as I could manage, 'that the titles of Bloch's French articles on hydrology are the same as the titles of Charles's articles he delivered at a conference here in 1939? When Gerald Bloch was in France?'

'Really?' Don was interested now, he reached for the file again and read it through.

I watched as the creases in Don's brow smoothed out, and he pushed his glasses up on his forehead and rubbed his eyes. He looked up at me with a grim set to his mouth and comprehension in his eyes.

'Thank you, Mrs Pearlie. You were right. This is very important. I'll take it upstairs immediately.'

He'd finally put two and two together, just as I had.

A G-man wearing a blue suit holding a fedora with a yellow feather stuck in the hat-band was waiting for me in my office. He was the same agent I'd noticed at Bob Holman's funeral.

'Ma'am,' he said to me, rising from a chair,

'I'm Special Agent Gray Williams, Federal Bureau of Investigation. Is there somewhere we can talk in private?'

Betty, Ruth and Brenda worked away, pretending to be oblivious.

This was it. I'd been found out.

'This way, Agent Williams,' I said. I tried to appear calm as I led the G-man down the hall and into the conference room. We squeezed ourselves into two chairs at the scarred conference table.

'Ma'am,' he said, 'I thought you should know, the Bureau has received complaints about you.'

'Really,' I said, trying to keep my voice steady.

'You see,' the agent said, averting his eyes and hesitating, as if he didn't want to bring up such an unsavory subject, 'a guest at the Wardham hotel let us know that, well, ma'am, you'd been seen behaving in a loose fashion, in the hotel bar, with a foreigner, a Frenchman.'

'Oh, dear,' I said, trying to appear embarrassed, 'I'd met Mr Barbier at a party, he seemed so nice.'

'You were seen again at the Shoreham on Saturday evening with the same man, and made quite a spectacle of yourself.'

'Oh, no,' I said, feigning surprise. 'I drank way too much champagne.'

'We investigated and you'll be glad to know that we saw no reason to suspect you of anything. On the contrary, your record appears to be exemplary.'

'Thank goodness,' I said. 'I assure you...'

Agent Williams waved off my assurances.

'You must understand that it is in the best interest of a government girl to maintain high social standards. Being seen out in public with foreign nationals is not acceptable.'

Condescending bastard.

'Yes, of course,' I said.

'The Bureau,' he continued, 'felt it would be helpful for you to know about this incident. For your own sake, you understand. As your record has been outstanding until now.'

'Thank you so much,' I said. 'I appreciate your concern, and I promise to be more circumspect in choosing my friends.'

'An excellent plan, ma'am,' Agent Williams said, settling his fedora on his head. 'I know my way out.'

From the doorway of the file room I watched him leave the building.

That was a close call.

I didn't intend to see or speak to Lionel Barbier again, which was why I was so irritated to find him at the drug store on the corner where I went for lunch. He rose from a booth from the counter and beckoned me over.

'What the hell are you doing here?' I asked.

'I know you lunch here often, and I needed to see you again. How fortunate that you chose to come here today.'

'I can't believe that you'd dare try to speak to me after what happened Saturday night.'

'Sit down, my dear,' he said, 'and don't look so fierce. It's not becoming.'

Angry as I was with the man, I was curious. Who was the FBI to tell me what to do, anyway? I slid into the booth.

'You're a snake,' I said. 'An FBI agent just cautioned me about you.'

'Really,' he said, stroking his chin. 'Interesting. Perhaps I should lie low for a time.'

'You couldn't get much lower than you already are.'

'*Chérie*, I know where there are the deepest of holes to crawl into. And remember, you did get that item you desired so much.'

The waitress appeared at the booth with her pad.

Once I realized the FBI wasn't going to arrest me, my stomach had unknotted. 'I want a grilled cheese and tomato sandwich, French fries and a Coke,' I said. Lionel wrinkled his nose. I figured he wouldn't eat lunch-counter food unless he was starving.

'Coffee only,' Lionel said. The waitress nodded and moved away.

'What luck to find you here,' Lionel said again. 'I was hoping you would come here for lunch today. I didn't want to risk calling you on the telephone.'

'Make it quick. After today I never want to see you again.'

'That is not in the cards, my dear. We must not see each other for a time, and we will never speak of your Monsieur Bloch again, but in a few months, we will meet at the Wardham again for another drink.'

'Surely you don't think I...'

'Calm down. Tell me, did you find what you needed in the file?'

I hated to admit it. 'Yes, I did.'

'Some good will come of it?'

'Perhaps.'

'Everything has its price. I did not collect the night we stole that file at my embassy. I risked much, you remember, to help you.'

'I know.' In other words I owed him a favor.

'I would be most interested,' he said, glancing around the room and lowering his voice, 'in knowing who your, ah, employer recommends to lead the Free French.'

So you can decide which side you're on, I thought.

So he knew, or guessed, I worked for OSS. Why was I not surprised?

I didn't answer him, and he didn't press me. I let him think I intended to do as he asked, instead of slapping him across the kisser like I wanted to.

The waitress brought our order. After cooling his coffee with cream Lionel gulped it down.

'Goodbye, my dear Louise,' he said, rising from the booth. 'In French we say *au revoir*, "until we see each other again".' I choked back the expletive I wanted to answer him with, but I thought to myself that it would be a cold day in hell before Lionel Barber saw me again.

He handed me his chit and walked out of the restaurant, leaving me to settle his account.

I arrived back at work in time to revel in the outcome of my venture into espionage. As I turned the corner I saw a crowd of OSS staffers standing on the front steps watching a couple of FBI agents, including Agent Williams, and two GIs lead Charles Burns away in handcuffs. I quickly ducked behind a tree and watched as they pushed him into a car and drove away. No one in the crowd on the steps said a word. I noticed Joan in the front row, eyes wide, a hand clapped over her mouth. Guy and Roger stood side by side, Guy with his arms crossed over his chest, Roger smoking a cigarette. I didn't see Don. He'd acted quickly, I had to give him that.

It was over, thank God. I'd realized why the Bloch file had been stolen, and who stole it, when I went through the stolen documents yesterday. The answer was right there, staring me in the face, evident even before I'd broken into the Vichy embassy. Charles Burns plagiarized one of Gerald Bloch's journal articles and presented it as his own at a professional conference in 1939 without even bothering to change the title other than translate it into English. I suppose he assumed that Bloch, a Jew trapped in France, would never have the chance to know what he had done. Burns must have noticed the file in Holman's office, realized what Bloch's freedom might mean to his career, and taken advantage of Holman's heart attack to remove it. The theft had nothing to do with the war or politics at all.

So my quest to help Rachel evolved into a trap for Charles Burns. I led Don to notice what I'd seen in the documents I gave him. Fortunately he did. I wondered what would happen to Charles, but I pushed him out of my mind, and thought of Rachel and her family. If the OSS thought Gerald could assist the Allies in North Africa they might still help his family escape.

Time was short. The Gestapo arrived in Marseille tomorrow.

The office was quiet as a tomb all afternoon. None of us dared talk about what happened. Don's office door remained closed. Guy and Roger sat together, talking easily, during coffee break. Guy even offered Roger a cigarette. I sipped my java with the other clerks, and we chatted about our Fourth of July adventures. I elaborated, with gusto, on my fictional afternoon at the Wardham Hotel swimming pool, to the point where I almost

306

believed it myself.

As we left to go back to our respective offices Joan pulled me aside.

'Let me give you a lift home today,' she said. Her face was pale and her eyes sunk deep in her face. I figured she wanted to talk about Charles.

'Sure,' I said.

The inside of Joan's car steamed like a coal boiler. We rolled down both windows and Joan pushed open the convertible top. I tied a scarf around my head to keep the hot wind from blowing my hair into a bird's nest. We didn't speak until we were blocks away.

'Do you know why Charles was arrested?' Joan finally said.

'Yes,' I answered. 'He stole the Bloch file, to save himself from a plagiarism charge. I wonder what will happen to him. What do you think they'll charge him with?'

'Murder.'

'What! Who was murdered?'

'Bob Holman.'

'But he had a heart attack!'

'General Donovan told me the whole story this afternoon. Don't breathe a word of this, Louise, but I have to tell someone. Charles murdered Bob Holman. When he delivered a map Mr Holman had requested that afternoon, he noticed the Bloch file on Holman's desk. Charles was terrified that if Bloch escaped from Marseille he would some day find out that Charles had stolen his work. Charles panicked and stabbed Holman with a letter opener so he could steal the file and prevent OSS from rescuing Bloch. OSS security and the FBI hushed up the murder while they investigated. Didn't want to warn off the killer.'

Killer. All this time I'd been pursuing a murderer and had no idea. It wasn't surprising, though. A man who was evil enough to condemn an innocent man and his family to a Nazi labor camp because of a few boring scientific articles would be capable of murder.

'The queer thing is, Charles told the FBI that he'd destroyed Bloch's file, but of course he didn't, because you found it.'

We'd stopped at a traffic light.

'When you returned the file and Don examined the documents he realized that Charles had killed Holman. He found Bloch's articles and evidence that Charles had used them as his own work. Don's some kind of hero for figuring all this out.'

I was angry that Don hadn't mentioned my contributions, but it was probably wise for me to let Don take all the credit. I didn't want anyone to question me about my role in all this. I'd broken way too many rules. Good thing I knew how to keep my mouth shut.

'Oh, and Dora Bertrand's back,' Joan said, 'she was a suspect, apparently, but the FBI reinstated her security clearance. General Donovan insisted.'

'The FBI suspected her of the murder? Why?'

'Well, Bob Holman was opposed to a second front in Europe, and Dora championed one. And because she's not the *Ladies' Home Journal* ideal American girl, I guess.'

'What crossed your mind when you heard Charles was arrested?' I asked.

'That I always seem to pick the wrong fellows to get crushes on,' Joan said, 'but this one was a doozy.'

'Let's go get a Martini. My treat.'

'Can't. Believe it or not, I have a date. A real date. He asked me.'

Joan let me out at my doorstep. I wished I'd had that Martini. I'd come to close to disaster, and I didn't mean getting caught breaking into the Vichy French embassy.

Knowing Charles killed Holman completely altered my perspective on his behavior. I'd been so naive to think he was romantically interested in me! When he'd asked me to dinner after our Monopoly game at Joan's, it was because I was so curious about Holman's death and the state of his office and he wanted to find out how much I knew, not because he was infatuated with me. Then when I'd visited him in his office with questions about the 1936 conference, he became truly worried about my

309

interest in Gerald Bloch. At dinner with Joan one night all he'd done was ask her questions about me. She thought he wanted to ask me out, but actually I was just too interested in the Bloch file for him to ignore.

So when Charles had picked me up outside Union Station the day I met Barbara, when he tried to 'take me to lunch' against my wishes, driven with me into quiet and empty Brentwood Park, I now suspected that he'd intended not to force himself on me, but to kill me.

I knew that I'd been playing a dangerous game, trying to help Rachel, but I'd had no idea my own life was at stake. Despite the heat I rested on the front stoop for a while, until I stopped shaking.

Phoebe and Joe were in the lounge listening to the radio.

'My dear,' Phoebe said. 'Are you all right? You look so tired.'

I leaned up against the doorjamb.

'I suppose I am,' I said. 'I didn't get much sleep last night.'

'Big day at work?' Joe asked. Was I being self-conscious, or did his voice carry a hint of deeper meaning in those words? Phoebe didn't act as if she detected anything in his tone of voice. I stared at him. He seemed completely absorbed in the radio and the newspaper on his lap. I must have been wrong. I badly wanted Joe to be one of the good guys, but I had no real proof that he was. Best to keep my distance in the future, I thought, after we went to that movie this weekend. I was considering *This Gun For Hire*.

'Have you seen Ada?' I asked.

'I believe she's in her room,' Phoebe said.

'So you see,' I said, gripping both of Ada's hands in mine, 'the FBI was watching me that morning, not you.'

'Oh, thank God,' Ada said. Tears streamed down her face, filling the creases in her skin with powder and mascara. I let her cry. I'd been scared when Agent Williams visited me, and I couldn't imagine how frightened she must have been. Instead it was me who had a file at the FBI, me and Eleanor Roosevelt.

'You will never tell anyone, will you?' she asked. 'About, you know.'

'Of course not,' I said. 'I know how to keep my mouth shut.'

She wiped her face with her handkerchief. It came away coated with make-up. 'I must look horrible,' she said.

'Go on and fix your face,' I said. 'Supper will be ready soon.'

Ada wasn't the only person in the house who got good news that evening. Madeleine, wearing the khaki suit with pink rickrack trim Ada gave her, floated into the kitchen right after dinner, full of the news she'd

311

landed a job with the Social Security Administration punching out Social Security cards on a special typewriter.

'The whole room was full of colored girls,' she told us in the kitchen, 'all high-school graduates like me. I'll be making twenty-one dollars a week!'

'What are you going to do when you get old, girl,' Dellaphine said, 'that's what I want to know. When you can't work that job no more, you be out in the street. I'll always have a home here in this house. The Knox boys will see to that.'

'Will you listen?' Madeleine said to her. 'Social Security, Ma!'

Dellaphine snorted. 'By the time you're old enough to collect it, there won't be none left.'

I was in Madeleine's corner. Unlike Phoebe, I didn't want life to return to the way it was before the war. I no longer had any intention of returning to Wilmington, North Carolina, except for an occasional Christmas visit. After the war I'd finish college and have a real career. My own apartment, too. If I met a man I wanted to marry that would be nice, but I wasn't planning my future around it. And as for Rachel, I felt at peace. I had, at last, done everything I could for her.

I went out on the porch alone. The evening sky rumbled, our usual afternoon shower on its way. I pulled the Lucky Strike I'd mooched off Dellaphine out of my pocket and lit it with the heavy marble table lighter I'd picked up off the hall table. I inhaled the calming nicotine deep into my lungs, then exhaled a cloud of smoke, relaxing with relief. I didn't care if my throat ached all night. I needed a cigarette.

Epilogue

Rachel awoke in the dead of night struggling against the rough grip of the man who loomed over her. She recognized George Barellet, son of the Hôtel Bompard's owner, from the odor of raw cheese and cheap red wine on his breath. He had one hand clapped across her mouth while the other pinned her to the floor.

'Be quiet,' he said. 'You are leaving here tonight. You've been ransomed.'

Rachel quieted, confused by the word 'ransom'. She'd heard that Barellet could be bribed to release internees, but the rumored price was so dear. Gerald, wherever he was, couldn't possibly manage it.

'Wake your children, quietly,' Barellet said. 'Come now, it will soon be too late.'

Rachel woke the children, shushing them as she pulled Claude to his feet and nestled Louisa into her shoulder. Claude was such a good child, he'd learned to be quiet without whining. The baby was sound asleep. Rachel had dosed her with a drop of the laudanum she'd bartered for the two packs of cigarettes from her Red Cross package. Barellet hoist-

314

ed her valise, already packed to bulging for the train journey east. They'd been scheduled for the first group to leave tomorrow.

Barellet led them through the crowded hotel room and down the filthy staircase. He unlocked the front gate and then they were outside in the street. Clean fresh air filled Rachel's lungs.

A cart loaded with shoddy household goods and a driver waited for them. The driver wore the rough clothing of a laborer, a stained felt hat pulled down over his face. The old mule hitched to the cart was too broken down for anyone to confiscate.

'Get in, and go,' Barellet said.

Rachel didn't hesitate, and didn't question the man who waited for her in the cart. She didn't know what lay ahead but it couldn't be worse than a labor camp in Germany. The driver reached for the children one at a time and laid them on a blanket behind the seat. Then he lifted Rachel next to him.

'You are my wife,' he said, 'you are exhausted and terrified.' Acting that part would be easy enough. 'We are moving to my parents' farm in the country. Do not speak, and cover your hair.'

Rachel wrapped her black hair, which she had cut short for cleanliness' sake, in a scarf and thanked God for her blue eyes. She turned to the children. The baby was already asleep again, but Claude sat up, wide-eyed.

'Lie down,' she said. 'Pretend to sleep.'

315

Claude promptly curled up next to his sister with his thumb in his mouth.

Vichy policemen stopped the cart twice on its way out of the city, poked and prodded at its pitiful cargo, but let them continue.

They plodded west, then south, for what seemed like many hours, until Rachel could taste the salt tang of the Mediterranean in the air. Down a sandy track they came to a rickety dock that jutted out into a lonesome bay. Another dozen or so ragged refugees already waited on the dock.

Her escort, who never told her his name, helped her and the children down to the dock, carrying her valise.

'Wait here, it won't be long,' he said, touching his hat as he left. Wait for what exactly, Rachel wondered.

Escape? She couldn't believe it.

Because of the moonless night Rachel didn't see the dinghy until it was nearly at the dock. The British seamen wore black, rowing with muffled oars. She and her children were in the first boatload to reach HMS *Splendid*, a British submarine out of Malta, she learned from the petty officer in charge of the dinghy. When she translated for the others in the boat they murmured with hope.

Seamen who tipped their caps to her and called her ma'am guided them below. The refugees spoke very little to each other. They all seemed stunned, almost to disbelief, to find themselves on a British submarine.

A young seaman brought them all blankets, sandwiches, tea, biscuits and cans of evaporated milk for the children.

The seaman told her the sub had offloaded supplies for the Resistance, small arms, food and clothing, and so had room to carry a few Jewish refugees to safety in Malta. She translated again for the others, and they all murmured in awe, *'En sécurité.'* Safety. How in God's name had this happened? Why had she and her children been spared from amongst the thousands penned up like cattle in internment camps all over the south of France?

She settled the children onto a cot to sleep. Once they were quiet she dug a thin pad of paper and a pencil stub out of her valise and began to write a letter.

'Dearest Louise,' she began. *'C'est un miracle!'*